PARISIAN GHOSTS 3

GHOSTS OF THE RESISTANCE

JANNA RUTH

A Note on Sensitive Topics

Dear Reader,

This is a book about ghosts, so naturally death plays a rather large part. If you don't like spoilers, and you're cool with everything, skip this note and start the book. If you want to be prepared, read on. I'm writing this because reading should be fun, not a nasty surprise.

In this book, Alix dives deeper into the conflict between the cataphiles, mainly the Chevalier and cataflics, mostly GoPol, exposing horrors on both sides, including murder, parental abuse, and necromancy. The latter includes depictions of deceased and reanimated animals.

Our heroine gets in a lot of trouble in this book as she is crushed between the sides. She'll be betrayed by those she trusts and outright threatened with death, while witnessing and learning some horrifying displays of power abuse. And she learns that not even her ghosts are safe. In addition, some of the terrors of Vichy France in World War II are mentioned, but not explicitly described.

The series is full of action with physical confrontations between the living and the dead, but our heroine is scrappy and will gain some strong supporters along the way.

Happy to tag along? Then join Alix in this new ghostly adventure on the streets of Paris!

Love, Janna

Grab your free copy

When an undead movie star asks you for a small favour, you know you're gonna be in deep trouble.

Seeing ghosts is just something I've learnt to live with. They're everywhere I go, especially since I chose to study history at the Sorbonne, one of the oldest universities in the world. While on a class trip to the Pantheon, where France's great men—and women!—reside, I get introduced to the fabulous Josephine Baker! One of her war medals has gone missing, and she wants me to find its whereabouts.

Who could say no to a flapper girl turned movie star turned war hero? Little do I know agreeing to do so will send me on a wild-goose chase across the country with a ghostly pet cheetah, hidden walkways, and a murder attempt.

Follow Alix on her first big ghost adventure two years prior to the events of Parisian Ghosts.

Sign up to my Story Seeker mailing list at <u>www.janna-ruth.com/ newsletter</u> and grab the prequel for free

Chapter 1

I'm in love with Gaspar. Absolutely, irrevocably in love with him. I love the way he smiles, his kindness, his devotion, the way he is with Malou, and the way he was with Petite Alix. And the way he is with me? Utterly amazing.

The minute I come home from work or school, he's there, welcoming me with a wicked smile. I close the door and it's all about making out with him from there. I don't care that he's technically dead or that no one else can see him. His hair is incredibly soft under my fingers, his lips are tender against my skin, and his hands are firm as he holds me in his arms.

My relationships before him were few and very short. I never had much experience when it came to the physical department. A few kisses here and there, an awkward touch, more accidental than intentional, and premature pressure to do more than kiss.

With Gaspar, everything is different. He kisses me in a million different ways; passionate or tender, cheeky or loving, with whispers of promises and declarations of love. Honestly, I could kiss this boy all day long.

Any doubts I ever had about the legitimacy of this relationship go out the window the moment our bodies touch. To be honest, there's not much to think about as I sink into his embrace, showering his beautiful face with kisses and exploring his body.

That is until I hear footsteps in the corridor.

Gaspar pulls back, barely out of breath—since he didn't have any to begin with—as he listens. "That's your Papa." He already recognises all my family members by the sound of their footsteps. "Again."

It's the only thing that puts a damper on our relationship. Amazing as it is, it's only real for me. Maman and Odile have no idea I even have a boyfriend. Malou couldn't care less, and I still haven't told Gaby about how physical my relationship with Gaspar has become—or that we're even back together. Now, Papa...

"I wonder if he's still having nightmares." I don't have to wonder for long, because from the sounds outside, he's throwing up in our toilet. "Let me check on him."

"Okay." Gaspar gets up, allowing me to leave the bed.

He stands by the door to my room, while I make my way over to where my father is currently emptying his stomach. I knock on the door, making the sliver of light coming through a little wider. "Do you need anything?"

Sweat covers Papa's forehead and the nape of his neck. Despite the weak smile he greets me with, he looks incredibly ill. "I'm good."

"Oh, yes. Very good." I feel terrible about the whole thing. If it wasn't for me, my father wouldn't be suffering from recurring nightmares. Heck, if I hadn't dragged him into my ghost business, he wouldn't have died. At least, that's what I think happened.

Somehow, Jacques de Molay, the last Grand Master of the Knights Templar, took my father's life and held it in stasis, or something like that, until I broke his hold. I don't claim to understand what exactly happened in the Boutique of Psychosis, but it left my father with recurring nightmares and the ability to see ghosts.

"Some water, perhaps?" he asks, amused.

"Coming right up." I go into the kitchen and get him a glass of water.

Gaspar is still standing outside my door, looking askance. I shrug, a guilty conscience weighing heavily on my shoulders.

My father being a ghost whisperer like me should've been a relief. Finally, someone I care about can confirm I'm not making it all up. But it comes at a terrible price. My own temporary death was so long ago that I didn't even remember it until I went looking for it. It's different for him.

I hand the glass to my father, then lean against the door frame and cross my arms. "Do you want to talk about it?"

"It's always the same. Dark shadows whispering and a burning searing pain, like flames engulfing me." He shudders and rubs his forehead. "My head hurts when I wake up. Doctor can't find anything, though." Papa gives me another weak smile. "I guess it's all in my head. It'll pass."

Hopefully, it will. I have no experience with whatever curse Molay put on my father. I didn't even know such curses existed. So I have no idea how to help him, or if he'll ever get better. "I'm sorry."

"For what?" He wipes his mouth and flushes the toilet but remains sitting on the floor. "I'm sorry I worried you, passing out in the catacombs like that. You must've been so scared."

"I about lost my mind." I really thought I was going to lose him.

"See." Papa reaches out to me. I take his hand and he rubs my fingertips reassuringly. "You had no idea this was going to happen. It was a risk I willingly took."

"Well..." I want to tell him that he had no idea what kind of risk he was taking, because I'd never told him about the ghosts, but then again, I had no clue either. And where would I even start?

"Seriously, Alix. I'm a grown man, an investigative reporter. I can handle the consequences of my own decisions. It's just such a shame I ruined your big find. We don't even have the photos."

The camera he took with him never made it out of the catacombs. "It doesn't matter, Papa. The skeleton was fake anyway. Just something the cataphiles put up for their pseudo rituals."

"Ah, yes. I remember reading about those. I'm sorry."

"It's alright. I'm just glad you're still with us."

"So am I." He toasts me with the glass and takes a few more sips. "Don't worry, I'll be fine."

"Okay." I let go of the frame and walk away.

My father's eyes widen as he notices Gaspar standing at my door. "I didn't know your boyfriend was staying over."

And just like that, he acknowledges the ghost in the room.

"Oh, yes. Is that a problem?"

"You're an adult, Alix. What you do with your boyfriend is none of my business." His eyes twinkle with amusement. "But maybe he could join us for dinner sometime?"

"Um... sure." Unfortunately, that won't possible, but maybe I can take him and my father out sometime. "Hope you get some sleep."

He grins. "You too."

With a heavy roll of my eyes, I return to Gaspar.

He puts his arm around my shoulder, and I close the door behind me. "You okay?"

"I..." I let out a small sigh and turn my attention to Malou, who's scurrying around her cage. Her food needs refilling. "We'll have to tell him about the ghosts."

So far, my father doesn't seem to realise that he's able to see ghosts. And why should he? If he's anything like me, they appear to him as perfectly ordinary people.

I fill Malou's trough and rub her belly when she comes to eat. Gaspar puts his arm around me and rests his chin on my shoulder. "Hey, he's in the best of hands with you. You'll figure it out."

"Thanks." I lean back, enjoying this quiet moment as much as the heated ones before.

Gaspar kisses me just below the ear. "Wanna go back to bed?"

Laughing, I turn in his embrace and wrap my arms around his neck. In the darkness of my room, his eyes are almost black. I kiss the tip of his nose. "Where were we?"

"Right here," Gaspar says, placing his lips on mine. "And here." He kisses my jaw. "And here." Another follows on my neck as I catch my breath. "And maybe here."

Giggling, we tumble back onto my bed.

CHAPTER 2

Classes at Sorbonne are starting to wind down for the Christmas break. Not that it stops our professors from giving us homework. And since exams won't be long after classes resume, in February, I expect to spend the majority of my break with my history books—or the ghosts from that time.

Gaby and I pack our things and leave the classroom. I pull my coat tight against the cold wind as we step into the muddy outside world. It snowed last weekend, and since the snow didn't last, there's brown sludge everywhere. Not exactly a winter wonderland.

"Coffee?" Gaby asks, already steering our feet in *Chambelland*'s direction.

I link my arm with hers and laugh. "Sure, why not?"

"So..." Gaby starts, "Don't kill me for this, but I had an idea."

Since there is very little I would kill Gaby for, I frown heavily. "What's the idea?"

"I want to ask Marie out."

"That's wonderful! What do you have planned?"

Gaby's cheeks redden slightly. "That's where you come in. I think it's time we celebrate surviving this year."

"That's definitely worth celebrating." I've never been in as much danger as this year.

"Agreed. So, there's a new club in the Marais that I want to check out."

"Oh, no." I groan softly. "A club?"

Gaby tugs my arm. "You already promised. We'll make it a girls' night out, and I'll invite Marie to join us. It's gonna be fun!"

I laugh at the intense look in her eyes as she tries to convince me. "If you say so."

"It's really chic. I'm not a monster, so I picked this one because—according to reviews—it's not filled to the brim, a bit classier, and queer-friendly. We'll have wine, maybe champagne."

"Oh, we can afford that now?"

"Cheap champagne," Gaby amends, making me laugh. "So, are you in?"

I owe Gaby so much more than this. "Yes, I'm in."

She squeals excitedly. "Oh, I can't wait. This is gonna be amazing. Like, even if doesn't work out with Marie," her voice becomes a little strained, "we'll still have a lot of fun."

"It'll definitely work out. Marie's always happy to see you."

"Yeah, happy and *happy* aren't the same thing."

I laugh. "You know that made no sense?"

Gaby clicks her tongue. "We still don't know much about her romantic preferences."

"I don't see how anyone couldn't love you, so don't worry. Once she sees you dancing—and after half a bottle of cheap champagne…"

Gaby hits me before I can finish the sentence. Then she looks at me curiously. "You're in an awfully good mood lately. What's going on?"

"Do you prefer me sad and heartbroken?" I ask, amused.

"Definitely not. So, tell me. What brought on the change?"

I take a deep breath. The exhaling air forms a white cloud in front of my face. "You won't like it."

"Alix." Disappointment slips into her voice, just as I expected. "How can I not like something that makes you happy?" When I give her a long look, her mouth forms a little 'o'. "You and Gaspar."

"Mhm." Any second now she's going to tell me how bad of an idea it is and that I need to move on from him. I won't do it, but I don't relish fighting my best friend for it.

"I thought the two of you broke up."

"We did." My shoulders sink with a sigh. "Gaby. He saved my life. But even without that, he's just perfect. You should've seen him with Petite Alix or with Malou. Malou loves him."

"Well, if Malou loves him…" It doesn't sound very convincing.

I click my tongue. "I know it's highly controversial, and that we don't have a future. We can't get married like Hélène and Cédric—"

Gaby interrupts me with a gasp. "You'd marry him?"

My cheeks start burning. "No, of course not. I'm just… What I'm saying is that I'm well aware that our relationship will never live up to society's standards. There's a ton of normal couple activities that we'll never be able to do. Like going out together. At least not without drawing looks. *But* I love him. And he loves me, and he makes me very, very happy."

Her face softens. Then she stretches her arms wide. "Come here." She pulls me into an embrace before I can say anything else. "I wish things were different. Mainly, I wish that this wonderful guy was alive. Because you deserve all the happiness in the world. And if that means a ghost boyfriend… honestly, there's much bigger red flags out there."

I burst into giggles. "What an endorsement."

She grins. "I love seeing you this happy," she whispers, "And I mean, honestly. If there's such a thing as ghost police, you can date a ghost. What's normal, anyway? I just don't want to see you get hurt."

"I know."

Gaby steps back and links her arm with mine again. "It's settled then. You and Gaspar. It's a thing."

Her acceptance makes me grin till my cheeks hurt. *Chambelland* appears in front of us, and I tug her arm again. "Let's make you and Marie a thing next."

Nervously, Gaby squeals again.

Chapter 3

Since my big blow-up at the Panthéon, things have been a bit tense at work. Napoleon's generals who helped in the fight against Molay salute me with earnest nods and questions about when we're going to do this again, but some of my regulars, like Voltaire, won't even look at me.

That's okay, because I'm still angry at them for their lack of care about living matters and the way they treated Gaspar. If it weren't for Victor and the generals helping in the end—and the fact that I really need the money—I would've quit my job. At least this way it's a lot quieter than usual. The ghosts probably have a couple of things they want me to take a look at, but none of them dare cross Voltaire. Not even Rousseau.

I'm just about to quit for the day when I see one of the regulars standing in the big hall. With his fedora, scarf, long coat, and slender suitcase, Jean Moulin makes for a striking figure. There's so many places, schools, and streets named after him that he rarely spends time at the Panthéon, which explains why he greets me with a tap to his head and a friendly smile. "Mademoiselle Dubois."

"Welcome home, Monsieur Moulin." He must have missed all the action. "How was your trip?"

He hangs up his coat in the locker room, where it vanishes into the ether the moment he lets go. "Informative, as usual. How have things been around here?"

I cross my arms and lean against my locker. "Not so good, but I'm sure Voltaire will fill you in soon enough and tell you what a preposterous person I am."

"You? Preposterous?" Moulin frowns heavily. "Care to elaborate?"

"I made the mistake of asking the Panthéon to help me with something."

"Not just something, little Miss." Voltaire strides into the room, clearly not keen on giving me any privacy. "You asked us to compromise the sanctity of this place. And not just once, but twice."

Voltaire is followed by a small gaggle of ghosts, among them Josephine Baker, who reprimands him straightaway. "Cut her some slack, Voltaire, the girl was heartbroken."

"That's no reason," Voltaire bellows. "She has no idea what kind of powers she's messing with for her own personal gain."

Moulin chuckles softly. "Is that so?" His amusement makes me feel a bit better about Voltaire's accusations.

"Don't make light of this, Moulin," Voltaire warns him. "I've only had eight cups of coffee so far today and won't suffer fools."

Moulin grimaces. "I'm hardly a fool."

Not interested in rehashing the fight, I leave the locker room without getting changed and withdraw to the crypt. It's pure reflex, searching for solace with Victor.

To my relief, Victor greets me with nothing but warmth. "Fleeing from Voltaire? I can't exactly blame you, kid."

With a sigh, I sit on the stairs to the crypt, not quite down there and not quite up either. "He thinks I'm the worst." Maybe I didn't know what kind of powers I was playing with, but it's not like any of my ghost friends explained anything.

Victor comes to stand before me, looking down benevolently. "You are far from the worst. Impulsive, and maybe too caring for your own good, but that's hardly a fault."

"Will you ever tell me what makes this place so special? Apart from all of you, that is."

He sighs heavily. "That's impossible." When I groan, he snorts. "It can't be apart from us, because we *are* what makes this place special."

Sometimes his conceited attitude is a bit too much to bear. I grit my teeth and force myself to smile. "Lovely."

"You don't understand—"

"I really don't."

Victor scoffs, slightly amused. "Will you listen now? That's usually a strength of yours."

A retort jumps to my lips, but I keep them closed for his sake and nod.

"You know how ghosts draw strength from their memory? The stronger our memory, the longer we're around. But it's not just that. A strong memory also gives us power. That's what makes this place so special. It's a concentration of well-known people... ghosts."

Surprised he's actually explaining it to me, I nod. "Like St Denis or Les Invalides?" Both were marked on the Chevalier's map.

"Yes. St Denis is full of the old kings and Les Invalides... we don't talk about Les Invalides." When I raise an eyebrow, Victor sighs. "Let's just say there's a reason Napoleon Bonaparte was buried within seven tombs like one of those Russian toys."

The explanation reminds me how well-secured Jacques de Molay was and makes me shudder. "He's not going to ask me for a favour or anything, right?"

"If he does, *run*." Victor takes a seat next to me, cocking his head slightly. "We never really talked about what happened in the catacombs. I know from the others that you fought and defeated Molay, destroying his ghost in the process."

What the Chevalier and I did still doesn't sit right with me. As terrifying as Molay was, it feels like I murdered him again. "He didn't leave us any choice."

"No, I suppose not." Victor nods to himself. "Before he came to you, he tried to force his way into the Panthéon. In vain, but we've never been challenged like that before. That's why Voltaire is still so angry."

"I'm sorry." There's no getting around the fact that I severely underestimated Molay and the lengths he'd go to.

"I take it you managed to free your father, though?"

Tears well in my eyes as I remember that frightful night in the catacombs. How I thought all was lost—even Gaspar—until Alexandre de Beauharnais and the Panthéon ghosts heeded my call for help. The fear about my father, a fear that still hasn't passed, because he's suffering even now.

"We got him out, yes, but..." I turn to him, suddenly overcome with the need to pour my heart out. "Somehow, Papa died down there. He can see ghosts."

"That's concerning."

"It doesn't make sense. And something's wrong. He's been having nightmares ever since we returned. I want to help him but I don't know how."

Victor frowns at me. I feel like he's battling the urge to say, "I told you so." Instead, he straightens his jacket and nods. "I don't know much about the true depths the Grand Master went to, but he had powers beyond any of us. After all, he was only one ghost and not a very well-remembered one. I wonder if your father can truly see ghosts because he died or because he had his eyes opened in a cruel and soul-tearing way."

I gasp. "Is that possible?"

He shrugs helplessly. "I don't know. We'll have to find a way to confirm he actually died."

For a moment, I'm too overcome with emotions to think straight. But then it hits me. "If he died, there should be a whisper ghost."

"A whisper ghost?"

I quickly update Victor on what I know about whisper ghosts, all of which I've learned from GoPol. "My own ghost is a toddler. Apparently, I drowned in the Seine when I was three."

Next to me, Victor tenses suddenly. "Is that so?" His voice is shaky, unlike ever before.

It takes me a couple of moments to realise why the thought of me drowning would upset him so much when it's obvious I survived it just fine. When it hits me, my heart overflows with sadness.

"I'm sorry," I say, hugging him tight, something we only do rarely. "I didn't want to remind of you Léopoldine."

Victor's oldest daughter and her husband drowned in the Seine at nineteen. Just like I almost did. In the wake of her death, Victor wrote many heartbreaking poems, never quite recovering from the loss. "I'm sorry."

He puts his hand on my arm. "Don't be. She's taken flight long since." He heaves a sigh full of century-old regret. "Drowning is a terrible thing."

"It is." Though I forgot about the instance initially, my confrontation with Molay has unlocked the memories.

Victor looks at me with so much love, as if it's his daughter he sees instead of me. "I'm glad you made it out of those waters to become the wonderful woman you are."

"I don't know about that," I mutter, flustered.

"Alix, I know we had a disagreement, but never once doubt your greatness. Don't let Voltaire hear it, but greatness comes in many forms and shapes. Even if no one else will ever acknowledge all you've done for us ghosts, we will remember."

"So, you won't shun me when I'm dead?"

He laughs softly. "I could never. You belong to the Panthéon, whether you're buried here or not."

Chapter 4

After three more nights of nightmares, I finally accept that my father won't be able to move on from this on his own. Rather than taking him to a psychiatrist, I invite him on a walk to Père Lachaise.

"The cemetery?"

"When was the last time you visited Grandma?" I purposefully don't add "grave" since that's not what we're going to visit.

My father rubs his neck, slightly flustered. "I'm not much of a cemetery visitor."

"Oh, she's noticed."

"What?"

I pat his arm as we exit the Métro at Alexandre Dumas. "There is something I need to tell you."

"Is it about that boyfriend of yours?"

I'm not quite ready to talk about *that*, though technically it is. "No, it's about what happened in the catacombs, and… about me."

He looks at me curiously. "I'm intrigued, carry on."

Together, we make the short walk to the Père Lachaise cemetery. "You know how when I was a little kid I wouldn't shut up about seeing ghosts?"

Papa laughs warmly. "Oh, yes, you had your maman pretty worried."

"But not you?"

"The ghosts never seemed to hurt you. I mean, sure, it was probably your way of coping with your grandmother's death, but any time you talked about them, you seemed excited. You weren't sad or anything, just telling wild stories."

"Well, I wasn't telling stories." He raises an eyebrow and I take a deep breath. "I never stopped seeing ghosts. I just shut up about it."

"What are you saying?"

"Look around."

Dutifully, Papa looks around the cemetery. Fresh snow has covered most of the graves, but that doesn't deter the flocks of ghosts moving around, some of them dressed as if it was the height of summer. "What am I looking at?"

Doubt enters my mind, maybe Gaspar was just a fluke, after all. "Don't you see all these people?"

"Oh, yes. There's a lot of them, right? I wonder if a tour bus dropped them all off for Jim Morrison or whether they're burying someone new here."

"They're dead."

The air leaves my father's lungs all at once. "Come again."

"All the people you see, well, most of them are dead. They're the ghosts of those buried here." I point to a group of ghosts who hang out around their graves like no living would ever dare.

Papa laughs nervously. "No, they're not. They're..." He pauses. His keen journalist eye is picking up on all the inconsistencies in the ghosts' dress, the different eras, the incorrect seasonal outfits, and the way they pay little attention to the path. At last, his gaze lands on the ground. "There are no footprints."

That's right. Despite countless ghosts moving about, the only footprints in the snow are those of my father and I, and another visitor and their dog. "Do you believe me now?"

"Alix? What's happening? Why am I seeing this?" His voice has become a hushed whisper, the fear lurking not too far from its edges. Straight to the point as always, though.

"Because something terrible happened in the catacombs. An event so dramatic it made you cross the line between living and dead. I'm sorry." With one glance I realise I need to be a lot more specific if I want him to believe me. "You've become a ghost whisperer, like me."

"Alix, you..." He pauses, and I know exactly what he's thinking. "You've been seeing ghosts all this time?"

I shrug half-heartedly. "I told you. No one believed me, though."

Papa breathes flatly, looking like he's about to pass out on me. "Does that mean…" He swallows. "Does that mean we're really going to visit my mother."

With a smile, I pull him along. "Yes. She's going to be so excited. She always asks me how you're doing, and she's so proud of all your articles. You've got a fan."

He chuckles softly. "She's always been a fan. I'm not quite sure ghosts read the papers, though."

"Oh, you have no idea what they get up to when they're bored."

Obviously, he's still a bit reluctant, but his job taught him to just roll with it, observe, and then come to a conclusion later. I know that a visit with a ghost he knows to be dead is going to convince him.

We arrive at my grandmother's grave, but she seems to be out. Only Beatrice is there to greet us, which is a curious sight as the two of them are usually joined at the artificial hip. She looks at me inquisitively, wondering whether I'll talk to her in the presence of someone else.

"Salut, Beatrice. Is my grandmother not around?"

Delighted, she claps her hand and comes to me. "Oh, Estelle is enjoying a late-night stroll."

"On her own?"

"Not exactly," she answers with a twinkle in her eyes. Then she takes a good look of my father who hasn't stopped staring. "You must be Rémy. I remember you speaking at Estelle's funeral."

"You knew my mother?"

Beatrice smiles warmly then pats her tomb stone. "That's mine, darling. We're plot neighbours."

I see the moment my father's heart sinks to his knees. He takes in the information on the tombstone, recognises that I called her by the name engraved on it, then finds out she died four months before my grandmother. "You're dead."

"Have been for a good fifteen years or more. I couldn't keep track of time when I was alive. It's only gotten worse since." Beatrice laughs, then looks at him with concern. "Would you like to sit?" She offers her gravestone. "Go on, Alix does it all the time."

When he staggers, I take his arm and gently lead him to the stone, so he can lean against it. "It takes some time to get used to." He didn't have the advantage of youth that I had. When I'd figured out some of the people I'd met were dead, it was just another weird thing in the life of Alix. But I was a child. We process things differently.

"That must've been so hard for you." Even completely overwhelmed he thinks of me first.

I shrug. "Some of it. Anyway, here she comes."

My grandmother is indeed strolling down the hill, but she's not alone. A familiar figure is leading her like the old gentleman that he is.

"Did she finally give in?" I ask Beatrice.

"A certain event made him seem worthy of a little indulgence," she says with much amusement.

"He promised not to tell."

"Oh, he didn't. But you know ghosts. We love to gossip. You didn't truly think something like that would stay quiet when several Panthéon ghosts and our favourite ghost whisperer were involved."

"Who's that with my mother?" my father asks, fortunately concentrating on the other matter at hand.

Alexandre bends to kiss my grandmother's fingers and bids her farewell.

"He fought in the Great Revolution and is buried at de Picpus."

"The Great..." Papa exhales sharply and holds on to the stone. "This is a lot."

"I know."

My grandmother strolls over, sighing happily. Her face changes dramatically when she sees who is waiting for her. "Rémy?"

"He can see us now, dear," Beatrice whispers. "It's all very new."

My grandmother searches my face, trying to understand how this could've happened. Since we've discussed my whisper ghost, she clearly knows what has caused this wondrous ability. A mother's worry washes over her. "Are you?"

"Alive," I say quickly before she draws the wrong conclusion. "Like me."

She staggers forward, looking upon her son in wonder. His eyes follow her similarly. At last, she runs her hands over his face, marvelling at the sensation of touch. "Oh, my boy."

Beatrice and I leave the two alone to give them some time to adjust. "He's been struggling a bit with what happened in the catacombs."

"And you?" Beatrice asks. "How have you been?"

"Surprisingly alright. Gaspar and I decided to give our relationship another chance."

"Very good. He's such a nice boy."

"Yes, he is."

My gaze wanders to the top of the hill where Abelard's and Héloïse's crypt is situated. The two ghosts are taking care of my younger self. I know it was the right decision, but I'm suddenly overcome with a deep sense of yearning. Petite Alix and I had no time to reacquaint ourselves with each other.

I think of Sébastien and Dix and how close their bond is. Technically, they're the same person, but they seem much more like brothers or best friends; if only they weren't after my whisper abilities.

There's a good reason Petite Alix is where she is, and I dare not endanger that, even though I mourn the lost chance.

Beatrice leans over and whispers in my ear, "You did well, my dear. You brought those two peace in a way they've never experienced."

That's true. Abelard and Héloïse deserve a chance at a little family. And Petite Alix deserves someone who has all the time in the world to look after an eternal three-year-old. My peace of mind must come second. First, I have to make sure my father is adjusting well to his new condition.

But as I watch him and his mother reconnect, cautiously happy, I feel he's on the right track at last.

I decide to give them some time and wander off. It's probably no surprise that my feet carry me towards Abelard and Héloïse's hill. I know I should stay away, but there's a longing inside me that I can't quite grasp. And burning curiosity. Have the three of them gotten used to each other? Did my plan work at all? Is she safe? Are they happy?

"Mademoiselle Dubois?"

Startled, I whirl around. In front of me stands a man I've never seen before, though perhaps "man" is a little too generous. He can't be twenty yet, his face still bare. His old-fashioned clothes identify him as a ghost, which makes me feel a little better. "Yes?"

"It's an honour, really." He tips his hat. Despite his young age, he seems much more mature than boys like him these days. "Pierre Roche, at your service."

His name tickles a memory, but I can't quite place it. An artist perhaps? Or a pianist? It's certainly not an unusual name. "Hello, Pierre. Do I know you?"

"We haven't had the pleasure, although you may have heard of me. Word on the street is you're familiar with our country's history."

Oh dear, this is going to be a test. I'm no fashion expert, but the long coat, the fedora, and the hair that's been smoothed down with a shiny pomade make me think he's from the '30s or '40s. "Were you in the Second World War?"

Pierre's face lights up. "Very good. But I didn't fight in the war."

"No." I've seen the soldiers. Those who died in the trenches often wear their uniforms and helmets. "Vichy France, then?"

He nods. "I'm not quite sure it's an honour, but I was the first Résistante to be shot on the streets of Paris."

"For what?"

"Cutting the telephone lines between La Rochelle and Royan."

It's all coming back to me now. He was just a footnote in the long struggle of the Résistance against Vichy France and the Germans. The first victim of the oppressors. "I'm sorry."

"Don't be. It was a worthy cause, and I would've died a million times over if it had helped my countrymen."

"Really?"

He cocks his head and for a moment I can see the sliver of the boy who thought he wouldn't get into trouble for his act of resistance. Not like this.

"I've had a long time to observe time. Did you know that ghosts helped the Résistance?"

Fascinated, I shake my head. "No, I didn't. How did they do that?"

"By passing messages between the different groups. If they had ghost whisperers like you. Of course, the Germans had ghost whisperers too, so some groups were compromised when the enemy ghosts found them."

I wonder how many betrayals weren't caused by defectors but by ghost spies. "This is all very interesting. Were you a spy too?"

"Indeed." He fills his chest, a proud gleam in his eyes. "Never got caught."

"Thank you... for your service, I suppose." I'm not quite sure what to say. The Second World War was a long time ago, and as interesting as this is, I'm not quite sure what Pierre expects. All I know is that I need to know more about him. "What brings you to me, Pierre?"

"Right. Got a little distracted there." He takes off his hat and clutches it to his chest. "Mademoiselle Dubois, I have a proposition for you."

"A proposition?" Is this another favour?

Pierre nods. "Your recent actions in the ghost world have led me to believe you'd make an excellent member of the Résistance."

"The Résistance?" It seems to me Pierre is still trapped in the world he lived in. There is no Résistance in modern France, and I can hardly join the old one retroactively. Not that I want to. I have enough problems in the present.

"Yes, you have the courage to stand up to those in power and protect those who can't protect themselves. As I said, an excellent choice."

Flustered, I feel my cheeks blush. "Thank you. That's very kind of you."

"Alix?" my father calls out in the night.

"I have to go but thank you for the offer."

"Think about it! We could use a whisperer like you."

I give him a noncommittal smile and hurry down the path, back to my grandmother's grave. "Are you ready to go?"

"Yeah, I think I need to lie down."

"Okay." I turn to my grandmother, who smiles at me. "Did you have a good talk?"

"We did, my dear. Thank you for bringing him to me."

We hug as my father looks on with a pained grimace. I say goodbye to Beatrice before following Papa. "How did it go?"

"I..." He breaks off and sighs. "This is all very confusing, Alix."

"Sorry."

"It's not your fault. I just... I need time. That's all."

"Of course."

Longingly, I look over my shoulder. The world of ghosts is magnificent, but he can't see it yet. The chance to reconnect with dead relatives, to learn about history straight from the source, or to meet new exciting acquaintances with strange propositions. Me, a resistance fighter... Only in ghost world.

CHAPTER 5

As promised, Gaby and I will go out with Marie. To make sure I don't bail, we're getting ready at my place. I let her take full control of the hair and make-up department since my experience is limited to a relaxed daytime look. Gaby has gone full colour for her own style: her blond hair is streaked with blue and red, as if we're celebrating Bastille Day and not Christmas in a couple of days. Her eyes are accentuated with glitter and tiny stars. It's a look that works incredibly well with her bubbly personality.

My own look is "more classy", as Gaby calls it. Some killer smokey eyes, eyeliner and mascara, with only a touch of gloss on my lips. All courtesy of her much steadier hand.

Gaby is just about to finish and move on to my hair when a knock sounds on my door. Without waiting for a response, Odile opens it. "Do you have time?" She pauses. "Oh, where are you going?"

"Out," Gaby says, leaving me wondering if it's an answer or an order.

Odile hops into the room and sits on my bed. "Where to?"

Gaby takes a deep breath. "Le Bibi."

Odile gasps. "I've always wanted to go there. Can I come?"

"What do you want, Odile?" I ask, saving Gaby from making that decision.

"Ugh." Odile groans. "We have a history exam next week. Like, literally three days before Christmas. It's so stupid." She lies down on my bed, all limbs stretched out like a starfish, as if the mere announcement of the exam has already defeated her. "It's all about the Second World War and the Résistance, and I just don't get it."

And there it is again, the Résistance.

While Gaby combs my hair, I say, "You have to be a bit more specific. Is it the lead-up to the occupation, the formation of the Résistance, or the civil war between the Maquis and the Milice?" It's been a hot minute since Gaby and I took 20th century history. Both of us are more interested in the 18th and 19th century and France's bloody path from an absolutist monarchy to a stable republic.

Odile looks at me. "All of that. Like, who organised it? I feel like there's a million different groups all doing their own thing."

"Because that's pretty much what it was until Jean Moulin brought the biggest groups of the Résistance together and united them behind Charles de Gaulle." And two months later, he was betrayed, tortured, and killed for it. Sometimes I forget what a horrible, horrible time it was.

Jean once told me that the worst thing was that his murderer lived a long life and was only held accountable at the very end. Did he regret any of it, I asked him once, putting his head out like that when he had the chance to flee? Not once.

"Can you talk me through it, just so I understand it, at least. I probably won't remember all the names and dates, but if I can show I've got an understanding of the events, it'll be enough for now."

"We don't have time for that," Gaby says.

"Not today, Odi," I say. "But maybe tomorrow."

That seems to pacify her a little. The smile returns as all thoughts of World War II are pushed away. "So, can I come?"

Gaby pauses, looking at me. "It might be good in case... you know?"

She doesn't need to say it. In case everything goes well for her and Marie, I'll have my sister around. "That's not exactly a draw."

"Oh, don't be like that." Gaby slaps my shoulder.

"Yes, don't be like that," Odile echoes. "Please. My friends are all busy learning, and I can't stay in this house another night listening to Papa toss and turn and moan in his sleep."

Despite reconnecting with his mother, it doesn't seem to have helped his condition. Not for the first time I wonder about his whisper ghost. If he exists, he'd still be in the Boutique of Psychosis. Maybe if I bring the two together, he can finally heal and move on. But that's a problem for another day.

Today, I don't want to think about ghosts or the nightmare that is the Boutique, and just dance the night away with my girl. Or rather, girls.

"Fine. But we're leaving in ten minutes."

Le Bibi is on the outskirts of the Marais. It has an outside terrace, which is completely snowed under and currently not in use. Although the temperatures are below zero, a line of freezing women and a few men wraps around the building. Odile has to prove that she's eighteen, but other than that we have no problems getting in. Inside, Le Bibi is decorated with subtle fairy lights for the season, and the bar is offering some sort of mulled wine cocktail. It's there that we meet up with Marie.

"Hey." Kisses are exchanged among the four of us, and I introduce Odile and Marie to each other.

"Shall we get drinks first or hit the dance floor?" Gaby asks, her eyes practically glued to Marie, who is wearing neon-bright fishnets, a tight dress, and reindeer antlers.

Marie takes Gaby's hand, grinning from ear to ear. "Let's dance!"

I elbow Odile, who's looking a bit confused, and follow the other two on the dance floor. "Who is she again?" Odile whispers.

"Marie."

"Marie who?"

My usual explanation that she's Gaspar's workmate would lead to too many questions. "Just a friend."

Odile frowns, but someone jostles her from the side, breaking the spell, and we finally join up with Gaby and Marie again, who are already swaying their hips and rocking with the beat. True to Gaby's promise, Le Bibi isn't completely packed. It's full, but people still have the luxury of personal space on the dance floor.

I usually don't care much for clubbing, but all that goes out the window as the music hits my ears and Gaby laughs. No one is watching or judging us, and soon I let go of all my inhibitions and lean into it. I'm not much of a dancer, but that doesn't matter. None of us are, and we're all just having fun, laughing as much as we're dancing.

After a while, it gets a little hot, and I know I need to take a break to hydrate. I lean into Gaby, letting her shimmy down on my body. "I'm gonna get a drink. Do you want one, too?"

"I'll join you in a minute," she says, already laughing and twirling under Marie's arm.

I leave them to it and make my way over to the bar to order a glass of wine that doesn't cost me an arm and a leg. While I wait, my breathing recovers slowly.

"Hey, there, pretty girl."

I nearly jump, but I'd recognise that voice anywhere. Gaspar is leaning against the bar in an open spot, wearing his usual obscure band hoodie, yet looking as if he belongs. It's the music, I decide.

"What are you doing here?" I mumble because I'm trying not to move my lips too much.

Gaspar moves a bit closer, watching the bartender as she hands me my glass. "Do you think I could stay away from a party?"

"It's a girls' night out."

He grins, now close enough for our shoulders to touch. "You look beautiful."

In all honesty, I absolutely love that he's here. Something about our first date at an underground rave brings back a lot of exhilarating memories. We had our first kiss after, long before I knew how complicated it would all get.

I turn around to lean against the bar and look for Gaby and Marie. "Oh, well, I suppose they no longer need me," I whisper as I put the glass of wine against my lips. In front of us, in the middle of the dance floor, Gaby and Marie are kissing, the music all but forgotten.

"Then can I have the next dance?"

"I have to drink my wine," I manage to say before bursting into giggles. "Yes."

Gaspar snakes an arm across my shoulder and holds me while I sip from my glass. "We should do this more often," he whispers, his lips brushing my neck. "I love the sweat glistening at your hair line. The flush of red on your cheeks."

If the heat in my face is anything to go by, my cheeks are only growing redder. "Stop it," I chide him, amused. "You're making me…" I bite my lip, avoiding someone's curious stare and drink again.

"Making you what?" Gaspar asks in an even softer voice, while he presses his lips to my shoulder and strokes my side with his other hand. I shudder in anticipation.

"Dance," I say a little too loud, before downing the rest of my wine and pushing off the bar.

Gaspar's husky laugh follows me. It's a sound that's going to get me into deep trouble.

I return to the spot where Gaby and Marie are still intertwined with each other, but don't make my presence known. I'm glad this plan of Gaby's has worked out just as she imagined. The wine I drank too fast is rising to my head, making me slightly dizzy as I start dancing with Gaspar.

Normally, I wouldn't be caught dead dancing on my own in a club, but technically, I'm not dancing alone. Gaspar is there, right with me, directing my movements with his own dance moves or pressing his body against my back. If anybody else is paying me attention, I don't really care. Let the Théos of this world think what they want to think about me. I'm having fun with my man under the flashing lights and hammering beats.

Time loses all meaning as one song flows into the next, much like it did back in the catacombs. When a rare slow melody comes on, Gaspar wraps his arms around me and kisses my neck. I lean back, almost losing my balance. I'm definitely losing my mind over these intimate touches that no one else can see, much less feel. Just as I'm about to fall deeper into it, an unbidden thought appears in my mind: *I wish this were real.*

I stagger forward, my head reeling. This *is* real. Why would I think anything different when I can still feel the burn of his kisses on my skin?

"Alix?" He touches my shoulder lightly.

"I need a break," I manage to say. After a short moment of orientation, I discover Gaby and Marie have moved to one of the seating areas, apparently locked at the lips. I'm jealous they don't have to worry about their affectionate display being odd to anyone. Not in this club, at least.

My gaze finds the restroom. "I'll be back in a moment."

The wine is definitely messing with my sense of balance. At least it feels like that in my head. I should probably get some fresh air after I make use of the toilet. But one thing after the other.

I use a hand on the wall to steady myself and make my way down some stairs. It's fairly dark down here and I can't help but wonder what it would be like to bring Gaspar with me and make out in one of the dark corners. *No, Alix,* I tell myself, *you're gonna embarrass yourself.*

But it would be hot.

It appears I'm not the only one with that idea. When I leave the restroom, half a river of pee and a couple of splashes of cold water against my flushed skin later, I hear snuffling behind the stairs. At first I want to go past, but then I realise the sound of crying is familiar. Not that I'm used to hearing it very often.

"Odi?"

I had all but forgotten about my little sister in all the excitement. Now I realise I hadn't seen her since I first went to get a drink. And truly, Odile is sitting in the dark behind the stairs, hiccupping. "What's happened?"

She clicks her tongue and wipes her tear-stained cheeks but struggles to breathe at the same time. "Gaby."

"Did something happen to Gaby?" How much did I miss?

"Yeah, well, *Marie* did."

"Marie... Oh." Realisation hits me suddenly. Surprised, I gasp. "Were you...? Did you...?"

Odile grimaces as if in pain. "Have a crush on her? For years!"

Think, Alix. This is important. "I didn't know."

"I didn't tell you," she snaps.

Of course she didn't. Odile and I aren't close the way Hélène and I once were. "I didn't even know you liked girls." I suddenly feel like the worst big sister in history.

"I like both, or everyone," Odile says with a shrug. "Doesn't really matter."

I finally get over myself and take a step forward. "Can I sit?" There's half a shoulder shrug and half a mumble, which I take it means no, but really, yes. Without further ado, I sit down and put my arms around her. "I'm sorry."

Odile immediately falls apart in my arms, resuming her sniffling and hiccups. "I thought we had something. She always texts me and she likes every post I do about Malou and comments with a heart."

"Why didn't you tell me?" Not that I could imagine Odile and Gaby together. In my mind, they're sisters, just like she and I are.

"Because you don't like me."

"What?"

Odile takes a deep breath and looks me straight in the eye. "You never tell me anything about your life. It's always Hélène or Gaby. Never me. And every time I go into your room, you tell me to leave."

"Oh, Odi." The guilty conscience is almost as bad as the wine. "I'm sorry I made you feel that way. Of course I like you. You might be annoying at times, but you're my little sister, and you can always, *always* come to me." Somehow I missed this, but I'm vowing to do better. I will not judge her like Hélène judges me, no matter what it is.

"I'm not annoying," Odile protests. Her tears have slowed down. "You're just weird."

I kiss her hair. "I love you too, Odi."

She wraps her arms around me and snuggles close, her actions speaking louder than any words could.

CHAPTER 6

"Did you make any progress with finding your whisper ghost yet?"

I've dreaded this text since we escaped the Boutique. I'm actually impressed it has taken Sébastien this long to start nagging. He must be bogged down with Christmas shopping or the paperwork my little excursion caused. Either way, my time is up. It seems everything the Chevalier told me was true. All GoPol cares about is finding my whisper ghost and removing me from the playing field.

Of course, I've long since found Petite Alix, but Sébastien isn't going to know that. Now I just need to find a way to get him off my back for good. As I walk home from the Métro station, I think about how to phrase my answer. How can I be blunt enough to be understood, but not make myself suspicious.

Finally, I type, *"Not really. Look, I've been fine without my whisper ghost for twenty years. I don't think I need her."* After all,

Sébastien has yet to come up with a valid explanation of why it's so important I should be followed around by a three-year-old.

He texts back almost immediately. *"It's important."* As usual, he's not even trying. *"Don't give up on it. We'll find her."*

I consider telling him how I don't *want* to find her but decide to just ignore him instead. I'll just have to pretend I'm too busy until he gives up.

It begins to snow again, and I quicken my steps to get out of the cold. Getting my key into the lock with gloves on is a bit tricky, but I make it into our stairwell. My shoes leave slush on every step as I climb to the fourth floor. They're almost dry by the time I kick them off in front of the door. As I search for a place on the rack, I notice Hélène's chic boots: faux leather with mid-sized heels and braided detail. It's almost enough for me to consider putting my shoes back on and going for a long walk around the block.

I convince myself that it's stupid. My sister is just worried about me and for good reason. If my heart-to-heart with Odile taught me anything, it's that I should put a little more effort into my relationships with my sisters.

As soon as the door closes behind me, Hélène ambushes me. "Finally. What took you so long?"

"Work." What's happened this time?

"We need to talk." She grabs my arm and pulls me into my room against my protests.

"What's the matter? Did you remember anything else or—?"

Hélène pushes the door shut with more strength than needed. "*I* just had a chat with Papa!" She's furious. "Care to explain why he can suddenly see ghosts? He told me you took him to Père Lachaise. To *meet* our grandmother."

"And they had a really nice chat." All my lofty plans about making an effort with Hélène go out the window. It's as if our talk the other day never happened. I'm the unreasonable one all over again.

"Alix! This isn't funny!" She nearly spits the last word. "You told me that the only way to become a ghost whisperer like you is to have a near-death experience. I know you took Papa down in the catacombs with you. So I want to know what happened! How did you get our father killed?"

I gasp at the accusation. "Excuse me?"

Hélène crosses her arms. "You heard me. How. Did. You. Get. Papa. Killed!"

"He's alive."

"He can see ghosts." Hélène looses her stance and rubs her forehead in desperation. "I'm sorry. You're right. He's alive, but he's obviously not well. Which... Please, would you tell me what truly happened?"

I'm not quite ready to move on as fast from her accusations as she is. "It's none of your business."

Her eyes nearly bug out. "*Excuse* me? This is *our* father we're speaking about."

"Yeah, whom you're accusing me of murdering in the cata-combs."

Hélène sighs heavily. "I didn't say you murdered him. Just... why did you have to drag him into your ghost things? Isn't it bad enough your life revolves around ghosts? Did you really need to drag him into this, too?"

She's making it incredibly hard to stay calm. Sure, some of it is valid concern, but it's delivered in such a way that I just can't answer without spewing acid. "I know you think my life is some horrible mess, but there's actually nothing wrong with talking to ghosts. Nor seeing them. I don't know why Papa can see them all of a sudden. He didn't *die.* But I'm going to fix this. So, take your prejudice and your accusations, and just leave me alone."

"Alix..."

"No. I've had enough of this. You didn't believe me until Cédric told you how wrong you were. I trusted you and you've thrown that trust in my face, gaslighting me at every step. What made my life miserable wasn't seeing ghosts. It was being repeatedly told that I wasn't normal and needed professional help." There, I've finally said it. How many years did I waste conforming my life to what other people thought of me? What Hélène thought of me.

Hélène pales. Her lips are shaking, but instead of actually lis-tening to what I'm saying, she lashes out. "Well, seeing ghosts *isn't* normal. It's real, I give you that, but it's a far cry from normal. And it doesn't excuse dragging Papa into it."

"Yeah, god forbid someone in this family understands me."

"Is that why you did it?"

"I didn't *do* anything," I spit. "The catacombs are dangerous in their own right and he chose to come along, because we're both adults." I'm so not getting into the whole Molay thing with her. Partly because I'm not sure I won't scratch her eyes out if we continue, and partly because I might have to admit that it's my fault after all.

Which is why I'm going to fix it. Alone.

"You can go now."

Hélène huffs. "You are so stubborn, Alix. Insufferable."

"Right back at you."

She almost stomps her feet but settles for an indignant glare at me before storming out of my room.

I let out a huge sigh and drop into my desk chair. A moment later, I feel my shoulders being massaged. An instant smile slips on my face. "Did you hear that?"

"Every word," Gaspar admits. "Man, I'm suddenly glad I'm an only child. Though I suppose my parents would give your sister a run for her money."

I put my hand on his, stilling the massage, and take a couple of deep breaths while I fight the tears in my eyes. It's in vain. "She's right, you know. I did this to my father."

"No." Gaspar walks around and kneels in front of me, holding my hands and looking up at my face. "Jacques de Molay did."

"But I—"

"You're not to blame. That's like me blaming myself for taking that bike route, for sleeping in that day, for not watching the traffic enough to realise a white van would run me over. It's useless. It was an accident. What happened to your father is the same. There was no way you could've known Molay would flip like that. Or that he even had those powers. This isn't your fault, Alix."

The tears fall despite his words. He's right, of course. If I'd known how dangerous Molay was, I would've never brought my father down there. Heck, *I* wouldn't even have gone there. It still feels like my fault, though.

"We need to go back."

Gaspar frowns. "What for?"

"To find his whisper ghost. If it doesn't exist, my father needs therapeutic help. If it does, then taking him from the Boutique might be what he needs to heal." While I don't believe Petite Alix can physically help me with my challenges, I'm craving the connection between us. It's probably the same for my father. He's missing half of himself. The half that died in Molay's grasp.

"Okay. So, we'll go—"

Gaspar is interrupted by a knock on the door.

"I'm done talking," I say, expecting Hélène to be back for round two.

The door opens nonetheless. "It's me." Instead of my older sister, Odile sticks her head in. "Can *I* come in?"

Initially I think of sending her out, but that would destroy any progress we made yesterday. So, instead, I wipe my tears and force a smile. "What's the matter?"

Odile comes in and closes the door behind her. "You and Hélène were pretty loud."

"Is that your way of telling me you were eavesdropping?"

Gaspar moves back a little to give us some space.

"It didn't take that much," she admits. "Ghosts?"

I groan. This is exactly what I feared. Odile will make fun of me for believing in ghosts, completely missing how real this is for me. But then I remember what she told me last night. That I never share things with her.

It's because of how badly I was burnt by Hélène. Perhaps I should give her a chance. "Sit."

Excited, Odile takes a place on my bed. In the meantime, I go to Malou's cage and lift her out. She's just waking up and eager to stretch her legs, but for now, I'll take whatever comfort I can find.

With Malou in my arms, I sit next to Odile. "You need to promise that you won't hold this against me. Like, don't make fun of me or tell me I need to see a shrink. No judgement. Swear it on Malou."

Odile's eyes grow bigger. Without hesitating, though, she gently puts her hand on Malou's spikes. "I swear."

"Okay. So." I rub Malou's belly while I try to find a way to explain my ability in a way that won't challenge her oath too much. "When I was three-years-old, I almost drowned in the Seine."

Odile gasps but keeps her mouth shut, eager to listen.

"Ever since then I've been able to see ghosts, though I didn't realise that until Grandma Estelle's funeral. To me, ghosts appear like normal people. I can talk to them, and I can touch them. It makes it really hard to recognise someone's dead. In the beginning, Hélène was all onboard. We visited Grandma together, and she made me talk to all kinds of ghosts. And then she grew out of it."

"Sounds like Hélène."

"Yeah. She's so grown-up. Well, as it turns out, there are other people who can see ghosts. Cédric's cousin even works for the ghost police, which is part of Interpol. So, clearly, I'm not making this up."

Odile shakes her head. "I never said you did."

"Yet." With another sigh, I let go of Malou so she can start her evening circuit around my room. "Anyway, after accompanying me to the catacombs, Papa has started seeing ghosts, as well, which has Hélène up in arms, because obviously, it's all my fault."

Odile bats at the air with a disgusted snort. "Forget that stuck-up prissy. She doesn't know what fun is."

"Ghosts aren't fun. They're just... ghosts." I glance at Gaspar, who gives me a reassuring smile.

Unfortunately, Odile follows my gaze. "Is there one in here, right now?" She sounds way too excited about the whole matter. "Tell me, please."

He shrugs, which I guess is supposed to mean I should go ahead. "Yes, there's a ghost here."

"I knew it! I heard you talking in your room before and it wasn't to Malou."

My cheeks are burning as I fervently hope she only heard me talking and nothing else. "Mhm."

"Tell her," Gaspar urges. "You've always wanted to introduce me to your family. Maybe there's a way."

Tormented, I grimace. I really want to introduce Gaspar to my family like a normal boyfriend, but as Hélène said, I'm not normal. On the other hand, it's one thing to believe I can see ghosts, quite another to get behind a ghost boyfriend. Even Gaby's struggling with that.

"Who is it?" Odile has moved up on her knees, wrapped up in excitement. She looks roughly in Gaspar's direction. "Please, I swore I wouldn't judge. I won't."

"Fine." I gather myself. Maybe I just need to plunge in full steam ahead. "His name is Gaspar—"

I don't get any further because Odile gasps. "Oh my god, is he your boyfriend? Do you have a ghost boyfriend?"

"Odi."

"I'm not *judging!*" she exclaims loudly. Then she breaks into a smile. "I love this. It's so unique. You just jumped several levels on the coolness scale." She sits back. "All this time, I thought you were so boring, but you had this secret life all the time."

I can't help it. Her enthusiasm eases the hold on my heart that has been there ever since Hélène turned on me. "Yes, he's my boyfriend. We've been together since... Well, we had a couple of hiccups, but I've known him since October."

"Is it your first?"

"Boyfriend?"

"Ghost boyfriend."

"Yes. And I didn't know he was a ghost when we had our first kiss," I admit.

"Sorry," Gaspar mutters.

I throw him a loving glance. It really wasn't his fault. "Anyway, that's what's been happening."

Odile nods, her eyes gleaming. "This is amazing." Then she hits my shoulder. "You should've told me earlier!"

"You really believe me?"

"Duh! This explains so much. Your obsession with dead things. Your weird anti-social stance. You prefer hanging out with ghosts, don't you?" It's amazing how quickly Odile hones in on my entire personality.

I shrug in response. "They're more interesting. And they don't think I'm weird." Slowly, I relax against the wall. "Most of the time

I do small favours for them. Fix a misspelling on their grave, deliver a message, find a lost trinket." The last one got me into all this trouble.

Odile shakes her head in awe. "That's seriously so cool. Are they all recently departed or do you also meet older ghosts?" Before I can answer, her eyes widen. "Wait a minute. You work at the Panthéon. Is it full of ghosts?"

"Chock-full of ghosts."

Another gasp. "So, do you *know* them? Like are you friends with Marie Curie or whoever else is in there?"

"I try not to get too close to Marie and Pierre. Their ghosts glow, and I'd rather not find out how ghost radiation will affect me. But I am friends with a couple of the others. Mainly, Victor Hugo and…" I guess I'm not friends with Voltaire at the moment. "Hey, that reminds me. Do you still need help with your history exam? Jean Moulin is buried at the Panthéon."

Her eyes widen. "Yes, please." She claps her hands excitedly. "Oh my god, can we talk to him? Like can you ask him all my questions? I wish I could see them myself."

"I can relay your questions. Just be mindful that he's still a human being, so some questions—"

"Are a bit insensitive. Got it. He's a person, not a history book."

I'm actually stunned. It's the most emphatic thing Odile has ever said. The most anyone has ever said about ghosts. Even

Sébastien could learn something from my little sister. Maybe we're related, after all.

"See, that wasn't so bad," Gaspar says, smiling happily.

Just as I return his smile, I notice Malou under my table. "Malou, no!"

The little hedgehog has gotten into my secret Christmas present stack, tearing the paper to shreds. Annoyed, I get up from the bed to pick her up and examine the damage. It's a total write-off. I'll have to wrap it again.

I pluck a piece of paper from Malou's snout before she can swallow it. "You are one naughty little hedgehog. Do you want me to replace your escargot with lumps of coal?"

"Malou can't actually talk, can she?" Odile asks, at last a little doubtful.

"No, but she can smell ghosts. Here." I hand her to Gaspar for a clear as day proof.

To me, I see Gaspar lovingly cradle Malou and rub her belly, but to Odile, my hedgehog is floating just above desk height, purring softly as she enjoys the attention.

"Wow!" Odile's eyes are wide again. "We can do so many cool stunts for her account."

"What?"

"Just imagine it. Your ghost—Gaspar?—holds her while she hangs upside down like spiderman. Or she abseils from the Eiffel

Tower." She squeals. "I've got so many ideas for action shots. Her account will go viral."

Well, I'm glad there's a practical application in all of this. I check with Gaspar, and he grins. "Sounds fun to me."

"He's game," I relay to Odile.

"I already like him better than Cédric." She stops herself to look at him. "Welcome to the family, Gaspar."

My heart explodes with joy. I couldn't have asked for a better reaction from my little sister. Maybe Gaspar is right and we can make this work, despite him being invisible to the rest of them.

CHAPTER 7

The next day, I leave straight after my lectures to enter the catacombs. My plan is to trek to the Boutique, find my father's whisper ghost, and get out of there before morning comes. I only do a quick pit stop at home to pick up Malou and change into proper cataphile gear.

I haven't told anyone about this. Gaby would try and stop me, my father would get upset, and I currently want to stay as far away from Sébastien and the Chevalier as I can. The only ones who know about this are already dead: Gaspar is coming with me, of course, while Alexandre de Beauharnais is on standby.

It should be safe. The Chevalier's ritual broke Molay's hold on the Boutique. His bones have been removed, and his ghost is no more. Still, the fear creeps in as soon as I enter the catacombs. As familiar as the dark walls are by now, they remind me of what happened last time.

I'm about half an hour in when I first hear steps behind me. Someone else is in this tunnel. I pause despite Malou pulling on the leash, and sure enough the steps pause as well. When I resume walking, I can hear them clearly. They're not just another cataphile; they're following me.

My heart races a million miles an hour, causing my headlamp to shake. I reach for Gaspar, who immediately takes my hand. He only holds it for a second before letting go.

After a tense few moments, he returns. "It's your sister."

I whirl around. My beam cuts through the underground and lands squarely on my sister's face. "Odile?"

She has the decency to look sheepish. "Hi."

"What are you doing here?"

"Well, I thought you were off visiting the catacombs. That style is"—she waves her hand towards my overalls—"not exactly flattering."

"It's not supposed to flatter anyone. It's supposed to keep me dry."

"Oh." Odile bites her lips. She's certainly not dressed for the catacombs, wearing flats of all things. "I didn't know there was water in the catacombs."

I wonder if she knows anything about the catacombs. "It's an underground system with multiple entries attached to the sewer and water reservoirs. Of course some parts are flooded."

"What about Malou? She can't swim, can she?"

"I'll carry Malou when it comes to that." I massage my nose, knowing that I'm focusing on the wrong thing. "Why are you following me?"

Odile catches up and tries for a winning smile. "You're doing a ghost thing, right?" When I don't answer, the smile wavers and falls. "I knew you'd never let me come along, but I wanted to see it. This thing you do. The catacombs."

"What makes you think I won't send you back?"

She crosses her arms and raises her chin. "Because I won't let you. I'm eighteen and well in my rights to be here."

"Technically, it's illegal to be here."

Her eyes bug out. "What?"

I sigh. "Odi, I'm not doing this for fun. The catacombs are dangerous, very dangerous. For one, you didn't even bring a lamp."

"I've got a phone."

"As if that's going to last." I doubt she even charged it before following me. "Second, there are people down here who want to harm you. I had someone shoot at me."

Her eyes grow even bigger. "And you're still going? With Malou?"

"I have business to attend to." And I sort of had a chat with the shooter, agreeing to a truce. Again, sort of. As for Malou, without her, I would've been lost. "Third, some of the ghosts of the catacombs aren't happy about the living treading in their space."

Odile leans in to whisper, "How many ghosts are there?"

"Right here? Only Gaspar."

He waves sheepishly, though Odile can't appreciate the gesture.

"Oh." She shrugs. "So, what's the problem?"

"The problem is I don't want to risk another family member's health."

She raises an eyebrow. "*Another* family member?"

This isn't good. My sister has to leave. Going back will lose me a lot of time. I'd have to postpone my visit by nearly a week. It can't be helped. The most important thing is that I get her back to safety.

"Come on, let's get you home."

Odile shakes her head. "Absolutely not. I'm here now. We're doing this together."

"You can't force me."

"Well, you can't force me to leave." Again, that triumphant chin raise. "I'll just have to explore the catacombs by myself." To emphasise her point, she starts walking down the corridor.

I'm so dumbfounded, I can only stare at her back. And Hélène says I'm the one who takes unnecessary risks.

Next to me, Gaspar raises his shoulders. "She won't get far without help."

"It's dangerous." Especially where we're going.

"You don't know that. Molay has been defeated. His bones were removed. The Boutique should be like any other room down here. The most dangerous thing is her getting lost in the dark." When

I'm still hesitating, he takes my hand. "I'll scout ahead, enter the Boutique first, and let you know if danger's lurking."

That does the trick. I pull myself together and nod. Gaspar leans in to kiss me softly, and together with Malou, we catch up with Odile, who's been marching straight ahead with her phone torch on full blast.

"Thirty-two per cent. That's going to get you far."

Odile ignores me, unappreciative of my sarcasm.

I remind myself how well she reacted to the ghosts. If we're going to spend hours in the catacombs together, I might as well tell her all the rest. "It was Papa I got into trouble."

That piques her interest. "You did some boring history thing with him, didn't you?"

"Well, it was more of a ghost thing, but it had to do with history. The reason I believed I found the bones of Jacques de Molay was because Jacques de Molay told me they were his bones."

In the low light, Odile flashes me a bright grin. "Sneaky! I like it."

"Well, it went south pretty quickly." I tell her the whole story. With luck it might deter her from this foolish idea of going any deeper. At worst, she at least knows enough to properly judge me, unlike Hélène who judges first and inquires later.

It takes me most of the way to the Banga to relay the story because Odile keeps interrupting and asking for more details. In the end, I not only told her about Molay but also the Chevalier, Sébastien, Dix, and the whole whisper ghost dilemma.

"So, you found your own ghost? Was that creepy?"

"It's definitely weird. Like, objectively, I know that she's me, but we're also so far removed from each other that I can't marry the two images. Petite Alix is a baby."

Odile nods thoughtfully. "Does she act like one? Like, I know she doesn't grow but it's been, what, like, twenty years?"

"She didn't grow physically or mentally, so yes, she's very much a baby."

"Well, how's that going to help you?"

I'm so glad she gets it instantly I let out a huge breath. "Exactly. It's so obviously a front for something else."

"So you think Sébastien has it out for you? That he's lying?"

"He's definitely not telling me the truth. Or if he is, it's a very small portion of it."

We reach the Banga. The light beam ripples over the water and all thoughts of GoPol are gone for the moment. This is the "make it or break it" point for many cataphiles. It'll definitely be my sister's, with her tights. "We'll have to cross that."

"That's a lot of water."

"There's a path through here, but the water goes up to your hip before it hits shallows again. You still want to come?" It would be a pain to turn back now, but I still feel uncomfortable with taking her to the Boutique. None of what I've said about Molay and Papa's condition has scared her off, but this just might.

Odile regards the water for a long time. "Give me a minute to take off my tights."

"You want to take them off?"

"Does anything live in there? Like, are there fish or is the ground covered with icky plants?"

I shake my head. "No, but the water isn't safe."

"I'm not planning to drink it." Odile takes off her shoes and tights and holds them up triumphantly. "Now I'll have something dry to wear on the other side."

Gaspar whistles softly. "I like her."

"Let's do this, then." Odile's pragmatism is admirable. I know she's planning on a gap year after high school, but for the first time since I'd heard of it I think she'll be just fine.

We make our way across the water together. Me in my water-proof waders, Malou in a bag on my chest, and she barefoot, never complaining even once. On the other side, she puts her tights and shoes on again, and continues as if we'd never met an obstacle. She even exclaims, "That was fun."

"Really?"

"Yes!" Odile is grinning in the pale light. "I love this stuff. When I go overseas I want to do all the cool stuff, like abseiling into a cave and exploring it. This comes pretty close. I am a bit mad at you, though."

"About what?"

"About keeping this from me. I would've loved to help you help ghosts, you know? Especially the adventurous favours like this one."

So, my sister is a thrill seeker. I'm not sure whether that makes me worried or relieved. I can't deny how exhilarating it is, though. Here's someone who appreciates the entire process. Much like Gaby, only Gaby won't crawl into a tight tunnel unless it's a matter of life or death.

"Like this Emily chick? Yeah, I would've gone with you."

"It ended with me being shot at."

"No, it ended with you uncovering a crime, escaping the catacombs, and giving that Chevalier something to fear."

That's not quite how I remember it. "I don't think he fears me."

"Alix, he went from trying to shoot you to courting your favour. He knows it's better to have you in his corner than on the opposing team."

"I don't think I'm in anyone's corner."

She links her arm with mine and leans into me over-enthusiastically. "Yes, you are. You're firmly in the ghosts' corner, fighting for their rights, like one of those résistantes."

It reminds me of Pierre Roche's offer. Do I really have the characteristics of a resistance fighter? As admirable as they were, I've never felt connected to them.

"The résistantes didn't fight for anybody's rights but their own. It was a fight of survival for our people and culture against the oppressors. They cared very little about helping any underprivileged groups, and if so, only singularly or by accident."

Odile rolls her eyes. "Yes, professor Alix. A revolutionist, then."

"Fine." I raise my chin in mock acceptance. "I can live with that." At least, I'd like to think that I would've been on the side of the revolution if I'd lived two hundred years ago.

"Speaking of the Résistance, though. Did you know a lot of them used the catacombs to hide from the Germans? They even had underground listening stations. And rogue radio stations."

"Radio stations?"

"To pass on important messages to the Résistance from London." We might as well help her study for her history exam while we're doing this. "They would play a few notes of Beethoven's Fifth, which happens to be the Morse code for V, victory. If the code didn't play, the station was compromised, and you knew the Germans had seized control of the message. The thing was a lot of the members didn't know about each other. That was to protect the efforts. They formed groups like 'Combat' or 'Liberté' and communicated via those messages. I know we all like to be heroes in the end, but at that time, a lot of people denounced their countrymen. I don't just mean members of the Résistance who got caught and tortured to betray their fellow fighters, but thousands who eagerly reported on their neighbours if they found anything suspicious. If it weren't for the French people itself, the Germans would've had a much harder time to keep their hold. As it was, they barely had to do any work."

"Which is why it's sometimes referred to as a Civil War," Odile chimes in, questioning.

I sway my head. "Well, that was a bit later when they formed the Milice and the Maquis started assembling."

We talk a bit more about the later years of the occupation and how the catacombs served the Résistance in Paris. We're almost to the Boutique when Gaspar arrives back at my side from his scout mission. "There's a group of cataphiles on your way."

I instantly tense. "Cataphiles?"

"What is it?" Odile asks. "Is there a ghost?"

We came across several ghosts during our walk, but none of them engaged with us. This group, though, seems to be alive. I can hear them chatting deeper down the tunnel. "No, it's a group of people. Should be harmless." The emphasis is on *should* because in my mind all cataphiles work for the Chevalier, and he's anything but harmless.

It takes another minute or so for the group to reach our spot. It's three men, all dressed in similar thigh-high waders as me. They look about ten to twenty years older than me: seasoned cataphiles.

"Hey, there!" the one in the front calls, smiling wanly.

"Hey," I answer cautiously.

He glances at Malou. "Is that a hedgehog?"

"Yes?"

"Now I've seen it all." He shakes his head. "Hope you're not planning to stay the night in the Boutique," he says, unprompted. "We just tried and let me tell you, all the stories are true."

My breath shallows. "The stories? You mean about the psychoses?" The three of them look pretty sound of mind to me, but who knows?

The middle one looks over his shoulder before he nods hurriedly. "We didn't stay long enough to catch one, but it's definitely haunted or something. We heard moaning."

"And whimpering," the third adds.

"It was so creepy, and I usually don't scare easy," the first admits.

Gaspar separates from us again, squeezing past the men to survey the area.

Before I can reply, Odile says, "We don't scare easy either. We're actually ghost hunters, so that sounds perfect."

"You're braver than us, then," the third says, sounding amused at Odile's boast. "I wouldn't risk it."

"Thanks for the warning," I say before Odile can compromise us any more. "We're not going to stay the night, just checking something."

The first one nods. "Well, if you find a ghost, tell them to leave. They're scaring good cataphiles out of a sleeping spot."

"Good luck finding another," I tell them.

"Good luck to you, too." The second one tips his head, and then we all squeeze past each other.

We're not much further along when Gaspar returns to us. "Did you find any ghosts?"

Gaspar nods, sending a chill down my spine. "It's your Papa."

Chapter 8

There is no keeping me away from the Boutique now. Obviously, it isn't our living father who's awaiting us there, though, I guess, in a way he is. Odile and I hurry down the corridor until we reach the little window. I have to brace myself and push away all the dark memories of that fateful night with Molay. Ironically, it helps having Odile there, since I feel like I can't lose face in front of her now. With one deep breath, I climb through the narrow entrance.

The first thing I notice is how different the Boutique is. There's no illusion of a fancy salon anymore, and while there's still a column of bones, the supporting full-size skeleton is gone. Somehow, it's lighter than I remember, even though we're still very much underground. A layer of dust and rubble covers the ground, only disturbed where I, the Chevalier, and Sébastien writhed on the ground. The faint lines of a pentagram can still be seen, but a plethora of footsteps crosses the lines. Either it was us who left such a mess or the Boutique is a more popular cataphile spot than I'd thought.

Right now, I don't see anyone else. For the first time, the Boutique feels abandoned. When I listen into the darkness, though, I pick up the faint sounds of crying.

"Papa?"

He flickers into existence so suddenly it frightens me. It's the most ghostly thing a ghost has ever done in front of me. Papa's whisper ghost is kneeling in the middle of the broken pentagram, holding his ears, and swaying back and forth as he whimpers inconsolably.

"What is it?" Odile asks, keeping just behind my shoulder.

I need a couple of breaths before I trust my voice enough. "It's Papa. I mean, it's his ghost."

"Good. That's good, right?"

Slowly, I pick up pleading whispers in the whimpers. "Please let me go. Don't do this. Not again. Not again. I can't take it anymore. I just want to go home."

I share a glance with Gaspar, who looks just as worried as I feel. "Give me a moment, okay?" I tell Odile and hand her Malou's leash. Then I steel myself and approach the weeping ghost. "Papa?"

Just as I stretch my hand out, he flickers out of existence again. Startled, I find him bound to the column once more, writhing and screaming. It's such a horrifying appearance, I can only stand and stare. It takes me a couple heartbeats to recognise what's happening.

"He's burning. Oh my god, he's burning at the stake." I can almost see the flames dancing around the column, consuming my father's no longer existent body. "Wh-what do I do?"

"Well, he's not really burning, right?" Odile asks. "I mean, I don't see any flames. Then again, I don't see Papa either. Can't you snap him out of it?"

Snap him out of it? Stunned, I continue watching my father. Even though I know the flames aren't real, I can feel the heat of them. "Papa!" I call loudly.

He ignores me.

"Papa! Wake up!"

His screams just get louder. The flames burn higher.

It can't be helped. I stride towards him, grab his arm, and pull him away from the column. At least, I try. My father barely budges, and the longer I have my hand in the imaginary flames, the hotter it gets.

"Together," Gaspar says, grabbing hold of his other arm. I nod as he starts counting. "One, two, three!"

Our concerted effort is enough. My father comes loose so suddenly, all three of us stumble away from the column. I land hard on my backside, which makes Odile giggle.

When I glare at her, she shuts up instantly. "Sorry, it just looked funny."

I don't care what it looks like to anyone who can't see ghosts. My father has returned to weeping, resuming his position in front of the column. This time, when I approach him, he doesn't jump away.

Gently, I put my hand on his back. "Papa? It's me, Alix."

His whimper breaks off. Slowly, he raises his head, though his eyes stare at me blindly. "Alix? I can't see you. Everything is dark. Where are you? Are you hurt?"

I cradle his face in my hands. "I'm right here with you."

He blinks and slowly, the fog lifts from his eyes. A shuddering breath of relief follows. "There you are." He touches my face as if he needs to make sure it's really me. "What time is it?"

"It's close to midnight. On the seventeenth of December," I add, hoping it doesn't freak him out too much that he's lost almost three weeks.

Papa blinks, working through the information one word at a time. "The seventeenth?"

I nod.

"That doesn't make sense." He gets up, shaking his head. "You were right there, talking to someone. And then..." Dumbfounded, he turns around. "I couldn't see you, but I heard you. I heard you yelling—screaming, really. And fighting. There was a fight. Just now."

"No, Papa. All that was three weeks ago."

"But I heard it. Again and again and again. Alix, why... When did you get here?" he asks Odile when his gaze lands on her. "Did you follow us?"

Slightly overwhelmed, I put my hand on his cheek and force him to look at me again. "Odi can't see or hear you."

"Why not?"

"She's alive."

Papa frowns heavily. "What are you saying? That we're not alive? Did you die? Did I?" He stumbles away from me.

"No... I mean..." I need to take a deep breath. "I don't know what happened. From everything I know about ghosts, you died. But you're also alive."

"You're not making any sense, Alix." I'm starting to lose him.

"That's because you're split. At the moment of your death, whenever that was, you split. One half was brought back. The other remained. You remained here. Stuck in Molay's dark memories."

"The fire." A flicker of recognition crosses his face. "Molay was burnt at the stake. Just like me." Irritated, he looks to the ground. "No, that's not right. I wasn't burnt. I was... What happened to me?"

"You died." I wish there was more I could say. But the truth is I don't even know if that's true. People don't die just like that. Or rather, people don't come back from the dead on their own. If my father truly died here, he shouldn't be walking around.

My father stumbles further back, but before he can return to the column, Gaspar steps in. "Easy there. We don't want you lost to the nightmare again."

"That's right, Papa. We will figure this out. Upstairs. Just come with us and—"

Suddenly, light floods the Boutique and Odile shrieks. I hear a clatter and Malou's squeak, then heavy breathing.

"Odi?" My eyes struggle to adjust to the sudden brightness. When I finally manage to make out shapes, I find my sister hanging on to the banister of the metal staircase and Malou's leash. The poor hedgehog is hanging from the steps like a bungee jumper, pedalling in the air.

But they're not alone. The shape of a man bends down. "Molay!"

"Leave my daughter alone!" Papa shouts, all madness leaving him as he rushes up the stairs and pushes the man.

The moment his attack passes through him, I realise it's not Molay. But I know this one as well.

"Monsieur Laugier?"

Paul Laugier, the custodian of the Order of Malta, shines a torch at me. "Mademoiselle Dubois. Why does that not surprise me?"

Chapter 9

"Come on up!" Paul says harshly.

I'm still a little disoriented, but Gaspar steadies me and helps me to the spiral staircase. Once there, we help untangle Malou, and the little hedgehog clambers into my chest, her heart pounding away. "It's alright. I've got you." Then I look at my sister. "Are you okay?"

Odile catches her breath and nods. "Who's that?"

"Marie's uncle." There's no point in going into all that Maltese history now.

All four of us follow Paul up the stairs and through a trap door. By the time he locks the door behind us, my eyes have fully adjusted to the light and our new surroundings come into focus.

It's a small room with packed shelves and artificial light. Shelves line the walls, full of boxes and unwieldy objects that look suspiciously like shields and weapons. The floor is covered by a large round seal, seemingly carved into the stone around the trap door.

Paul is standing on it wearing a night robe, hastily thrown on trousers, and a stern frown. "You!" he bellows, almost as angry as the Nexus woman who came after me. "You're the one who messed with the Templar bones."

"W-wait, what?" When we first met Paul he was an interesting but unassuming chap. Someone with an interest in the history of the two knight orders, but also someone who feigned to have no knowledge of what had happened to Jacques de Molay. "You knew Molay's bones were down there?" No, more than that. "Your church is on top of the Boutique of Psychosis?"

"Is that what they call it?" Paul asks. "I try not to go down there very often, just to strengthen the wards, but I guess there's no use in doing that now. What did you do with Molay's bones?"

I know he's angry but so am I. He could've said something earlier.

"Look, I have no idea what you two are on about," Odile chimes in, "but maybe we could have this conversation somewhere else? That door leads somewhere, right?" She's pointing at a normal cellar door.

Paul sighs heavily. "You're right. It's too late to reverse what you've done. We might as well discuss what to do next over some tea. Follow me. Try not to disturb the sigil. Little does it matter now," he mutters.

Odile follows the priest out of the room without second-guessing it. I look at Gaspar, who simply shrugs. Meanwhile, my father is still standing near the trapdoor, which has four heavy bolts securing it to the floor and more sigils inscribed on it. He's sweating, his presence flickering.

I stretch out my hand. "Come on, Papa. We're almost home. You're safe now."

He hesitates but then he takes my hand, instantly solidifying, and nods. "Take me away from here. Please"

"I will." But not before I have a talk with Paul.

The priest seems to think the same, curiously looking at our intertwined hands—or rather mine. He doesn't say anything, though, and leads us to the same little room he entertained Gaby and me before. From what I remember, this little storage room must be located right under the altar.

On the way, a door opens and a sleepy Marie appears. "Uncle, what's this... Alix?"

Paul looks at her. "Marie, go back to... No, actually, I need to talk to Alix alone." He nods towards Odile, who looks more distressed to see Marie than she was about Paul's sudden appearance.

Marie blinks, taking a moment to orient herself. "Yes, of course. Odi, was it, right?"

"Odile," my sister says icily.

"Odile, of course, come with me. We'll make some tea and I can show you around or read your hand, if you want."

My sister looks at me, silently begging me to intervene. Knowing she'll be fine in Marie's care, I nod at her and trust her with Malou once more. "Go with her and make sure Malou gets some treats and water. I'll tell you later."

With the most dramatic sigh, Odile joins Marie on her way to the kitchen, while Paul opens the door for me, then glances at my hand again. "Alone, please."

Gaspar steps in. "I'll take care of you, Monsieur Dubois. Shout out if you need help." He kisses my cheek and gently leads my father away.

Paul nods to himself and steps into the room. He waits until I've taken a seat before closing the door behind us. "You're one of those who can see ghosts," he says in a weirdly accusing manner.

At least I don't have to keep that secret any longer. "And what are you?"

"A Knight Hospitaller and a priest. It is my sacred duty to guard the remains of one of the most devious people the world has ever seen. Remains you stole. Where are they?"

"I don't have them," I answer truthfully. "But before you get all righteous on me, let me tell you that I did it because his ghost was holding my father hostage. It was the only way to free him from Molay's grip."

Paul sits with a heavy sigh. "You have no idea what you released."

"I didn't release anything. His bones were scattered or so I was told."

"Did you see them being scattered?"

For the first time, doubt creeps into my body. "No."

"Then we can't know for sure it happened. Those chains that bound him were there for a reason." Again with the accusations.

I'm so tired of being everybody's punching bag, while at the same time not being trusted with relevant information. "I came here first. We talked about Molay. At no point in that conversation did you tell me about his skeleton being secured under your church or that the allegations of devil worship were true."

"You wouldn't have believed me. Like every modern historian, you eschew magic and religion and apply your contemporary lens to events of the past."

I bristle at the baseless assumption. "The fact remains that you could've done more."

"And you could've done less."

Our standoff is interrupted by a knock. Marie enters with a tray holding two cups of tea, sugar, and a delicate teapot. "There you go." She sets the tray down and says, "It's my own mixture. It calms and relaxes, opening you up to the world around you." Her words seem pointed at her uncle. "Alix means well."

"It's my sacred duty."

"Which you guard jealously, even from me," Marie says, not unkindly. She turns around and winks at me. "Find me afterwards."

Once the door closes behind her, Paul sighs. The anger leaves his features as he pours the herbal tea into the two cups. "Sugar?"

"A spoonful, please." I'm not a huge tea drinker but this one is quite nice. It carries notes of chamomile and something else. Sage, perhaps. "So, Marie knows too?"

"No. As you just heard, I don't confide much in her. She knows our family has guarded this place since the fall of the Templars and that she's not allowed to enter the cellar. She also knows a bit about holy sigils, but no more than the basics."

"Does she know about ghosts?" After Paul's shock reveal, it wouldn't surprise me if Marie had kept this from me as well. I'll have to have a serious talk with Gaby if so.

Paul shrugs. "Not the way you and I know about ghosts. My niece has a strong spiritual interest. She studies the old crafts—palmistry and horoscopes. If I had to guess, she probably *believes* in ghosts. But I don't think she knows the extent of their existence." He studies me. "So, your father fell under Molay's spell? He's a ghost, yes?"

"Uhm, no. It's more complicated than that." I guess we can both be a bit more forthcoming with information. I'm just not used to people taking me seriously. Otherwise, our last meeting would've been much different. It could've saved Papa. "My father is alive but he stood under Molay's spell, if you want to call it that, for twenty-four hours. When we rescued him, I didn't realise it immediately, but something had happened that made him a ghost. There are two of them, one alive and plagued by nightmares, and one dead trapped in Molay's memories."

I knew I was right to trust him when Paul just nods, dark eyebrows knitted together. He doesn't refute me or tell me that's the worst story he's ever heard. No, he believes every word I say.

"Before I explain my role in this," he says, holding up a hand, "I need to know how Molay first got in touch with you. He's not supposed to be able to leave his prison."

"Prison?" Cold washes over my arms. If Molay was confined to the Boutique of Psychosis, then he was able to leave it long before I came across him.

Paul is still waiting for my answer. If I want to know more about the Knights Hospitallers' role in this, I need to help him understand. "Do you know about the Boutique of Psychosis?" Judging by his frown, not really. "It's what the cataphiles call Molay's resting place. Legend has it that if one spends the night in the Boutique, they wake up with a psychosis, sometimes so severe it costs them their life."

"I had no idea," Paul exclaims, looking utterly dismayed. "I mean, I knew the cataphiles managed to get into the room a decade or two ago. Foolish thrillseekers but harmless. I tried to discourage them, but I can't watch the room every day."

"You were there when I first stepped into the Boutique," I realise. Molay had enhanced the truth until it became a horrifying vision, but the voice I'd heard was real. "I heard that the ghosts of Nexus, a cataphile organisation, were meeting there. It wasn't until I found the Boutique that I met Molay. He... he asked me for a favour."

"And do you usually grant favours to ancient ghosts?" Paul asks.

I shrug. "I don't discriminate between ghosts and living, and his favour seemed innocuous enough. All I had to do was introduce him to the ghosts at the Panthéon. They, however, told me later that they won't meet with any ghost in *their* sacred hall unless the ghosts were interred there. And that's when I started looking for ways to find and move his bones, because I thought they belonged in the Panthéon, not in some macabre display in an underground cell. And before you admonish me, he came to me twice outside the Boutique. Once to remind me very *strongly*. And another time after I'd met with the Panthéon ghosts, again to press the importance of that meeting."

"His power must've been growing after all those years feeding off the fears of foolish cataphiles," Paul muses. "And then you came along." He sighs again. "I'm glad the Panthéon ghosts refused him. If he'd had access to their power, his reach would've extended far beyond the Boutique. Imagine the effect he'd have had on all those tourists."

I feel myself paling. Paul had managed to express the issue Victor and Voltaire had with Molay's request far better than the ghosts ever did. The Boutique was creepy enough. To imagine the same on a much bigger, much more public scale gives me shivers. "I didn't know."

"Yes, child," Paul says mildly. "I gathered as much. I'm sorry I've been so harsh on you. It was my own mistake for not seeing what was happening. Molay should've never been able to get into your head. That's on me. My failure as the custodian."

As much as I appreciate the apology, I want to know more. "You said you'd explain everything to me."

"Very well. What do you know of the Quarry Department?"

"The Quarry Department?" It takes me a moment to remember. "They're the ones who built the catacombs. I mean, who gathered all the bones and sorted them into what's generally known as the catacombs to tourists."

Paul nods. "Do you know why they did that?"

I had an entire lecture series on that. "Because of the dead slowly suffocating the city, multiple collapses, and maintenance issues. The stacking was an economic choice."

"It was so much more than that." He looks at me, as if trying to appraise me. "You said you scattered Molay's bones?"

The connection becomes clear immediately. "They scattered the bones to dispel the ghosts. But why? They weren't like Molay, were they?"

"Most of them probably weren't, no. But as you said, they were starting to suffocate the city. Six million dead. Six million ghosts. The quarries were overflowing with their energy. The collapse that finally spurred action on the side of the city planners wasn't called Devil Eruption for nothing. Horrible things happened, things that were obliterated from all records. It fell to the Quarry Department and the Knights Hospitallers to fight those evils, but the only thing that truly stopped them was the disassembly of the majority of the ghosts."

"Wait, you work with the Quarry Department?" None of what he just said has made it into my history books. Whatever rumour remained was dismissed as a product of that time's imagination.

"The Order of Malta generously offered their help to the Quarry Department in making sure the ghosts wouldn't retaliate and hinder their removal. We had experience with fighting such evil." Paul throws a look over his shoulder, as if he could see into the Boutique from here. "Jacques de Molay once tried to raise the dead to overcome the king."

"Really?" I can't help it. Even though Molay attacked me, I can't imagine the entire obliteration of the Knights Templars to be actually justified. "You said you took in surviving Templars."

Paul nods. "We did. Many of them were innocent, some even fought the evil that was spreading in their lines. And, I suppose, Molay had a very good reason. Well, not a *good* reason, but a reason. The king was coming for his order out of greed. But the way he chose to fight Philip was despicable. He betrayed everything the order once stood for." There's so much anger in his voice, as if he was there. "He was rightfully apprehended and burnt. Then his bones were delivered to our order to dispose of, but we knew about the ghosts. And thus, he was chained in iron and by our holy power. A church was built on top of his burial chamber to keep people from accidentally stumbling into his grave. It worked… until this century."

All of this is extremely fascinating. I wish I could take notes and dig into the historical sources to hunt for hints. "Wow. Does GoPol know about this? Are they involved too?"

"GoPol?"

"The ghost police?"

For the first time tonight, Paul seems amused. "The ghosts have formed a police?"

I guess that answers my question. "No, they're actual police, made up of people like me."

He frowns. "I didn't know such a force existed." He shakes his head. "No, this is a secret that has been kept between the Quarry Department and the Order of Malta. We quietly ensure the safety of Paris without any interference from the police."

"By controlling the number of ghosts?"

"Yes. Too many dead are not good for the living."

"But what about the ghosts? Do you know what happens to them after you scatter their bones?" When he shakes his head, I recount my first visit to the catacombs. "They remember just enough to exist, but not enough to appear as they used to. Three legs, a missing body, abandoned heads. It's cruel."

"I'm sorry to hear there's much suffering. I would've thought they'd moved on by now."

I snort. "They would've—if the Quarry Department had left them in place. A ghost's span of existence isn't eternal. They pass on when they're no longer remembered. The Panthéon ghosts will be here forever, but most normal people pass on a few generations after their death. By collecting all their bones in a single space and making it a place of interest, you called them back from... well, from wherever they go afterwards. But only partially."

Paul nods thoughtfully, his brows knitted together again. "I see. That sounds unfortunate."

"It's horrifying, actually—when you can see them. I can send you my essay on the dignity of the dead I had to do for class."

"I'd be very interested to read that."

"I guess I'm just saying that not all ghosts are evil beings that need to be banished or secured. Most of them have valid concerns and needs."

"But they're dead," he says softly.

I swallow heavily. "And that makes it easy for most people to ignore them, but when you see all their suffering, when you talk to them... They were all people once and they still are. They still have dreams, aspirations, wants, and needs. They can love." Not that I'm going to tell him about my ghost boyfriend.

"I hear you, Alix. But we all have a limited time on this Earth. I'm more concerned with the living than those who've already lived."

"What gives us the right to decide that? That we're more important than them?"

"Life does."

"As I said, easy to say when you don't see them."

Paul smiles wanly at me. "Your heart is in the right place. Men more experienced than either of us have argued this. I've never been much of a philosopher, myself. Just a man with a sacred duty. One you've relieved me of."

"Sorry."

"It wasn't done out of maliciousness or stupidity. I know that now. I hope your friend truly scattered the bones as promised. Molay cannot be allowed to rise again."

"Agreed."

"Wonderful." Paul rises from the couch. "Well, now. It's quite late. You're welcome to stay, of course. We have guest rooms available. My niece will show you to them."

I get up, feeling the early hour deep in my bones. Now that I've remembered them, I can't quite shake the memory of the catacombs ghosts with their disassembled bodies. Did I do the same to Molay? It turns my stomach to imagine him like that, and I still feel bad about the destruction of something of historical value, but in the end, Paul is right. My living father is more important. The sanity of living cataphiles is more important. My own sanity most definitely is. As much as I want to, I can't please everyone. But completely disregarding the ghosts' needs doesn't sit right with me either. If only I knew the right way with the same surety everyone else seems to.

Outside, Gaspar's at my side almost immediately. "How was it?" he asks, taking my hands in his.

"I learned a lot."

Paul gives me a curious side glance. "Your father?"

"Another ghost."

"You're quite peculiar, Alix," he says, not without a smile. "I don't think I've ever heard of a ghost whisperer quite like you."

Because none of the others ever truly picked ghosts over those alive.

I follow him to Marie's room. He knocks softly and tells her goodnight before leaving me there.

Marie pulls me inside as soon as he's gone. "I'm so sorry about that. Uncle Paul can be a bit pigheaded sometimes. Things have always been done this way, you know. They can't possibly change."

Her words immediately put a smile on my face. That's right. I might be looking at history through a modern lens, but that's not necessarily a bad thing. After all, we study history to learn from the past. Just because things have always been one way doesn't mean they have to stay that way. Not even ghosts.

Marie's room is a comfortable size with a big bed, a desk, several shelves, a couch, and a low table on which a matching set of teacups have been placed. Malou is shuffling around in a cardboard box with a small bowl of cat food and water, while my sister is curled up on the couch and seems to be fast asleep, a wool blanket draped across her. "Oh, yeah, she was exhausted. We talked a little, I read her palm, and then she started dozing off."

"Thanks for taking care of Odi." I'm glad to hear there was no big drama. Either Odile is over Gaby or she knows she's not going to win any favours by getting her claws out.

"No worries. I hope my uncle wasn't too harsh? I've never seen him this... angry, I suppose."

Paul told me that Marie isn't really part of the Order of Malta. She wouldn't know anything about Jacques de Molay and the sigil in the cellar. "A bit of a miscommunication."

Marie laughs. "Turning up in a church in the middle of the night with your sister and a super cute hedgehog in tow requires quite a bit of miscommunication. Did you get the time wrong or something?"

"I never planned to turn up here." I sit down next to my sister, while Gaspar settles on the armrest to my other side. After a quick scan of the room, I find my father standing at the wall, facing it. I sigh. The sooner I can unite him and Papa the better.

"Do you want me to read your hand?"

"What?" I blink at Marie who has settled on the other side of the table. It's only now that I notice a tarot card deck and several gems in her reach.

She follows my gaze. "Would you rather have the cards? I find palms easier to read, but I can give it a try."

"Right. About that. You read palms?"

Marie chuckles. "I know, not exactly what you expect from a future lawyer. Then again, my parents never expected me to become a lawyer." She picks up the cards and makes five piles.

"Why *are* you studying law?"

She shrugs, puts the cards together, and shuffles them without looking at them. "Why not? I know, I'm supposed to have a really good reason, but I enjoy the text work, like finding some tiny loophole or an obscure law you could draw from. And I like the idea of it. That everything has a place. Following the same rules. Or rather, if you don't follow them, there will be consequences."

"So, you're a rule-stickler?" I ask doubtfully.

Marie bursts out laughing. "Kind of the opposite, but I know how to get away with it." She winks at me, then puts the cards away. "Give me your hand, palm up. I owe you one."

"What for?" Nevertheless, I give her my hand.

"Ever since you reached out to Gaspar's spirit, I feel him around the shop." She takes my hand, holding it gently, and runs her fingers over the lines on my palm.

"About that…"

"You have a strong connection to the spirit world," she says stroking the area just below my index finger. "But we knew that already." As she studies my hand, a sharp vertical line appears above her nose. "Your life line is interrupted. Right at the beginning, maybe one or two years in."

I snort. "Three. I almost drowned and had to be resuscitated."

Her eyebrows crawl upwards. "That makes sense. Since then, you've lived your life close to the other side. The two lines are intertwined until you can't actually tell which is which."

This is frighteningly accurate. Unlike Gaby, I've never believed in horoscopes and all the other woo-woo, but this hits a little too close to home.

"Are you okay?" Marie asks, looking up with concern.

"Why do you ask?"

"Well, there seems to be a lot going on. Teetering on the edge of death, big life decisions, an array of friends and foes, and a double love line so faint I don't know whether it's because you'll never love deeply or because the one you love is lost."

I hiccup so suddenly I scare myself. "The latter."

"Gaspar," she whispers. Then she shakes her head. "But how? You said you guys only had the one date."

Gaspar has put an arm around my shoulder and presses me against him, knowing exactly why I'm so upset. "You might as well tell her."

I sniffle slightly and nod, then take a deep breath. "I never met him."

"What?"

"Not while he was still alive."

Marie's eyes widen. "You... How? I don't understand. I..."

I take another deep breath. "Since my drowning, I've been able to see ghosts. I met Gaspar at the site of his accident, but I didn't realise that until much later, until I had already... well, fallen deeply in love with him."

"I love you too," Gaspar whispers, and I wish we could've done this somewhere else. Somewhere with just the two of us.

"He's here, isn't he?" Marie seems to have gotten over her initial confusion. Her eyes glisten, but she doesn't cry. "With you?"

Tentatively, I put my hand on his knee. For Marie, it's hovering in the air. "Most of the time, yes."

"You can talk to him? Like, actually ask him questions?"

"What would you like to know?"

"Where do we keep the extra set of keys?"

So, it's a test. Gaspar answers, "Under a loose cobble stone under the freesia pot," and I relay the answer.

Marie chuckles. "Okay. Wow. When Gaby said you were some kind of medium, I didn't expect you to be this good. Does she... does she know?"

"Gaby? Yes, I told her two-and-a-half years ago. She didn't believe me at first, but I managed to convince her." It only took a dead movie star, one ghost cheetah, and Malou.

"Good. Because I can see you cultivating strong friendships," Marie says, poring over my hand again, "which you'll need because... I'm sorry, Alix. Life is going to be tough. I mean, it's just lines on a hand. Everybody's life is tough, I suppose."

"What do you see?" I ask calmly.

Marie takes another deep look. "Threats, betrayals, death. You're toeing a narrow line between the worlds, and it's only going to get harder."

"Only harder?"

"Perhaps... I don't know, Alix. I think you need to carve out your own space because, right now, the world doesn't have one for you."

Gaspar's embrace tightens around me as I stiffen in shock. I knew I was taking some risks but hearing that there's no space for me in this world or the next brings up old feelings of inadequacy. I'm okay with being in between; I'm not okay with being nothing.

"Sorry. That came out a lot harsher than it should've. What I can see is that you're in control of your fate. Your decisions will determine whether you'll succeed or whether you'll go under." She smiles. "That's a good thing. And you *do* have strong friends by your side." Marie closes her fingers around my hand and looks me deep in the eyes. "You're not alone."

CHAPTER 10

The next morning, the four of us return home. Maman has some choice words for me and my sister, complaining about the lack of communication from either of us as to where we spent the night. Of course, she completely ignores Gaspar and my father's ghost.

As soon as she leaves for her work Christmas function, I knock at my father's bedroom door. "Papa?"

Though it's already early afternoon, he's still in bed. Or rather, he's lying on the bed, fully dressed.

"Are you okay?"

With a groan, he turns to me, looking at me so hauntingly it makes me shiver. "You went back, didn't you? To that place?"

"Yes, but it's alright. The ghost that plagued you is... well, I guess, truly dead now."

"He's gone?" he sounds a little hopeful.

"Has been since we left."

The hope flees from his eyes again. "Oh. I thought... Alix, the nightmares won't stop."

I figured as much. "Which is why I went back. You started seeing ghosts because a part of you separated from the rest." That sounds better than dying, doesn't it? "I went to get that part. Papa, meet... um, Papa, your whisper ghost." Gaspar leads my father's ghost into the room, reassuringly patting his hand.

Papa shoots up into a sitting position as soon as he sees his ghost. "What's this?"

"Your whisper ghost. He is... you. Up until the point of... our visit." I feel like I'm making a mess out of this, but how else do you introduce someone to themselves? "Since it happened so recently, the two of you are practically the same, only you're alive and he's a ghost. My own whisper ghost is a three-year-old."

"Alix!" his voice is so brittle it seems to fall apart around my name. "I'm not—... This is not—... I cannot—"

"I think it's pretty neat," Odile chimes in, sticking her head in next to me. "Having a ghost double. Just imagine the two of you investigating your next big case. You can send him out whenever your informant holds back information."

Papa's ghost looks a bit pained, almost mirroring my father's reaction. "Please don't let me burn again," he whispers, then wets his lips. "I just want to go back to my job and..."

"It's no longer your job," I tell him softly. "Though, Odile is right, you can always help Papa. I mean... This is confusing. We need a name for you. What was your middle name, Papa?"

"Antoine," Odile says.

"Perfect. Antoine and Rémy. Or Papa."

My father has been slowly getting to his feet but only to retreat to the back of the room. "Take this away."

"This? Papa, this is you! He's not an it. He's a real person."

"A dead person," Odile clarifies.

"I'm dead?" Antoine asks, eyes wide.

Gaspar pats his arm. "It's really not the worst thing in the world. I died and I can still—"

"You're dead?" my father exclaims.

Concerned, I turn to him. "Look, I can explain. Gaspar and I—"

"Your boyfriend is dead? You—... No, no." He clasps his forehead with both hands, looking down. "This is wrong. All of this. You're kissing someone who's dead. My own ghost. Your ghost. Alix, what is this?"

My mouth has gone dry. Next to me, Odile gnaws her bottom lip, no longer so forthcoming with ideas. "It's the truth. The true state of the world. Ghosts are real."

"Nonsense!" Papa declares. "Ghosts are—... If ghosts exist, then they're spectres, energy, a whisper in the wind. They're not—... They can't be"—he looks up at me and the two ghosts—"this."

I don't really get the logic behind this. He's ready to accept creepy storybook versions of ghosts but not the representations of who those people really were. Not even if the truth is staring him in the face. That's so unlike my father that I wonder if I got him and his whisper ghost mixed up.

"Papa," I say gently, taking a step towards him. "It's okay if you need a little more time. I understand that it's a big change."

"Take him," he interrupts me. "Take him away from me."

"This is my bedroom," Antoine protests.

Gaspar grabs him by the arm. "Not anymore. Come on, let's go for a walk." He throws me a glance, letting me know he'll take care of Antoine.

That leaves Papa for me. "If you want to talk more about this—"

"No!" He sinks to the ground, burying his face in his hands. "I don't want this. I never asked for this."

"Papa..."

"Please leave."

His reaction makes me taste bile. I want to fix this so badly, but everything I do just seems to make it worse.

Odile puts her hand on mine, tugging slightly. "Let's go and make some cookies."

I don't want to make cookies but I follow her, nonetheless. The last thing I see is Papa crouching near the wall and sobbing—just like his ghost did in the Boutique of Psychosis.

"What do we do now?" asks Odile, looking just as spooked as I am.

I don't want to admit that I'm at the end of my rope. I'm fresh out of ideas. Only one remains. "I need to talk to the expert."

CHAPTER 11

It's no surprise to me that Sébastien agrees to meet me straight-away. He suggests the Marché de Noel Notre Dame at Square Viviani as a neutral meeting ground, which gives me the opportunity to shop for presents for my family.

Contrary to the big and loud Christmas market along the Champs-Élysées, this one is a little more magical, with little chalets in front of the famous church, and a wide array of hand-crafted gifts and delicate food items. I pick up some roasted chestnuts on the way in and meet Sébastien at a vin chaud stand.

He's come alone, wearing a wool hat against the cold that does little for his nose, which has already turned a bit redder than the surrounding area. We exchange kisses and he invites me to have a mulled wine, while I feel obligated to share my chestnuts with him. When our hands are full of hot drinks and food, he leads me to a round table.

I put my bag of chestnuts in the middle and wrap both my hands around the mulled wine to savour its warmth. "Thanks for meeting me today."

"I was actually hoping you'd call," Sébastien admits. "There's something I need to talk to you about."

Hopefully, he's not going to bring up Petite Alix again. "Sure, what's on your mind?"

"Later. You said you needed help with your father?" He takes a sip from his wine and seems to regret it quickly as he nearly spits it out and then frantically blows on it.

I can't help but laugh. "Still too hot?" There's a reason I'm using the cup as a tiny heater rather than drinking it.

"Very much so." After blowing on the wine a bit more, he finally manages to take a small sip. "It's good, though."

The smell is tempting enough to believe him. I let go of my cup to peel another chestnut, letting it cool slightly in my hand before nibbling on it. "So, my father... uhm, it seems as if he died while he was under Molay's influence."

"You mean he's started seeing ghosts?" Sébastien surmises, surprisingly fast.

I nod. "Yes, he can see Gaspar. I also took him to meet his mother on Père Lachaise. He's definitely a ghost whisperer now, though I have no idea how that could've happened."

"There's a lot I'm still trying to figure out about the Boutique. Admittedly, I've only been doing this job for five years, but I've never even heard of a ghost having that kind of power—or intention. I don't like it, but the Chevalier might be onto something. Have you talked to him since then?"

I shake my head. As it stands, I don't trust the Chevalier any more than Sébastien, but unlike the young special agent, he hasn't been constantly bugging me. I'm not ready to take up his offer of help, and he seems to respect that.

"Hmm, I hoped he'd have more insight. Never mind. If your father has become a ghost whisperer, then he must've left behind a—"

"Whisper ghost, yes." I take a sip from my wine, managing not to burn my tongue. "Already ahead of you. We found him lingering in the Boutique and recovered him." Sébastien raises his eyebrows, but I don't let him chime in. "But here's the thing. Both my father and his ghost seem to be... extremely distraught over what they experienced in the catacombs. I thought reuniting them would heal them, but... How do you deal with new whisperers at GoPol? How do you acclimatise recruits who are completely new to this?"

Sébastien's jaw tenses, and I'm suddenly afraid the answer is, "Not at all, we just eliminate them". But that's not what he says. "It takes time. Obviously, not everyone is cut out for this. Very few of us have lived through something as traumatic as your father."

"I'd argue almost dying would be traumatic for anyone."

He shrugs. "Surprisingly not. I mean, I'm not saying that people are unaffected by it, but many see it as a blessing. An inspiration to make better choices, for example. And those are the ones who can adapt the fastest. Honestly, my advice is to take small steps. Like, don't dump everything you know about ghosts on him in one sitting, for example."

Yeah, that's pretty much exactly what I did.

Sébastien chuckles softly. "I'm too late, am I?"

"I might have been a bit too excited about having another whisperer in my family."

"I understand." He drinks the rest of his wine and leans his forearms on the table as he peels a chestnut. "Look, just give him some time to come to terms with this. If you want, I can have a chat with him."

That's what I feared. "I don't think adding yet another person to the mix will help the case."

Sébastien nods thoughtfully. "True." He leans back. "Well, the offer stands. You're probably right, though. Give him some time to come to terms with it." Shuddering slightly from the cold, he rubs his bare fingers. "Shall we walk a bit?"

"Don't tell me you get cold easily?" I ask, amused that he's not infallible after all.

"I'm a summer guy. Thirty degrees is my optimal operating temperature."

Surprised, I laugh. "I'd die!" Unless I'm at the beach, anything above thirty degrees would reduce me to a puddle.

It's astoundingly pleasant to spend time with Sébastien. We walk the market together, contemplating over what to gift our relatives, and pick out the worst possible present for Cédric and Hélène: a pair of hand-painted wooden clowns in nutcracker optic, with wonky eyes and creaky limbs. Sébastien convinces me to buy it and we split the puppets between us, promising to pretend it'll be some great coincidence.

"You know she's never going to speak another word to me?"

"That'll get you out of the wedding," Sébastien quips. "Cédric asked me to be his witness." He shudders mockingly.

At this point I'm sure Hélène is regretting she ever asked me. "Same." I raise the bag with the creepy clown. "Do you think this will ward them off?"

"If this doesn't, I don't know what will."

"So, what's the deal with you and Cédric? Any real dirt or just a general sense of antipathy?" The latter would be me. I know I haven't really been fair to him, and that he might not be half as bad as I make him out to be.

Sébastien groans a little, as if it's such a chore to remember. "We've had our ups and downs, spending a lot of time together at family meetings when we were younger. Everyone always expected us to be the best of friends, but instead, we competed constantly. I usually won despite being the younger one, and he didn't take that very well. I didn't like him much because he always tried to be best buddies with my father. It was annoying and Papa never indulged him."

It sounds a bit like Odile's early teenage years after my sister moved out. "I suppose it's only natural to challenge the hierarchy. Even between cousins."

"Maybe. But I remember one day keenly. We had a fight, I don't know about what. Perhaps a wrestling match gone wrong or something like that." Sébastien doesn't look at me, his mind completely engrossed in the memory. "And he stood there, fists balled, and said to my face, 'I bet your maman left because she hated you.' I broke his nose for that, and from then on, I refused to go to those meetings." For a moment, Sébastien's face distorted, but now he shrugs and shakes it off. "So, yeah, I never forgave him for that, but he's forgotten. Or I don't know. All his attempts at being best friends just seemed so fake to me afterwards."

I watch him with deep pity. The cold way he tries to disassociate from the comment, as if it hadn't cut bone-deep and left a scar. I don't blame Sébastien for holding a grudge. "How old were you when your maman left?"

"Six." The number is so firmly stuck in his head he doesn't even have to think about it. He throws me a glance and scoffs. "I know you're going to ask, 'so, why did she leave?'" He shrugs, again shaking it off as if it was nothing but droplets on his waterproof skin. "It had nothing to do with me. Papa and her just didn't get along anymore. She couldn't deal with his job and disapproved of his partnership with C—... his whisper ghost."

"Was she a ghost whisperer as well?"

He frowns, as if he's never asked himself that. "I don't think so. Anyway, she moved to Algeria with her now-husband. I think they had an affair while she was married to Papa. She wasn't interested in gaining custody of me, and I didn't want to leave Paris or Papa, so it all worked out in the end."

Did it, though? From the way Sébastien talks about her, they don't seem to have much of a relationship now that he's an adult. Cédric might have been wrong about the reason his mother left, but he wasn't too far off about Sébastien's feelings about the whole affair.

"I'm sorry," I say softly, brushing his elbow instinctively.

He snorts. "For what? I know not all relationships last. It's also been twenty years since then, so old news really."

Are you ever too old to miss your maman? He obviously doesn't want to talk more about it, so I let it slide. It's not really my business anyway. "Isn't Cédric from your mother's side?"

"Mhm. Her sister still lives in Paris. I don't see her much these days, but she tried to keep the relationship intact. For a few years, at least. Anyway, can we please talk about something else?"

"Sure."

While talking, we somehow make it out of the Christmas market and onto the promenade. Darkness has fallen and the lanterns are alight, casting their orange glow on the river next to us. It takes me a moment to recognise the spot, but when I do, cold drips down my spine. "Why did you bring me here?"

"Huh?" Sébastien looks around to get his bearings before he pulls out his phone to check something. "Right. So, listen, I know you've been struggling with finding your whisper ghost. You had a lot going on, so I did some digging through old records and I found this."

My insides freeze. Dark waves crash over my head. Breath evades me. "You..." There's not enough air in me to protest.

He studies me. "You feel it, don't you? The place where you drowned?"

A ginormous lump has formed in my throat. I swallow heavily to speak. "It happened here?"

Of course it happened here. This is the exact spot where I stupidly jumped into the water to try and save myself last month. The spot where Petite Alix drowned.

"I hope you don't mind, but I sent Dix to have a look for your ghost." Sébastien closes his eyes for a heartbeat, and sure enough, Dix strolls down the walkway to meet us. To my great relief, he's alone. "Did you find anyone?"

Dix shakes his head. "Nope. Not a single soul. I mean, there are some other ghosts who've drowned in the river, but none look even remotely like Alix or fit the description." He turns to me and grins. "Hey, History Girl."

Sébastien seems confounded. "That's unusual. I'm sure this is the right spot. You feel it, don't you?"

I need to think fast if I want to keep my secret. "I don't know what I feel, but now that you say I've drowned, deep water always made me a bit uncomfortable."

Sébastien buys my explanation, nodding in commiseration. "Look, I don't want you to unearth buried trauma or anything like that, but try to find her. Think of her and try calling her. She might not hang around much, but I'm sure your connection will be the strongest here."

Without meeting his eyes, I step towards the edge of the water. My toes hang slightly over, and I feel dizzy. Too close. I'm too close.

Sébastien grabs me by the elbow, narrowly avoiding a repeat of last month's events. "Careful."

"Sorry." I stare into the choppy waves and pretend to call Petite Alix, but in my mind, all I repeat is *stay away, stay away.*

At last, I step back from the edge, letting out a breath of relief. "There's nothing."

Sébastien frowns heavily. "That's unusual. Maybe if you remembered it more clearly."

"I thought we weren't unearthing traumas," Dix quips. He winks at me, suggesting he's on my side.

As so often when Dix doesn't display the necessary gravitas, Sébastien stiffens. "I wasn't planning on forcing her to remember, just thinking out loud."

"Maybe it's just not meant to be," I probe carefully. "It doesn't matter, either way, does it?"

"Well, see," he scratches behind his ear, "after what happened at the Boutique of Psychosis, my father has expressed some interest in having you join our force."

I stumble back, nearly tumbling over the edge after all. "What?"

Dix shoots forward to grab me and drag me to safety. "No need to kill yourself. You're already a whisperer," he quips.

His choice of words doesn't make it any better.

I push the dark waves from my mind and try to focus on what Sébastien just said. "Your father wants me to join GoPol?"

"You exhibited a range of desirable talents and kept your cool. Without you and your ghost friends, we wouldn't have made it out of the Boutique alive. GoPol would be lucky to have you."

As outrageous as the idea sounds, hope soars through me. If I join GoPol, I'd get to keep Petite Alix and my powers. I wouldn't have to give up on Gaspar or my dear friends all over Paris' necropolises. I could stop this ruse and embrace what I am. Even get paid for it.

"But I'm a historian," I blurt out.

Sébastien shrugs. "People change careers all the time. How many of your classmates do you think will work in the field? Five per cent? Ten?"

He's not wrong. History isn't exactly a field that ensures job security. I might be better placed than most with my Panthéon job, but that's only part time. Plus, I can't imagine being a tour guide forever, repeating the same old details day in and day out.

"GoPol is an excellent employer. The work is interesting, the pay is good. He wants us to partner up."

I'm not quite sure if that's supposed to be an advantage or just an extra fact. "Partners?"

"We usually work in pairs. And since I currently don't have anyone… It makes sense. You need someone experienced on your side."

He's really trying to sell it now, which makes me more hesitant about the whole thing. "I'll think about it."

"Well, if you want to have a look, I can always show you around the premises. You could meet my father, have a chat to other ghost whisperers." Sébastien raises his hands. "I don't want to pressure you, just putting it out there. I think this could be a good thing."

"A good thing?"

The right corner of his lip twitches. "I mean, I don't hate it."

I snort. "That must mean a lot, coming from you."

"She said it, not me," Dix chimes in, grinning wildly.

I glance at him, trying to gauge what he thinks about the proposal, but his face is unreadable, any true emotion hidden behind that cheesy grin. "I'll think about it."

"Alright." Sébastien smiles gently. "Give me a call if you want that tour. Or if you need anything else."

When I leave him, I'm not quite sure what my decision will be,
but surprisingly, I don't see myself exactly hating it either.

CHAPTER 12

Someone who *does* hate the idea, though, is Gaspar, who meets me back at Notre Dame where I left my bike. Or rather, he hates Sébastien. "I don't get why you had to meet him here."

"What do you mean. What's wrong with this place?"

"Nothing."

It's quite dark now. Huddled as I am at the side of Notre Dame, no one pays me much attention. "Come on. Don't start keeping secrets from me now."

Gaspar rolls his neck with a groan. "A Christmas market? Drinking mulled wine and eating roasted chestnuts, picking out family presents..." When I fail to see what the problem is, he says unhappily, "It was a date."

Surprised, I laugh. "That wasn't a date. I was with Sébastien." The thought hadn't even crossed my mind. "That's not what this was."

"I know that it wasn't, but it wasn't coincidental either." He steps forward to put his hands on my elbow, imploring me. "He's interested in you."

"No, he's not."

"Believe me. I've seen his face. And look, I can't blame him. You're obviously a catch." Doubt flickers across his face. "And I guess... well, he's alive. So he's got that on me."

"Gaspar, stop!" Gently, I push his arms down and take his hands in mine. "I don't care if he's interested; I'm *not!* The only one I love is *you*." I lean in to kiss him, but just then, a couple walks past and I take a step back, swallowing my disappointment.

"See?" Gaspar whispers. "I don't get to do these things with you. We can't have dates. We can never stroll across a Christmas market, hold hands, share food, and goof around."

Rebellion wells up inside of me. "Says who?"

He laughs awkwardly. "Everyone? It would be too strange for you, looking as if you're talking to yourself, holding out your hand awkwardly." He cups my face, a sad smile on his lips. "I can't bear the thought of people thinking you're somehow less than you are. Because you're so much more than anyone knows."

What he's describing does indeed sound awkward. Defiance broils in me. I want to laugh in the face of all the Théos in the world and go on a date with my ghost boyfriend. But how can we have a romantic date if everyone keeps staring at me?

Gaspar kisses me. "Let's just go home."

"I want a date with you," I whisper.

Just then a couple goes past, holding hands and laughing. Gaspar takes a step back and offers me his hand. "It doesn't matter, anyway. We've got more important things to do, like talk about what Sébastien told you."

"Let's go to Gaby. I need her opinion, too." And besides, I don't have to worry about hanging out with Gaspar at her place. I get the fleeting idea of a double date. Sure, it'll look like I'm the third wheel, but a group might provide just enough cover. Then again, I'm not ready to make out with Gaspar in front of Gaby and Marie either, despite both knowing he's there.

Marie happens to be at Gaby's. Despite them insisting that we're not interrupting, I notice the bowl of popcorn and the open wine bottle. They were watching a movie in bed—not because their relationship has already progressed that far, but because there's no space in Gaby's apartment for a couch.

"No, come in!" Gaby drags me inside. "What were you doing out?"

"Hey, Gaspar," Marie greets him. "He's with you, right? I'm not just imagining it?"

Gaspar snorts. "And here I always thought she was a little kooky with her tarot reading."

"Palmistry," I correct him. "She prefers palms."

"That's right," Marie says with an awkward smile, as she struggles to make the connection. "Can't read a hand I can't see, though."

"There's not much future to read for a dead guy, anyway."

I elbow Gaspar. "You've got a future." Then I finally pay proper attention to Marie. "Yes, he's here, and he's in a bit of a funk, so uhm..."

Gaby throws back the blanket of her bed. "Settle in. We're watching *La vie d'Adèle*. Not sure if that'll lift his mood, but it's romantic and..." She giggles and leans into Marie.

I love seeing Gaby so happy. Hopefully, this one will last, not like the others. I climb in next to her, leaving enough space for Gaspar. It's a rather tight fit and Gaspar needs to put his arm around me to avoid tumbling out. I'm not complaining.

"This is strange," Marie admits as she regards the empty space beside me and my slightly unnatural posture, "But on brand for you, Gaspar. You've always been a weirdo."

Just for talking to Gaspar as if he was still alive, Marie gets all the brownie points she needs to be approved of by me.

"Tell me about it," Gaspar mutters, his nose nuzzled in the crook of mine. Then he whispers in my ear, "I'm having a lot of bad ideas."

I'm glad his mood has improved, but I'm not ready for this. "Did you get Hélène's invitation?" I ask Gaby.

My sister and her fiancé are throwing a New Year's party, location yet to be announced, which is supposed to double as an engagement party. It's just like Hélène, throwing some fancy party months after the fact. At least, she's invited Gaby as well.

"I did. Are we going?" she asks me.

"The whole family is, so I don't see how I could get out of it. The party is going to be full of people from Hélène's office, so there's a big chance I won't have to talk to her. It says we can bring a plus one, though."

Gaby turns to smile at Marie. "Want to come?"

Marie giggles. "Whose party is this?"

"Alix's older sister. A total bore but she'll throw money at this. So there's gonna be champagne and fancy canapés." Gaby turns to me. "Do you think there'll be caviar?"

"Undoubtedly." Not that I was looking forward to eating some, but it's totally something Hélène would serve.

Gaspar kisses the nape of my neck. "And who's your plus one gonna be?"

I shudder excitedly, a grin forming naturally on my lips. "Malou, of course."

He retorts by poking my ribs and I twitch, nearly knocking my elbow into Gaby.

"You should totally bring Malou," Gaby says, grinning. "I bet Odi's already looking forward to making a little cocktail dress for her."

I make a mental note to prepare Odile for Marie's presence and urge her to bring one of her friends from school.

"A cocktail dress for a hedgehog?" Marie asks, prompting Gaby to show off Malou's Instagram account. It doesn't take long for Marie to exclaim, "Oh my god, she's adorable in those!"

Gaspar uses their distraction to plant a row of kisses on my chin. "I'd never dream of getting in the way of Malou having a grand time."

Flustered, I lean back into him. "She's small. She can fit in my handbag, while I"—I put my hand on his arm—"will hold on to this."

Gaby looks over, an eyebrow raised. "Do I want to know what you're holding onto?"

My hand is far above Gaspar's nether regions, but I still blush heavily. "His arm, Gaby. His arm."

Both Gaby and Marie start laughing. Then Gaby pats my other arm. "I know, ma puce. Even so, Hélène will throw a fit."

"Let her," I say grumpily. "She can no longer pretend it's not real. Not with Officer Cédric on my side these days."

"That's so weird." Gaby wrinkles her nose before explaining to Marie, "Cédric is Hélène's fiancé."

"I gathered as much."

"We call him Officer Cédric because he's... well, he's a police officer and loves pretending to be on duty during family gatherings. It's never funny." Gaby rolls her eyes.

Marie chuckles over that. "Oh, well, then I'm definitely coming. Someone needs to save you from his unfunny jokes, and with Alix making out with Gaspar on the dance floor, you need me to be that person."

"I will *not* be making out on the dance floor." As mortifying as it would be for Hélène, it'd be even more embarrassing for me. "But I'm sure there's a corner I could vanish to."

"I'll scout the place," Gaspar whispers in my ear, while his hands wander south, causing heat to form in my belly.

Meanwhile, Gaby shrugs. "Well, if Hélène has a problem with any of it, she can take it up with GoPol."

"Speaking of GoPol," I say a little too intensely, grabbing Gaspar's hands before they can go any deeper under the blanket. "They want me to join."

Instantly, he frowns.

"They do?" Gaby asks, surprised.

"Who is *GoPol*?"

Gaby turns to Marie. "Oh, it's short for the ghost police. They're made up of ghost whisperers like Alix and do cool ghost reconnaissance work."

I don't know about cool but, put like that, it doesn't sound too bad. "Apparently, I impressed the big boss with my work at the Boutique, so now he wants me to join the force and work with Sébastien."

Gaspar's grip on my waist intensifies slightly. Hopefully he's not still jealous about Sébastien.

"I thought they wanted to eliminate you… I mean your powers," Gaby corrects herself.

"From the sounds of it, they changed their mind." I'm glad they did. I don't think I could live without my powers. The world would be so much emptier without my ghosts, never mind losing Gaspar. "I just… I'm not sure I want to work for them."

"Why not?" Gaby asks. "Look, I know you and Sébastien didn't get off to a perfect start." She pauses to frown. "Honestly, that's not true. He's been pretty reliable and always courteous. You like him more than his cousin."

Next to me, I feel Gaspar tense, prompting me to say, "I don't care for him."

"I didn't say… Oh." Gaby understands and rolls her eyes. "She's yours, Gaspar. Heart, body, and soul."

"But not life," Gaspar whispers. "Never that."

"It's just a job. And as a workmate, Sébastien doesn't sound too bad, in my opinion." Gaby shrugs. "Just think about it. Joining GoPol means you get to stay a ghost whisperer *and* get a job with ghosts. Like a real, paying job with all the added benefits. We've only got one more year at uni, so you're already doing better than most of us. Plus, I'm gonna be envious, because being a special agent would be damn cool."

Marie nods excitedly. "I only understand about half of what's going on, but if someone offered to pay me to spend time with ghosts, I'd take it. What's bothering you about it?"

They actually bring such good arguments, I struggle to answer straight away. The truth is, I *did* like Sébastien—and Dix—but that was before the Chevalier told me what they were really planning. Only... I pause for a moment in my thoughts. What if he got it wrong? Sébastien doesn't want to take my powers away. On the contrary, he wants me to join his agency. Why am I believing someone who tried to shoot me over someone who went out of his way to clean up my mess?

"I guess the only thing I don't like is how they see ghosts as tools. They rely heavily on their whisper ghosts, treating all others as flaky. They don't see them as the humans they once were."

"But they're not asking you to change your attitude," Gaby says. "In fact, seeing how you bond with ghosts could inspire them. I mean, when you say their boss was impressed with your work at the Boutique, that means he liked what *you* did with the ghosts."

"True." Maybe this whole thing is a good offer. One I should consider instead of letting some criminal's words get into my head.

Gaspar slings his arms around me, pressing me against his body. "You could revolutionise that place. Maybe even improve things for us ghosts. Just imagine how much easier fulfilling certain favours would be if you had GoPol's connections at your disposal.

It could be the first step in changing how the world sees us ghosts. And then maybe... maybe one day we could go on a real date."

I don't know about changing the world, but that doesn't stop a wild spark of hope from fluttering inside my stomach. "I guess it wouldn't hurt to check them out."

Gaspar and I get home after the movie is done and it becomes clear that Gaby and Marie would prefer some privacy. It might not have been a real date, but we had fun, laughing and teasing, while trying not to get too hot and bothered by some people's invisible boyfriends.

It left me eager to go home and continue what we started in the privacy of my bedroom. I've just hung up my coat and unzipped my boots when my father walks into the corridor. "Oh, hey Alix. Did you go out with Gaby?"

Irritated, I check with Gaspar who's standing there in plain sight. "Yes. And Gaspar." He doesn't need to know about Sébastien. That will only lead to the wrong conclusions again.

"Right, Gaspar. Your ghost boyfriend. Is he with you right now?"

I can't quite tell if he's pretending not to see him or whether he actually can't. Gaspar picks up on my confusion and walks towards my father, waving a hand in front of his face. Nothing.

Cold fingers close around my heart. "Papa. What did you do?"

"What do you mean?"

"You can see Gaspar, can't you?" I refuse to believe anything else.

He shakes his head and smiles. "It doesn't appear so."

"What. Did. You. Do?"

"Uhm, there's a place you can go where they fix that. It was really easy, painless. I just had to sign a piece of paper and then they took that other—well, you know, *me*—away, and half an hour later, it all went away."

I feel like I can't breathe, a million knives piercing my lungs. "They took your ghost away?" I don't need to ask who *they* is. It seems obvious.

My father smiles again. "It's for the best, Alix. We're not meant to see ghosts. This is more natural."

The bitter taste of bile fills my mouth. "Just because you can't see them any longer doesn't mean the ghosts went away." Gaspar is standing right there next to him, looking as dismayed as I feel.

"Well, my ghost has." Papa shrugs, and I can't deny that he looks better than he has in weeks. More himself again.

Sébastien.

My eyelids flutter as a wave of nausea hits me. Oh, wasn't he so kind and understanding? Magnanimously, he offered to help, and I believed him. I believed him when he didn't fight me for making the decision to do this on my own. Because why bother winning me over when you can just go behind my back and take my father's ghost away?

I can't believe I didn't see this coming.

I can't believe I just considered taking his offer. To join this organisation that controls who can and who can't see ghosts.

But most importantly, I can't believe I trusted him.

Chapter 13

That night, Gaspar and I enter the catacombs and make our way to the Crossroad of the Dead. As usual, the crossroad is full of ghosts passing through. I don't see any cataphiles lingering, so I take the stairs to the Chevaliér's unofficial office. As expected, he's there, poring over his maps with another woman. *The woman whose ghost pretended to shoot me.* Though this one is a little older, closer to the Chevalier's age than mine, with beautiful tight, black ringlet curls.

She stiffens at my sight. "What are *they* doing here?"

The Chevalier looks up with knitted brows but smiles when he recognises me. "Alix! And I assume you brought young Gaspar as well."

Which further proves that the woman is a ghost whisperer. Little surprise there.

"What can I do for you, ma chère?"

"I'm not your sweetheart."

He grins cheekily. "No, no, that would be Gaspar's." Then he comes around the table and walks towards me. "To what do I owe this pleasure?"

"You said I should come to you when I'm done with GoPol." I spread my arms, my mouth still full of bitterness. "Well, I'm done." There's no way I'll forgive this betrayal.

Delighted, the Chevalier checks with the woman. "See, I told you Alix is one of us."

The woman massages the root of her nose with a sigh. "She's a kid. You really trust her not to change her mind next week? Or once she knows what she's signing up for?"

Righteous anger brought me down to the catacombs, but now I'm wondering if I didn't jump from the frying pan into the fire. "What is it you're doing?"

"I fully intend to win her over," the Chevalier declares before turning back to me. "But I'm forgetting my manners. Alix, this is Samara. It wasn't too long ago that *she* started working for me." It appears to be a reminder for her rather than information for me.

Samara lowers her hand with an exasperated expression. "Lovely. Just lovely. I don't trust her."

"Neither do I," the Chevalier announces cheerfully. "But that's where we all started. I have no doubt Alix is keen to earn our trust."

What am I getting myself into? "Earn your trust?"

"Well, the thing is I want you on our team. I know that you're not. How could you without knowing what this is all about?" The

Chevalier spreads his hands. "Why don't we start with what made you come down here?"

"Sébastien took my father's ghost away." I should probably back up a little. "After our fight with Molay, my father started seeing ghosts. I still don't know what happened there, but there was a whisper ghost. I was going to help him adjust to his new reality, but when I told Sébastien, he went behind my back and took my father's ghost away." And thanks to me, he didn't even have to crawl into the Boutique to do so.

The Chevalier nods, eyebrows drawn deeply into his face. "That tracks, unfortunately."

"The worst thing is he offered me to join him at GoPol, all the while planning on how to betray me as soon as we parted." That two-facedness is what I struggle with most. That he could be funny and charming one minute and a calculating bastard the other. Did he open his heart to me to lull me into a sense of security? Who does that? What kind of person uses their own trauma to trick others?

The kind of person that gets recruited by GoPol. Which is why I'm here and not there. In the end, the Chevalier is the lesser evil. I can't risk getting torn between them, so my choice falls to him.

"They want you to join GoPol?" the Chevalier asks, quickly exchanging a look with Samara.

"Or so they say." How can I trust any of it being true?

The Chevalier digests the information quickly, then returns to his table to roll up his map. "Come with me."

"What are you doing?" Samara looks at him in panic, as if he just declared he was going to blow up the GoPol building. Maybe he has.

Instead of giving either of us a satisfying explanation, the Chevalier walks down the stairs, expecting us to follow. Since there's little else we can do, we follow him. With Samara taking up the rear, it feels like I'm getting marched off somewhere. I reach for Gaspar's hand, and he squeezes it reassuringly.

"You're shacking up with a ghost?" Samara asks as we turn to the left, walking down one of the underground boulevards I've never stepped foot in.

My cheeks flush with heat. "We're not doing that." Though our make-out sessions have been getting more physical and the promise of more has been hanging in the air.

"Told you, you're nothing but a child."

Way to shame me for not jumping into ghost sex. I make the decision to dismiss anything she says. After all, this is the woman who has no scruples about pointing a gun at my face or firing at me in the dark of the tunnels.

Instead, I concentrate on my surroundings, noting when we veer off the boulevard and pass through twisting corridors and abandoned rooms. So far, the path is quite accessible. There's no water to cross and no tight tunnels to squeeze through. Wherever the Chevalier is taking us, it can't be the secret lair I'm expecting.

That is until we stop by a manhole. Instead of being above us like all the others, the manhole is down here, in the catacombs. The Chevalier takes out one of the skeleton keys sewage workers carry around and bangs it against the manhole in several quick and slow turns. A secret signal? Or an actual Morse code? Then he inserts the key and turns it.

"After you." He lifts the manhole cover and nods towards the hole.

My heart is practically tap-dancing in my chest as I search for the familiar hand and footholds and lower myself into the hole. Part of me thinks the Chevalier is going to shut the cover and lock me in darkness, but I try to tell myself that wouldn't make any sense.

It doesn't take long for my feet to hit the ground, yet I'm still surrounded by walls. Panic rises in my throat as claustrophobia seizes me. My hands roam across the walls, desperate to find some space to go from here, when they suddenly come across something. A door handle.

Fingers wrapped around the cool metal, I push. The door opens and I'm blinded by light. Before my eyes can adjust, someone jostles me from behind.

"Don't block it," Samara hisses.

I stumble sideways, blinking furiously. Slowly, the room comes into focus. The light isn't actually that bright, but it comes from several plain bulbs on the walls of the room. They're hanging above giant consoles with a wide array of buttons, screens, and headphones, all in pristine condition. On the other side, behind the column I climbed down, is a bunk area with at least eight spartan beds. I've seen some of this before in a history book.

A bunker. We're in an old WWII bunker. Only, it doesn't look old. The machinery is still in action and has been upgraded with computers and laptops. And it's not abandoned.

A small group of people mills around the room. A few are sitting on the lower bunk beds, while two are currently manning the computers. Some of them are wearing 40s dress and hairstyles, like the familiar figure of Pierre Roche, but there are others in more modern clothes, and two in centuries old fashion. Besides Pierre, there's only one I recognise: Samara's whisper ghost.

"Are these all ghosts?" I whisper, unsure whether the three people in modern clothes are dead as well.

"No." The Chevalier startles me when his hands fall on my shoulders. "Welcome to the Monastery of Bears. Guys, meet our new probational member, Alix. Alix, meet the Résistance."

You'd make an excellent member of the Résistance. Pierre's words echo in my memories. "What are they resisting?"

"GoPol, for example," the Chevalier says nonchalantly. "Or generally, society's notion of ghosts and ghost whisperers. Some call us Nexus, but we've evolved so much further from that. That's as much as you need to know before you pass the test."

I swallow heavily. "The test?" I've got a million questions swirling in my head, mixed with excitement and dread. Who are all these people? What are they really resisting? Why are they gathering in an old WWII bunker? Why are they still using the equipment? Who are they listening to? Or are they broadcasting? And why is this place called the Monastery of Bears? I don't see any effigies of bears hanging on the wall, nor anything that looks like it could've been part of a monastery.

"Yes, you see, the work we do here is highly secretive. We can't risk word of this getting out to government agencies. I knew I needed to show you something to make you believe me, but before we can proceed any further, we need to make sure you're really on our side."

"How?" I wish I had time to think about whether I *want* to be on their side.

The Chevalier steps into the room and turns around to face me. "Join GoPol."

"What?" It's safe to say, I didn't expect that.

"I know it seems counter-intuitive, but we need someone among them. You have a rather convenient invitation to join them. Take them up on it and report back."

Spy work. He wants me to spy on GoPol. "That sounds dangerous." I hate how cowardly that makes me sound.

"This is the Résistance, Alix," the Chevalier says rather harshly. "Our work *is* dangerous. It's your choice if you want to join us, but remember this: the alternative is GoPol, who will take your ghost away."

"Not if I join."

"Maybe. In that case, they'll take your soul away." That's not what Gaby said, but I only have to think of Sébastien to know it's true. Despite being dead, Dix is the lively one, while Sébastien is dead inside, able to betray me with a smile on his face.

The Chevalier shrugs. "Look, I'm not going to force you, just take it from me. GoPol have been abusing their power for decades. They hold a cruel monopoly on ghost whispering and they'd do anything to keep ghosts small. How many people do you think they've robbed of their ghost powers? They've got agents stationed in hospitals across the country to swoop in the moment someone has to be resuscitated. I'm not going to lie to you. While your powers are still intact, it's either us or them."

I don't like this. It feels too much like an ultimatum, but then I only have myself to blame. It was me who put myself on GoPol's radar. And me who crossed the Chevalier's path. I believe him. I believe that my life has come to this crossroad where I have to choose. Join a corrupted agency, join a dubious organisation of the underworld, or lose my powers, the latter being no choice at all.

"So, by joining GoPol, I'll prove myself?"

The Chevalier winces. "Not quite. Here's the actual test. Infiltrate GoPol, report on any actions that seem to be directed against us, and to make sure you're really on our side, steal a copy of the Coullier file from Charles Roubert's office."

My heart skips a beat. "Steal?" All of this sounds terribly dangerous and overwhelming. I'm not ready to trade my somewhat normal life of being a history student who happens to be friends with ghosts for one of danger. But then I don't want to trade it for a boring one without ghosts either.

Gaspar's hand closes around mine. "We can do this. Together."

That's right, this isn't just about me. I'm fighting for him and our relationship as well. And it's not like I'm being held at gunpoint—for once. I can still wait to make a decision, because honestly, I don't yet trust this so-called Résistance or Nexus, either.

I wet my awfully dry lips. "I'll give it a try."

That's all I can promise for now.

The Chevalier nods contently. "Great. Let me walk you out of here."

CHAPTER 14

I leave the catacombs with a head full of questions and fears. One thing's clear, I'm in way over my head with this one. Again. But I've learned from my mistakes. Instead of trying to solve this by myself, I turn to the ones I can trust. In short, I need to talk to my ghosts.

Once I finish work and have sent Philippe home, I settle down in the crypt, surrounded by those who still care about me. Victor is right there, as he always is, while Jean Moulin leans against a column, fedora tipped down. Josephine Baker is sitting on the bench in a sparkling fringe dress, her bare legs crossed elegantly as she listens attentively.

It doesn't take very long for the others to creep closer. Some of the writers are hanging in the back, while the generals from above start crowding the stairs. Jean-Jacques Rousseau slips into a space near Victor as if he always stood there, and I even see Voltaire hovering at the edge of my field of vision, looking on grimly.

They all listen quietly as I tell them about the offer from GoPol, Sébastien's betrayal, and finally my subsequent visit to the catacombs. As soon as I finish, Voltaire grumbles and disappears into the shadows. Guess even insatiable curiosity won't make him forgive me.

"So, what now? I can't risk losing you." Surrounded by all the ghosts I hold so dear, the very thought of it is suffocating. "But this... I'm not a fighter, neither for the resistance nor GoPol. I'm just... I just want to study history and live my life." I know how pathetic that sounds, but despite my love for adventure, this adventure has gotten a bit too big and scary.

"This so-called Résistance," Moulin asks, "Who are they? Do you have any names?"

I assume that he's looking for the names of the ghosts in the bunker, not the living people, but Pierre Roche, the Chevalier, and his ghost whisperer are the only names I've got, and even those were given without surnames.

Moulin nods thoughtfully. "Naturally, they wouldn't part with their real names. Too much risk attached. I would love to meet them, though. See if I can catch up with some old faces, gauge how sincere this new Résistance is."

"Of course they're not sincere!" Voltaire bellows. Apparently he hasn't quite retreated as far as I thought he had. In his volatile manner, he strides back into the group, his blazing eyes finding me. "Résistance! What are these people even resisting? We're not at war. Not even a civil one."

As if called upon, Rousseau speaks up. "I believe it's human nature to always be at civil war with those in power, whether the majority is sympathetic to the cause or not. If these people are burdened by unhappiness, then their cause is valid."

"Horseshit!"

As Voltaire and Rousseau descend into one of their usual spats, I turn to Victor. "What do you think?"

"I'm worried for you. It seems to me like you're choosing between two hungry beasts, each eager to devour you."

"What you need is information." Moulin kicks off the column and saunters over. "Play both sides until you know their true mechanisms."

Victor shakes his head. "It's too dangerous."

"It seems to me like Mademoiselle Alix is already in a great deal of danger as is. What she needs now is the courage to forge ahead onto the path she's chosen."

I sigh heavily, not feeling courageous at all. "I suppose lying low is out of the question?"

Moulin shudders, as if the mere thought offends him. "Oh, absolutely. Don't let them scare you into submission. You need to stay true to your beliefs and fight for what you hold dear in whatever way you can."

"I'm not a fighter," I repeat softly.

He smiles softly. "None of us were. What makes us fighters aren't weapons and training. It's choice: the choice to stand up for our beliefs, even in times of adversity. *Especially* in times of adversity. You stand to lose too much of yourself, otherwise."

How true that is. I take a shuddering breath, my eyelids fluttering as I feel the future overwhelming me. I already knew that lying low was not an option. Since I cannot escape GoPol, it will just see me stripped of all I hold dear, what I'm left with are two impossible choices.

Risk selling my integrity by joining the legal, orderly ghost police or join a mysterious rebellion with goals yet unknown to me.

"Which one would you choose?" I ask Moulin. I feel someone as heroic as him would know something about picking the right side.

But Moulin shakes his head. "My choices no longer hold consequences. None of ours do. Which is why I'm telling you to get more information."

Victor clicks his tongue, looking grim. "You can't advise her to become a double agent. If someone discovers what she's doing, she'll be in big trouble."

"Not if she plays her cards right. Look, everything's already in place. Alix has the offer from GoPol and the Chevalier asked her to spy for them. They *want* her to go behind enemy lines. All Alix needs to do is to play along." Moulin turns around to speak to me directly. "As long as none of them asks you to engage in active combat, you have little to fear. And I'll be here every step of the way. I will investigate this Résistance, see what intel I can gather."

"And I will help you navigate that government agency," the warm voice of Josephine Baker chimes in. She smiles at me. "Moulin often forgets that not every act of resistance is about hiding in dark tunnels, attending clandestine meetings."

Moulin chuckles softly. "Au contraire, I would never forget the valuable services you provided. It's a shame we never had the pleasure of crossing paths during the war." He nods at me. "Josephine is an excellent source for more subtle manners of espionage."

I get what he means. After all, Josephine isn't just a celebrated actress and singer, but also a decorated war hero for aiding the Résistance. Her status as an artist gave her a certain immunity that allowed her to attend enemy functions and escape more thorough body searches. She smuggled hundreds of notes back to the Allied Forces.

"How do I pull this off?" At the moment, I'm more inclined to join the Chevalier's side, as unthinkable as that was only a few days ago.

"Oh, it's fairly easy," Josephine says. "In this situation, be the ever-attentive student. Speak little, listen lots. It's ridiculously easy when you're a woman. Note down everything you can remember as soon as you're alone. You don't know what parts of the conversation could be important. It might be the mention of a meeting or a name. Sometimes something as arbitrary as a pet's shenanigans."

"And how do I steal that file?" Just thinking of it sends my heart racing.

"Opportunity," Josephine muses. "As Moulin keeps harping on, you need information. Use your little friend to scout ahead. See if he can find out where the file is kept and how it might be protected. You're a ghost whisperer, Alix. Make use of it."

If only GoPol wasn't full of ghost whisperers as well. Then again, they barely use ghosts to their full potential. I'm the one with the ghost friends, with all these people who are the best of the best. Josephine, the experienced war-time spy. Moulin, the courageous politician-turned-resistance-fighter. The generals who came to my aid, and my moral compass, Victor.

"If you tell me to back off, I will." Part of me wants him to say it.

Victor heaves a sigh, sadness filling his eyes. "I'm but a sentimental man, worried for one I hold as dear as my own flesh and blood." He bows his head. "But Moulin's advice is sound. As much as I hate the thought of you venturing in the lion's den, I see the necessity. To love is to act. And you must fight for what you love. And whom," he adds with a soft smile.

That settles it. I'll play both sides until I get a clearer sense of which will allow me to continue my life of ghosts without compromising all I believe in.

Chapter 15

Despite an intense coaching session by Josephine Baker and Jean Moulin that even involved role-playing sessions with other ghosts, I'm nearly peeing myself while waiting for Sébastien at the Place de la Madeleine. Further down the street I can see the colourful lights of the conjoining Christmas markets from the Champs-Élysées and the Tulieres gardens. In comparison, the stark-white columns of the St. Madeleine Church, that looks more like a Greek temple than Christian church, are a calming influence.

And I need it. Not only will I walk into the lion's den, as Victor said metaphorically, it's also the first time I'm seeing Sébastien since he betrayed me. If I want to pull this off, I can't let him see how hurt I am. And then there's the whole matter of spying on GoPol for the Chevalier that makes my heart beat a hundred miles an hour.

My nerves turn to instant anger when I see Sébastien making his way over to me, accompanied by Dix. His face lights up at my sight and he leans in to kiss my cheeks, as if he hadn't twisted the knife between my ribs only days ago. "Glad you called."

"Well…" I don't get much further, my mind blanking as the anger rolls over me. I swallow hard, burying the choice words I have for him.

"Shall we?" Sébastien nods towards a standard apartment building with beige walls, grey roof tiles, and narrow windows.

I manage a sharp nod and join him stiffly as he crosses the street.

"You good?" Dix asks softly.

My face twitches. "Just nervous."

He gives me a commiserating shrug. "I'd be, too."

Sébastien looks over his shoulder. "There's no reason to be nervous. Today is just a tour. We'll show you around the office and answer whatever questions you might have. No pressure to sign the contract today."

There's no need to respond as we reach the entrance. The array of doorbells proclaims two medical specialists, a lawyer, and three floors of GPF, which I assume stands for GoPol France.

Sébastien lets himself in with a key and leads me up two flights of stairs past the medical practices—a GP and a surgery—and a public relations lawyer. Contrary to the entrance below, the GPF door on this level requires a swipe card. A scratchy hum welcomes us in.

I don't know what I expected from the offices—something small and cramped perhaps—but it's not what awaits me behind the doors. After a short corridor, the space suddenly opens up into one big enough to fit my family's entire apartment and then some. On the left is a well-lit corridor and a spacious open kitchen. On the right, two parallel corridors lead deeper to more office spaces. On the opposite side, there's a stationery room and staircase, which leads both up and down. Between the two, someone has put up a Christmas tree and hung red and green garlands. Presents have been placed between the roots, though I can't tell if they're real or just nicely wrapped Styrofoam blocks.

My mind struggles to process the sheer amount of people. At least five are bustling around the kitchen, others are in a lounge area I've only just noticed. People cross the open space to go from one office to another, while there's a three-way discussion blocking off access to the corridor on the left. The noise from all the conversations is enough to blow my mind.

I don't know why, but in my mind, GoPol consisted only of Sébastien, his father, and maybe three or four other whisperers. Now I realise how silly that notion was. Five or even ten people would never be enough to serve an entire country, not even if they were only responsible for the Greater Paris area. Despite the public notion that ghosts don't exist, this is a big agency hidden in plain sight in what looks like a standard apartment complex.

They probably don't just have whisperers working for them but an equal, if not larger, number of admin staff.

"This is it?" I ask, unable to keep the awe from my voice.

"Surprised?" Sébastien asks amused, before raising his hand in greeting at another young man.

I quickly adjust my face. "A little. You made it sound a lot smaller than it is."

Sébastien frowns. "I did?"

Anger still churns in me now that I'm over my initial surprise. I don't want to talk with him, but that's not what Josephine advised. I manage a noncommittal shrug. "You just don't seem like the kind of person who..." I stop myself before I can say something offensive.

Sébastien's mouth quirks up, so deceivingly amiable. "Go on, tell me what kind of person I am."

"A solitary one." I'm embarrassed that's what I come up with, because it's the first thing Cédric said about him.

He scoffs, the mirth fleeing from his face. "You mean a loner?"

"She's not wrong," Dix says before Sébastien has the chance to refute my claim.

Sébastien closes his eyes for a second and takes a deep breath. "I prefer working alone in the field, but that doesn't mean I can't socialise."

"He can't," Dix whispers to me at a volume that doesn't conceal anything from Sébastien.

"Hush," Sébastien says, sounding more like he's warning him than reprimanding him.

I don't have much time to wonder about the weird inflection since an older man is approaching us with a confident stride. His looks instantly identify him as Sébastien's father. Though his hair is more grey than blond, his eyes are as strikingly blue as his son's. Contrary to Sébastien, he wears an easy smile, with deep creases around his eyes and his mouth.

"Mademoiselle Dubois. We meet at last." He stretches out his hand and grabs mine the moment it twitches in his direction, kissing my cheek. "Charles Roubert. Welcome to GoPol."

His jovial demeanour is the opposite of what I expected from Sébastien's father, who is an even bigger workaholic, according to his childhood tales. This is a man who enjoys being around people, as evidenced by the amount of people who shout out to him or wave a hand. A gesture he returns without ever looking tired of it.

When he's finally dealt with all the well-wishers, Charles stretches his neck a little, as if trying to look behind me. "No ghost?"

Sébastien throws his father a long look. "I told you. We haven't found her yet."

Surprised, I look at him. Since when was there a *we*? Is this one more attempt at making me feel included and appreciated so he can figure out another way of driving a knife into my back?

"Ah, right. I forgot we're still waiting on that." Charles makes a half turn, inviting me to step into the room with him. "Well, then, let's give you a quick tour."

I'm glad I no longer have to pretend to like Sébastien despite his betrayal. We leave him trailing after us as Charles starts walking slowly around the room.

"We moved into the building about eight years ago because we needed more space," he says. "This right here is our social area. As you can see, we've got a lounge space and big kitchen, which, in my opinion, is just a fancy word for an embarrassingly large ugly mug collection."

Now that he points it out, I can see that at least three long shelves are filled with mugs, and that doesn't count the ones drying on the counter.

"Down that way there's also some quiet spaces, meeting rooms, a parent room, and our stationery storage, which is about eighty per cent copy paper and printer cartridges."

I'm unable to stop a little chuckle escaping my determined lips. Charles makes it all sound so incredibly mundane.

"You'd have no idea how much paperwork ghost matters require. All kinds of permissions, transcripts, and records." Charles waves a hand. "I'm quite glad I can pass most of that off to my small army of assistants. The perks of being the boss of this whole mess."

"So, are all of them familiar with ghosts?" Josephine told me to appear interested but not push the conversation too much. I figure a certain amount of curiosity is expected of me. I just need to be careful not to get carried away.

Charles shakes his head. "Oh, no. There are a few layers within our organisation. Everyone working here knows that we're an intelligence agency, but only a small portion, our whisperers and some support staff, know about the ghosts."

"What do the rest do?"

"Keep the agency running, communicate with InterPol and the gendarmes, write reports. As I said: a lot of paperwork. That said, we value all our employees' contributions and try to foster community spirit, like our Secret Santa over there." He jerks his head towards the Christmas tree, which must mean those presents are real.

I'm low-key impressed. I thought the organisation was a lot more hush-hush, bare minimum of staff, all secrets, and each out on their own. This doesn't look as scary a workplace as I thought it would be.

"Do the whisper ghosts take part in Secret Santa, too?"

Charles laughs a deep belly laugh that turns a couple of heads. Judging by the smiles he gets, it's not unusual. In stark contrast, Sébastien's face doesn't even twitch and Dix has vanished altogether. I wonder when that happened.

"You're funny," Charles says at last and claps my back. "What would you gift a ghost?"

A favour. It burns on my tongue, but I just force my lips into an awkward smile and pretend to laugh about my joke that wasn't a joke.

Last year, I created a special fun-fact tour for the Panthéon, sharing little-known details about our ghosts that made them feel seen as humans rather than just a bunch of achievements. I've already built a dub-step playlist for Gaspar that I'll listen to, despite it not really being my kind of music. He'll appreciate it greatly since he can no longer choose his own. It's not impossible to make ghosts happy.

What I take from Charles' reaction, though, is that while the human employees are valued, the ghosts are not.

Chapter 16

We take the stairs next to the Christmas tree and go up through another card-secured door. The layout is very similar, though what is an open space downstairs is split into meeting and training rooms here. Less people loiter. The only two I see is a guy entering the gym and a woman behind a desk in an office.

"This is our field agent area," Charles explains, then starts pointing out rooms. "We've got safety gear in that one, weapons there, locked with a triple access key, and our own fitness gear. A gym membership is basically one of the perks of this job."

Not a perk that means much to me. I'm perfectly happy with the workout I get from riding my bike, even if I can't do much of it at the moment. "Is it required?"

Charles sways his head uncertainly. "Yes and no. We don't log our agent's work-out hours, but a certain fitness status is required for field missions and agents are encouraged to keep their fitness up. But don't worry, unlike the gendarmes, you don't have to pass a fitness test to join. We'll just get you up to speed after that. And it's not just cardio or muscle training, we do regular sparring classes as well, teach you hand-on-hand combat. It's fun."

It doesn't sound fun.

"I'm happy to be your sparring partner and teach you all the tricks," Sébastien says.

I ignore him, grinning at Charles instead. "Well, I've always wanted to take some self-defence classes." If it ever crossed my mind, I've never followed through with it.

"There you go. It's all inclusive here. Now, down there we have our labs." He points down a corridor.

"Labs?"

"Spectral research. In order to improve our intelligence work we need to understand why ghosts are the way they are, where they appear, and how they can be managed."

My heart flutters as I inadvertently think about the split-up bones in the catacombs. I want to ask whether they work closely with the Quarry Department and the Knights Hospitallers but remember that Paul didn't know about GoPol. Unless he'd been playing dumb yet again.

Instead, I strike a different path. "You can be a researcher?" Despite everyone's encouragement, the special agent job doesn't sit right with me. I just don't see myself as someone like Sébastien.

But a researcher is something I could be. Something that wouldn't even be that far from what I've always wanted to do.

"What was it that you do again? Physics?"

"History," Sébastien answers.

"I don't think there's much ghost history to work with," Charles says, amused. "They don't exactly have records."

I could point out how that might be even more reason to establish one. Contrary to normal history, which relies on written records, the ghosts are still here. I could interview them, build up the sample size, and establish timelines, but apparently there's little interest in *actually* understanding the ghost world.

"True. I hadn't thought of that." A nervous laugh is all I can manage. I don't want him to dwell too long on my awkward suggestion, and ask with what's hopefully just the right amount of curiosity, "So, what are you researching then?"

"I'm no scientist myself," Charles admits, "but much of our research is centred around the nature of ghosts, measuring ghost activity, and whisper ghosts, which seem to be an entirely different kind of spectre. That said, our research team is fairly small. Most ghost research is done in the UK or overseas."

I wonder if those bigger research centres would be more open to other faculties or if all they're interested in are the biological and physical properties of ghosts. If it was up to me, there should be research on the psychology of ghosts, on their social bonds, and yes, their history. But that would require seeing them as dead humans and not alien spectres.

"Anyway," Charles is slowly regaining his smile. "Your talents would be wasted in our research department. We need you out in the field."

"You do?" I want to know what makes me such a perfect candidate.

Charles nods. "Sébastien told me what you did in the Boutique, calling on highly qualified ghosts to aid you in a fight. How did you do that?"

"The calling?" There doesn't seem to be any harm in giving away that information. "Well, I've noticed that ghosts appear when I think of them with intention."

He waves me off. "We know that. It's how we work with our whisper and partner ghosts. I meant calling these particular ghosts and getting them to help you."

His question confounds me a little. "They're my friends?"

"Friends?"

Oh, that's what we're struggling with. "Yes, friends. I—" I stop myself before I can launch into a little rant about how ghosts should be treated. Smile and listen, Josephine had said. Ask questions but offer nothing of substance. Or, at least, nothing they don't already know. "I work with them at the Panthéon."

"Fascinating." Charles' eyes sparkle with curiosity. "I can't wait to talk some more about this once you're truly one of ours. I've never thought of making friends with a ghost. My real friends are flaky enough as it is," he jokes.

I giggle along, hoping it comes across somewhat naturally. "Well, it worked for me."

"And that's why we need you," he says, with the kind of smile that makes me feel incredibly appreciated.

Sébastien's father is truly a force to be reckoned with. Even as anti-GoPol as I currently feel, he's starting to charm me. Sure, his views are a bit archaic, but those could be challenged. And if he's hiring me specifically because of my relationships with ghosts that should indicate that he's at least open to alternative ways.

"Come on. Let's have a closer look at the training facilities."

The next couple of rooms are two high-standard gyms, a mat-covered room used for sparring, and a high-tech VR room for simulated fights. "For real shooting practice, we go to the police academy and use their facilities," Charles explains as he lets me try out a gun simulation. "I wish we had the space to have our own, but these are good enough to train your reflexes and aim. Here."

He takes the gun controller from Sébastien's hand and gives it to me, then proceeds to show me how to hold it. Sébastien looks slightly dejected, once more reduced to being the third wheel on this tour.

The controller is surprisingly heavy, probably to simulate the weight of a real gun. My breath quickens as I think of the previous few times I've been faced with a gun. Now I'm on the other end, and even though this is just a game, the implication is that I'm training for the real thing. I bet any other candidate would've loved this chance to prove themselves, but my fingers are shaking. I don't like guns. I neither want to get shot by them, nor do I want to shoot them. Not even if the bullets are replaced by salt. Perhaps especially then.

But I'm here to keep an open mind—or at least attempt to look like I'm enjoying myself, so I put on the visor and let Charles guide me through the set-up. To my great relief, I'm not shooting people in the game but standard target practise. And while the gun-shaped controller still gives me the ick, hitting the target is surprisingly exhilarating.

"You've got some nice steady arms there," Charles says when he takes the equipment off me again. "You'll pick up shooting in no time." When he sees me swallow heavily, he chuckles. "Don't worry, as Sébastien can surely attest, it's extremely rare the guns get any use outside the firing range."

Sébastien opens his mouth but I pretend not to have seen him. "That's good. I'd rather not have a repeat of the Boutique anytime soon."

"I've got to be honest with you," Charles says as he leads me from the room, disregarding his son as well, "I've never heard of anything like that before. That a ghost should be strong enough to attack a human? I mean you hear of people claiming a ghost pushed them down the stairs all the time, but we've never been able to prove it. Physical altercations are very rare in our line of work. Our main objective is to remain secret after all; gather information, protect our country's assets, and hand over to Interpol if there's anything that requires action."

That makes me feel a bit better. GoPol's main line of work is espionage not detention. I've just had a bad run so far, but that might change once I start working here.

Charles raises a hand, suddenly struck by an idea. "You'll love what I'm going to show you next. Come."

My curiosity is piqued. I follow him past closed-up offices to the very end of the corridor where a plaque at the door announces the archive. Sure enough, excitement hits me.

Charles grants us access with his swipe card and holds the door for me. "The archive. Every mission report ever submitted to the Paris branch, plus copies of important national and foreign cases."

I step into the room with awe. It's not huge when compared to the library at Sorbonne or even our history library, but it's still an impressive size. There are hundreds of little notebooks, some more worn than others, all sorted by agent name, and even more folders labelled with years and locations. I immediately spot an entire shelf labelled 'catacombs'.

My feet lead me to the shelf without consciously making the decision. I run my finger across the back of the folders, amazed at how far back they go. There are reports from the late nineteenth century, roughly around the World Exposition. What a wealth of information. I could've used them for class.

"Can I read these?" I ask over my shoulder.

"Once you've obtained the necessary clearance," Charles says with a warm smile.

"Which would be when?"

He laughs. "Well, first, I would suggest a trial month, shadowing one of our more experienced agents." He nods at Sébastien—little surprise there. "And then once you've signed the contract, you'll start as a junior agent. Depending on your performance, you could be promoted to senior in as little as five years."

Five years is a very long stick for the dangling carrot. "And then I can access the archive."

"Yes, though of course you can always request individual reports. Depending on the nature and justification behind it, you should be granted access as soon as you start working on your own cases."

"I see." With a longing glance, I turn away from the historical reports and leave the room again. If I truly make it to five years at GoPol, I'll spend every waking moment in this room and read those reports. Put that way, I'd probably withhold access from me for as long as possible as well.

Charles nods and locks the door behind me. "Alright then, shall we proceed to the next floor?"

"What's that?"

"It's dubbed the command centre." He laughs again, as if it's some grand joke. "It's nowhere as fancy as that, but it's where the mission controllers and I have our offices. We even have our own pool table up there."

"Well, now I've got to see it." Pool sounds more fun than the clichéd golf strip other big offices have. But the main reason I want to see the office is the Chevalier's request. If I can get inside, I can at least see where the file might be. Or if there are any special security measures I need to be aware of.

We make our way up to the third floor where the offices are fewer and larger. Charles shows us the hangout space for the agency leaders, which does indeed boast a pool table, several extremely comfy couches, and even a bar.

"Wow."

"A few amenities for those that put so much work into our nation's security," Charles says with a wink. "Come, my office is right down there."

It's by far the biggest of the lot, with a view of the Eiffel Tower. There's another seating group and a large meeting table, but the heart of the office is the massive oak-wood desk with its rows of pictures and small piles of files.

I start when I notice that the room isn't empty. Someone's sitting behind the desk.

"Oh, I should've probably introduced him first. This is C-Trente, my whisper ghost."

The man behind the desk looks a lot like Sébastien, though contrary to him, he wears a short beard. He's leaner than Charles and glowers at me, which makes him look much more like son and less father. At the mention of his name, he gives us a sharp nod.

"C, this is Alix, Sébastien's new find."

I shudder at being called anything of Sébastien's, especially since he betrayed me so easily, but I keep my smile intact and wave. "Nice to meet you, C-Trente." Another name, another number. Just one of the many tools in GoPol's arsenal.

"Someone was snooping," C-Trente says with a slow drawl. "A ghost."

My heart grows cold. While I've been getting the grand tour, Gaspar made his own way here. We thought it would be the easiest way to locate the Coullier file, falsely assuming the office would be empty.

Charles raises an eyebrow. "A whisper ghost?"

"Normal. And local."

"Local?" Charles frowns. "So, not an enemy ghost then?"

C-Trente shakes his head slowly, his expression growing even colder. "That remains to be seen."

"Remains to be seen?" I repeat inadvertently. With a nervous laugh, I try to mask my anxiety. "What does this mean?"

Charles raises a hand towards his ghost. "We'll talk about this later." Then he puts a hand on my shoulder, gently leading me toward the door. "There's nothing to worry about, Alix. Sometimes ghosts wander into our premises. We just need to make sure that they're not following enemy orders."

"Enemies?" I swallow heavily.

"Well, the European Union isn't the only government that employs ghost whisperers in their intelligence service. But don't worry. The ghosts are harmless. We just don't want them to gather any information."

"So, what do you do with them?" The way C-Trente phrased his answer, I'm afraid he somehow caught Gaspar.

"Salt them," Charles says instantly. "That scatters their mind and usually wipes the information from them. When they gather again, they only remember their life and nothing of their afterlife. It's like a cold reset."

I suppress the urge to swallow in front of him. Did C-Trente get Gaspar? Did he just memory wipe our entire relationship from him?

"And that concludes our tour. Do you have any questions?"

My mind is swirling with questions about Gaspar's well-being. I need to check up on him, but I don't know how. Then it hits me. "One urgent one, right now." I laugh in a supposedly awkward manner. "Could you point me to the restroom please?"

"Absolutely." Charles points down the corridor. "It's right over there. Once you're finished, join us in the lounge, and we'll have glass of wine to discuss this further."

"Great." I do my very best not to run, walking as calmly as I can.

As soon as I'm in the restroom—a fancy one on this level with brass armatures—I lock the door behind me and flee into one of the two stalls. After locking that one too, I think of Gaspar as hard as I can. "Come on, Gaspar, please. Appear. Come to—"

I nearly scream with joy when he appears next to me. After the initial bout of relief, concern hits me. Gaspar is sitting on the floor, holding his side, and wincing. Bruises cover his chin and eye. Bruises on a ghost.

"What happened?" My voice feels too loud. Even as far away as I am from the door.

"It wasn't empty." He grimaces in pain.

I drop to the floor next to him and cradle his poor maltreated face. "Are you okay? Do you remember who I am?"

A corner of his mouth lifts. "Of course I remember who you are—" I hug him so tight he groans in pain. "Careful."

"Sorry." I let go of him again. "So, you weren't *salted*?"

Gaspar shakes his head, slowly letting go of his side. "I'm okay."

"No, you're not."

He chuckles softly. "Fine. I'm going to be okay. These wounds will pass. I just remember the pain. Not that I've ever been beaten up before. Or thrown out a window."

"You were thrown out a window?"

"I can't die, remember?" He tries for another laugh but fails miserably. His voice softens. "It's fine, Alix. You don't need to worry about me. Don't cry."

He pulls me close as I try to swallow my tears. The wounds will fade. They're nothing against what he endured at the hands of Jacques de Molay. He's okay. He still remembers me.

"We'll try again another time," Gaspar promises. "How are you?"

"I'm good."

He looks me deep in my eyes, searching for the truth. "Really?"

I nod. "Yes, it's been... alright." Too much information to process right now. "I'd better get back to them. We'll talk at home."

Gaspar smiles at me, then kisses my forehead. "You've got this."

After another hug, I let myself out of the cubicle again and face the mirror. Quickly, I splash some water on my face to wash away the tears and counteract the redness of my eyes. Hopefully, Sébastien and his father won't notice. There's no good explanation I could give them.

I do another splash and look up to check the effect, finding Sébastien staring at me from the mirror.

My heart jumps into my throat and I let out a little scream. Or I would've, if Sébastien hadn't stepped forward and clamped his fingers around my mouth. "Don't."

CHAPTER 17

After the initial shock, I realise it's Dix and not Sébastien. He looked so serious, I didn't recognise him immediately.

I push away his hand and whirl around. "What are you doing? It's really bad form to follow a woman to the toilet."

He shrugs, unabashed. "It's a unisex toilet."

"You knew I was here."

"You didn't go to the toilet."

My heart is still racing. Dix knows about Gaspar. How much has he heard? "How long have you been here?"

"Just a minute. I heard you crying." His voice softens. "Are you okay?"

My voice hardens. "Yes, I'm fine. You don't need to worry about me." Now that the shock has worn out, anger floods my system. I turn back around and pretend to check my make-up. It's barely existent, as always. "What do you want?"

"What are you doing here?"

"In the bathroom?"

"At GoPol." He sounds petulant.

I look over my shoulder. "Haven't you heard? I'm Sébastien's new find. Your father wants to recruit me."

Dix's mouth thins. "No, he doesn't."

With a pointed look, I say, "He's giving me the tour. You were there. And then you weren't." I frown at him. "Why did you vanish?"

"Because Séb told me to scram."

"Why?"

Dix scoffs. "I can't keep my mouth shut when I'm near dear old Papa. He doesn't appreciate it."

Charles didn't seem like a strict father, but it's a good reminder that the smiling face I got to see today might not be his real one.

Satisfied with my appearance, I turn back around. "Well, I need to get back. Can't have them wondering where I am."

Dix only steps aside reluctantly. "Don't trust him, Alix."

That's rich, coming from him. I smack my lips, anger crawling under my skin. "It's you I don't trust."

Okay, maybe I've just blown my cover. I've very likely done that, but it can't be helped. Not here, not after the scare I just had, not with Dix.

He frowns. "You mean Sébastien?"

"Isn't it the same?"

I push past him and release the lock. Stunned, he just stands back and lets me go.

Without wasting any more time, I return to the lounge with a big fake smile on my face. "Sorry, that took so long. I shouldn't have had two coffees before I came here." Now that I've said it, I actually have to pee.

To my surprise, Charles and Sébastien haven't been sitting together. The boss of GoPol sits comfortably on the couch, while his son stands near the window, as if he were some bodyguard and not Charles' own flesh and blood. Despite what Sébastien told me about his childhood, there doesn't seem to be much love left between the two.

Interesting.

Charles answers my smile with one of his own. "Never rush a lady." He waves me closer. "Sit, sit. Wine, Sébastien?"

Abruptly, Sébastien turns and gets two glasses and a bottle, keeping none for himself.

"You're not drinking with us?" I ask.

"I'm at work," is all Sébastien has to say.

Charles chuckles lowly. "We usually encourage our employees to keep the drinking to after hours. But this calls for an exception."

"Indeed." I take my glass and smell the rich bouquet of red wine.

"Have you already made your decision?" Charles seems surprised.

I lower the glass again and give him a girlish little shrug. "Everything I saw today was truly inspiring. I don't know if I am necessarily a good fit for GoPol, but if you still want me, I'd love to give it a try."

Charles puts his glass down with a thud, giving me a strong nod. "Of course we want you. That's why we invited you here. Well then, let's not beat around the bush. How about you come here on the twenty-seventh and Sébastien can run you through the basics? You will have to sign an NDA, of course, in case it doesn't work out."

"Of course." Just the thought of signing a contract, and one that effectively puts a muzzle on me, gives me the shivers.

"Let's toast to that. Once again, my dear, welcome to GoPol."

As our glasses clink together, I can't keep myself from stealing a glance at Sébastien. For the first time since we entered the building, he's smiling with relief. It makes me feel like I just made a deal with the devil.

"I'm confused," I tell Gaspar as soon as I arrive home.

He already looks a lot better. There's no more swelling and he's not cowering in pain, but a purple shadow still graces his face.

Before I can continue to explain my conflicted feelings, the door opens, and Odile slips in. "What now?"

She's got Malou in her hands and is returning her to her cage. "Don't look at me like that. We had to do a fitting." Then she takes a place on my desk chair. "How was GoPol?"

"Don't you have an exam to study for?" It comes out harsher than I intended.

"Wrote it today and I think I did pretty well." She smiles. "Thanks for the help."

Exasperated, I stare at her, unable to bring myself to care. Gaspar comes up and puts his arms around me, holding me securely, and I let out an anxious little breath.

"Sorry, Odi. That's wonderful."

Her forehead creases with concern. "You don't look too good. Was it that bad?"

"No, yes, I don't know." I rub my face, while Gaspar massages my shoulders. My visit to the GoPol offices was overwhelming and that's about all I know.

"Your shoulders are—... Never mind. Shall I leave you alone with Gaspar?" Odile asks, pretending to avert her eyes.

"Are you going to eavesdrop?"

"Probably."

"Then stay." I'd rather have her in the room as a visual reminder, than forget she's listening in.

I sit on my bed with Gaspar, who keeps a hand on my leg, stroking it comfortingly. "The tour was actually really interesting. It's not what I expected, but then again, it was also *totally* what I expected." I give them a quick rundown of the different things I was shown, ending with the archive.

"It was amazing. There's such a wealth of information in there. But even if I stick with GoPol, it'll be five years before I gain access to the archive without having to ask somebody else." I sigh. "You know, the thing is, I could totally see myself working for GoPol, just not where they want to place me."

Odile cocks her head in confusion. "That makes no sense."

Annoyed, I click my tongue, thinking about how I could make it clearer. "GoPol doesn't just gather intelligence. They also research ghosts, and they've got these archives, which apparently no one has ever worked through. They're so mission oriented that they're not making use of what they already have. If I got offered a job to catalogue and research those hundreds of years of ghost reports, I would take it instantly."

"But that's not what they want you for," Gaspar says softly.

I nod. "Exactly. They want me in the field with Sébastien. Or what I really think is that they don't actually want me. They want my connections."

Gaspar grimaces. "Yeah, that's probably it."

Meanwhile, Odile bites her lip. "But isn't that more interesting? I mean, you love working with your ghost friends."

"I love *spending time* with my ghost friends," I correct her. "That's the other thing. Everyone at GoPol sees ghosts as tools only, even their own whisper ghosts."

"Whisper ghosts, you mean like Papa's ghost?" Odile asks. "Antoine?"

"The one Sébastien took away, yes."

Her eyes widen. "What?"

"I stupidly told Sébastien about Papa, hoping that he'd know how to help him, but instead, he came over at the next opportunity and convinced Papa to give his ghost away. Now he can no longer see ghosts."

"Not even Gaspar?"

I shake my head, my eyes burning suddenly. "No, not even him." For a short time, someone in my family was just like me. I was able to introduce Gaspar to my father. And now he's going to pretend ghosts—and thus, Gaspar—don't exist.

"So, your whisper ghost, Petite Alix, where is she hanging out?"

As much as I love my sister, this is not information I trust her with. "She's safe. Sorry, but..."

"You're keeping her location secret, so they won't take her away." Odile nods thoughtfully. "I just thought that you needed her to join GoPol. I mean, they can't take your ghost away if they want to hire you, right? Don't you need to keep your powers to be of value?"

"That's my whole problem. The Chevalier said they'd take them away, that Sébastien is only concerned with finding her because of that. And sure enough, he took Papa's away as soon as he knew about it." The thought is making me angry all over again. "But, contrary to what the Chevalier said, GoPol now wants to hire me. At least, I think they want to." I mean, I'm going to sign a contract and all. A contract I intend to read very carefully, but a contract nonetheless.

"Yeah, but the problem here is that it's either work for them or lose your power," Gaspar adds softly. "They're not offering out of kindness. They're offering because they want to use you. Just like their ghosts. And if you don't agree, they'll come after your powers."

A chill runs down my back. There's that, of course.

Odile nudges me. "What did he say?"

I relay Gaspar's argument, noticing that it doesn't feel any better the second time around. "In the end, I don't have much of a choice. At least overtly. As long as I play ball, I get to keep my powers."

Odile pulls a face. "What if they aren't actually that bad? I mean, yes, the all-or-nothing sucks, but beyond that, they do this to keep us all safe, right? They're some kind of secret service, and as such it makes sense that they need to make sure their assets are protected. It's probably a huge risk to have unregistered ghost whisperers running around."

"About as dangerous as having anyone run around. We could all be spies, ghosts or no ghosts. I mean, all I'm doing is studying, going to work, and talking with extremely interesting people who died a long time ago. I'm not spying on anyone, I'm not extorting information, I'm not working against my own country. Nor do I ever intend to."

She raises her hands. "I wasn't saying that. Just that I understand the secrecy. The thing is you already know too much. Of course they want to hire you. They probably wouldn't care if you'd never met Sébastien."

"Too bad he took his job so seriously." I want to vomit.

The memory of our first meeting tastes bitter now. I was so happy to meet someone who understood what I'd been dealing with all my life. But all he was interested in was keeping me close, so he could use and betray me. "Gosh, I hate him."

"That makes two of us," Gaspar says softly.

I snort at him. "You're just jealous."

But Gaspar shakes his head. "Not any longer. I'm angry. He betrayed you. All his special interest in you just so he could deliver you to his father. Remember when he had you followed around by Dix?"

Dix's supervision saved my life, but it hadn't felt very good. "You're right. He's no friend of mine. He's his father's creature through and through." And harder than his father. Completely dedicated to his line of work.

I sigh. "So, what should I do?"

"Do you have a choice?" Odile asks.

Gaspar puts his hand on mine. "Play along for now. Take that trial month. If by the end of it you're absolutely sure that you don't want anything to do with GoPol, then turn to the Chevalier for protection. His Résistance has means you don't." He gives me a warm smile. "Remember, you're not alone in this. You've got friends. Living and dead."

Grateful, I lean against him and take a couple of deep breaths. "Guess I'm starting a new part-time job." As if I wasn't busy enough.

Chapter 18

The next day, Hélène invites me over to discuss her wedding plans. I know what it really is: an excuse to mend the rift between us. But she's got éclairs and macarons, so I figure I might as well take the olive branch. After all, she's still my sister.

"I'm still struggling to find a place," she complains after the first round of sweets and coffee. "I mean, I know it's my fault. I started planning this engagement party far too late, but now I've sent the invitations and people are asking where the party will be."

"Can't you move it?"

She shakes her head. "No. I'm starting a new project in January and will be extremely busy at work. I won't have time again until mid-February, if then. And with the wedding in March, well, I might as well not have an engagement party at all."

Personally, I think that would be the right choice. Nobody needs an engagement party at New Year's, but I know Hélène's already got that firmly locked in her head and I don't want to start a new argument. "Where have you looked?"

"Literally everywhere. Unsurprisingly, lots of people plan New Year's parties, so all the good, big spaces are already gone. I've got the catering sorted, thanks to a friend, but she needs an address, too."

"You should ask GoPol," I say flippantly. "They've got a huge open space at their office."

Hélène cocks her head. "They do?"

"Oh, yes. The entire first floor—well, not all of it—is open plan. There's a couple of seating groups, but those could be moved." The thought of my sister approaching Charles with her silly engagement party amuses me. "Just kidding. I mean, yes, the space is there, but I don't think they hire it out for private functions." That doesn't quite fit with the whole secret service theme.

But it's too late. A dangerous glint has entered my sister's eyes, and her lips are slowly curling upwards. "I'll ask Cédric." She leans forward and hugs me suddenly. "Thanks, Alix. You're the best witness ever."

"Uhm." Her gratitude is quite unexpected. "Do you really think they'll give it to you?"

She pulls back. "Why not? That's his uncle and cousin. They've both already confirmed they're coming."

Great, I get to see Sébastien in private too!

"I'm sure they'll be happy to help us out."

"Did you meet them?"

Hélène rolls her eyes. "In fact, yes. I know that Sébastien and Cédric aren't the best of friends, which is sad, but his father is really nice. He welcomed me to the family and mentioned he was looking forward to working with you." She smiles widely all of a sudden. "I heard you got a job offer from them."

"Yeah, about that..."

But I don't get to voice my doubts because Hélène squeals. "Let me get the champagne." She jumps up to grab two glasses and a bottle of champagne, which appears to be something she just has lying around these days.

"This is so exciting," she says as she pops the bottle and pours the glasses. "I didn't know there were jobs around ghosts. And such good respectable jobs. Government jobs are the best: proper renumeration, good benefits, and the ideal job security. I mean, you definitely have that, because how many other people can see ghosts?" She laughs then hands me my glass. "To my little sister, who will have a phenomenal year ahead with her first full-time job."

I clink my glass, still too stunned to react differently. It takes me two sips before my thoughts appear in the right order again. "Well, there could be lots more people who could see ghosts if GoPol wouldn't take their whisper ghosts away. Like they took Papa's."

A little subdued, Hélène sits down again. "Yes, but Papa wasn't coping very well. He tells me he's been sleeping much better now that his ghost is gone." She quickly regains her steam. "But *you* are different. You are extremely comfortable with ghosts, which makes you the perfect GoPol candidate." She squeezes my knee in excitement and squeals again. "I'm so proud of you."

Proud or relieved I got a job she deems good enough? I drink half the glass, making myself a little dizzy.

Hélène laughs and reaches out to lower the flute. "Slow down. I don't want to get you drunk."

"You brought the champagne."

"To celebrate." She takes a sophisticated little sip. "I'm glad, Alix. I'm really glad that you've finally found your place. Granted, I haven't been the most supportive in the past, and I'm sorry about that. I truly thought you were making it all up. But now, I'm so happy for you. You don't need to compromise yourself and get to do what you love, while being paid handsomely."

I refrain from pointing out that we haven't actually talked about salary yet. I don't even know if my trial month includes payment or not.

Instead, my sister's honest words soften me towards her. Lately, I've been incredibly harsh towards her and Cédric. And she was only looking out for me, and for Papa. For all of us, really.

"Is Papa really doing better?" Sébastien's betrayal still sits deeply, but maybe it's time to acknowledge that my father was struggling immensely, and that in his case, removing his whisper ghost was probably the right course of action. I guess I just would've liked to have been consulted.

Hélène nods. "Yes, I called him this morning on my way to work and he said that he didn't even have a nightmare last night."

"That's good." It sounds like whatever hold Jacques de Molay had on my father was broken when his carbon copy of a ghost vanished. Perhaps "*Antoine*" was never a real whisper ghost.

"It is."

There's the sound of a key in the lock. Cédric is home. "I'd better get going."

"Already?"

"It's getting late."

The door opens and Cédric appears. "Ha, I knew I recognised those shoes. Bon soir, Alix."

"Bon soir, Cédric." I get up, taking another look at Hélène, her éclairs, and her champagne. "This was nice."

"Going already?" Cédric sounds sorry to see me go.

Hélène stands and hugs me. "It was very nice. Thanks for coming by. Hey, it's already dark. Why don't you let Cédric drive you home?" She throws an apologetic glance at Cédric. "If you don't mind."

He answers with a smile. "Absolutely not. It would be a pleasure."

I suppose that settles it, then. "Would you mind dropping me off at Père Lachaise?" I ask. "I was planning to visit Grandma before

Christmas." Gaspar and I have agreed to check on Petite Alix to make sure she's still safe and sound—and well-loved.

"Of course," Cédric agrees instantly. "I'll drive you there, no problem."

Hélène sighs. "I don't think I'll ever get used to you going to cemeteries after dark. But hey, it worked out for you, so who am I to complain. See you Sunday for Christmas dinner?"

"Of course."

We exchange kisses and I follow Cédric down to the car. "Sorry for making you go out again." It's drizzling slightly, not exactly the greatest weather for a visit to the cemetery.

"As I said, it's a pleasure."

Cédric got lucky and found a parking lot only two streets away. He holds the door open for me and waits until I sit to close it, not noticing how Gaspar has taken a place in his back seat. I throw him a quick glance while Cédric walks around the car, and he grins.

"You didn't think I'd leave you alone with Officer Cédric."

I chuckle inadvertently, forced to turn the sound into a cough when Cédric gets in. He shudders slightly. "You sure you want to go to Père Lachaise?"

"Yes, please."

"Are you really going to meet with your grandma?"

"We're close. Death didn't change that." If anything, it made our bond stronger.

"Very well." He pulls out of the parking lot, which no doubt will be filled when he returns, and enters the traffic. "So, how is the old lady?"

"You never met her," I point out.

Cédric shrugs good-naturedly. "Hélène told me a bit about her. All about the living person, of course."

"Of course."

He throws me a glance. "Hey, don't be so harsh with her. She feels awful that she didn't believe you."

"It's alright. We've made up."

Surprised, he raises an eyebrow. "Really? That's awesome. Now if that isn't a Christmas miracle, I don't know what is." Cédric laughs softly and turns on the wipers when the drizzle increases in frequency.

"You know, she's been stressing a lot about the wedding," he continues after a short while, his forehead creased slightly. "She wants everything to be perfect. And life has thrown her a few curve balls."

"Curve balls?"

He looks at me again before turning. "Learning that ghosts truly exist. Worrying about you. Worrying about her father. Sometimes, I worry she'll drive herself crazy."

"She's always been crazy."

"Spoken like a true younger sister."

I can't help it and laugh. "I know what you mean. Hélène has always worried too much. But that's because she thinks she has to take over every responsibility. Like being a parent to Odi and me when we already have two perfectly fine parents." I take a deep breath before admitting, "I'm sorry, too. It wasn't my intention to add to her stress."

Cédric smiles. "Well, now that the two of you are good again, she can stop worrying quite so much. Thanks for that."

The gates of Père Lachaise appear in front of us. "No worries. She's my sister. I care a lot for her."

"You and me both." He halts the car. "Well, here we are. Do you want me to come along, so I can drive you home later?"

That would be the stuff of nightmares and kind of defeat the whole idea of my visit. "No, I'm good. Go back to Hélène and tell her everything will be alright."

"I will. Goodnight, Alix."

"Goodnight."

I get out of the car and wait for him to pull away, under the guise of waving farewell. Gaspar has gotten out, too, using his jacket to shield me from the rain.

Once the car has well and truly left, I turn to him. "So, what do you think?"

CHAPTER 19

"What do I think of your future brother-in-law?" Gaspar raises an eyebrow.

It's the first time he's been in Cédric's presence. My own feelings for Cédric have considerably mellowed in the last few weeks. I'm warming up to him and it confuses me enough to ask for an independent opinion.

Gaspar scoffs. "He has terrible taste in music."

"Music? I didn't even notice any music." As hard as I try, I can't recall what was on the radio as we drove.

"Exactly."

I burst into giggles. Gaspar wraps his arm around me, and together, we make our way towards the cemetery.

"In all honesty, though, he seems alright. I mean I only had a short experience of him. He truly seems to care for your sister and, by extension, you."

"He cares a little too much about me." I sigh. "Well, at least, I used to think so. Now I believe it had more to do with Hélène caring so much about me. I mean, he always tried to help me out one way or another. I found it overbearing, but I suppose I've got my sister to thank for that. She must've told him how worried she was that I'm not doing my Master's in a promising field."

Gaspar huffs. "Little did she know it's the most promising of all."

I laugh again. "True. But I didn't know that, either."

He kisses my temple and I lean into him. "Look, I know I said before that your sister would fit in incredibly well with my parents, but I don't think that's true. They would get along well, don't get me wrong, but she cares. All my parents cared for was *their* reputation."

"True. Hélène might have bougie aspirations, but she only wants the best for me and Odile. And Cédric seems to be good for her." I struggled with that for a long time. Now I can see how supportive he's always been, even adopting her worries and concerns for her younger sisters. "It no longer feels like he's taking her away from us."

Gaspar makes a pitying sound. "Is that how you felt?"

I shrug. "Maybe? We were so close as kids. And while Cédric had nothing to do with her pretending ghosts don't exist, he's like a symbol of her distance. I think I was kidding myself that she'd return to us if he didn't exist." I shake my head with a laugh.

"It's silly. Hélène's just growing up. She was always going to move out first, get a job first, marry first." Suddenly, I have to swallow. "Damn. Call me silly, but I just realised I'll never marry."

Gaspar hugs me tighter. "That's not true. You're still young and have a lot of life ahead of you. I'm the one who'll never marry."

I know I'm being ridiculous. If Gaspar and I were in a normal relationship neither of us would even be thinking about marriage at this point. It's only because Hélène is planning hers and we can't ever have that. Not now and not in five years either.

"If you think I'll just leave you behind, you're sorely mistaken," I say with as much force as I can muster.

Gaspar smiles, yet what he says is, "You will, eventually."

"Don't." I take his hand and squeeze it tightly. "I don't want to think about the future. We're together *now*. And we don't need fancy parties to show off our relationship." Defiantly, I raise my chin. "And maybe you're wrong. Maybe one day you and I will just get ghost married, with a big party right here on Père Lachaise. We could have Chopin play our wedding song."

The idea makes him laugh. It's such a beautiful sound that I stop walking and pull him to me instead, stealing a wet kiss.

"I don't need an official paper or the world to acknowledge my relationship," I tell him. "All I need is you."

He slings his arms around me and holds me close as he drops multiple kisses on my face. "I love you, Alix. Now and always."

My heart nearly overflows with happiness. I bury my fingers in his soft brown hair and pull him into another deep kiss. The melancholy taste of rain fits our relationship perfectly. It's not ideal, but it's worth fighting for.

Hand in hand, we quickly show our faces to my grandma and Beatrice before making our way up the hill to visit Abelard, Héloïse, and my own whisper ghost, Petite Alix. We're only halfway there when I pick up a child's laughter.

Excitement bubbles up in me, and I half-drag Gaspar the rest of the way. On the hilltop, a couple of puddles have formed around the mausoleum of the two historical lovers. Both Abelard and Petite Alix are jumping into them with great glee. The little girl giggles hysterically every time she gets splashed.

Normally, I'd worry about a child jumping in puddles and getting completely soaked on a blistery winter day, but Petite Alix has nothing to worry about. Her clothes stay completely dry, and all that remains is the childhood memory of careless days in the rain.

We find Héloïse sitting on her gravestone, watching the two with an immeasurable fondness. She looks up when we come closer and smiles. "Alix."

The little girl looks up. "Yes, Maman?" She has well and truly adopted her new ghost parents.

Héloïse laughs. "Not you, sweetheart. The big version of you."

At the mention, Abelard looks up and gives me a wave. Then he dives down, picks up Petite Alix, and whirls her around. Petite Alix's squeals even make me laugh.

"Looks like she's adjusting well."

"Oh, she's a little ray of sunshine," Héloïse says. "She brightens up our days and nights. Abelard is a changed man. You made him so happy. And by extension, me."

I'm glad to hear that. It felt a bit like giving a part of me away, but it couldn't have gone to a more deserving couple. "Did you have any trouble with...?"

Héloïse shakes her head. "No, nothing. No one has expressed any interest in her. I mean, a lot of ghosts have. They're all drawn to our new addition. But no one alive has come looking for her."

"Good." My secret is safe for now.

Abelard brings Petite Alix over, who surprises me by instantly stretching out her arms. Until I realise it's Gaspar she wants.

"Hey, little one." He takes her gently and strokes her head. "How's your new Maman and Papa?"

"They're super nice," Petite Alix claims. "They don't ignore me like my old ones."

"That's good. Really good."

Petite Alix looks at me questioningly. "Where's Malou?"

"I didn't bring her today."

"Why not?"

I laugh softly. "Because I came here from my sister's. You remember Léni?"

"Léni! I want to play with Léni!"

Abelard takes her back and kisses her forehead. "We'll play with the other children here. It's almost time for the big hide and seek."

The distraction works and Petite Alix squeals excitedly.

"There's a hide and seek planned? Isn't it a bit late for that?"

Abelard shrugs. "Ghost children don't go to bed. And hide and seek is more exciting at night."

It should make me sad that there's even such a thing as a ghost child, but of course, the cemeteries are full of graves for the young ones. Death makes no difference. Despite the sadness of their existence, I'm delighted. Instead of centuries of wailing, the ghosts are taking care of the young ones, and the children do what children do best and play. It shows me that death isn't the end of it all. There's still so much to explore in this world. So much left to experience.

I lean against Gaspar, my head against his. "Next time, we'll bring Malou." Contrary to what Sébastien told me, there's no grand connection between me and Petite Alix. Just now, she showed very little interest in me. Even Hélène is more important to her. And why should she care for me? I'm a stranger to her, someone she never got to know.

"Alright. The rain is getting heavier, so we'll head off. Have a lovely Christmas, you three."

"We will," Abelard promises. "The best in eight centuries."

Yes, this was a very good thing.

I take Gaspar's hand, and together, we stroll down the hill again. "I'm glad it all worked out. Petite Alix is safe and Abelard and Héloïse have the child they've always wanted. They seem so happy."

"That's because they *are* happy." Gaspar pulls on my hand, so I stumble into him, then cups my face, and kisses me softly.

Raindrops fall from his hair onto my nose, and yet I can't imagine a better place to be than in his arms. I close my eyes as I savour his cold kiss, balanced by the heat building in my stomach.

"Let's go home," I whisper, making Gaspar laugh. Filled with happiness, we resume our walk, only to stop short.

A lone figure is waiting on the path downhill, face turned towards us, striking bright eyes full of intelligence.

Dix.

Chapter 20

The happiness leaves me in one big swoosh. Cold fingers grasp my throat, while my heart beats up a storm. My thoughts crash against my skull. *He's here. They found us. I'm gonna lose Gaspar. I'm gonna lose everybody.*

"Dix," I try to say as we reach him, but it comes out as a strangled whimper.

"Salut."

Gaspar glowers at him. "Are you following us?"

Dix buries his hands in his jacket and shrugs. "Yes?"

He admits it! Just like that. I'm so screwed. I feel dizzy. My breath is quickening and I need to sit down.

Gaspar catches me before I fall. "Careful. It's slippery." I know he's trying to cover up for the fact that I'm close to fainting, but what use is that? They're going to take Petite Alix away and that will be the end of everything.

"What are you doing here?" I manage to whisper, hoping against hope that it's for some other reason, that he doesn't know what's hiding at the top of the hill.

Dix looks to the ground, then up again. His face is twitching, as if *he's* the one struggling with emotions. "I had a feeling you'd already found your ghost. Even before we tried to find her in the Seine."

I close my eyes as he confirms my biggest fear. My knees buckle from under me, but Gaspar holds me upright.

"So I came here and asked around." Dix swallows. "It's a beautiful thing you've done."

"What?" I must have misheard.

He laughs softly. "Everyone's enamoured with your little self—just like everyone's charmed by the bigger self." Irritated, he waves it off. "They told me the story of Abelard and Héloïse and how you healed their pain. Perfect parents for your little self, and a perfect child for heartbroken lovers. As I said, it's a beautiful thing."

"A beautiful thing you're going to enjoy destroying," I say, my voice slowly regaining its strength.

I'm not prepared for the look of hurt that flashes over Dix's face. "Destroy?"

"Isn't that why you and Sébastien have been pestering me so much about finding her? So you can take her from me, along with my ability to see and converse with ghosts."

The guilty look in his eyes tells me it's all true. But then he looks up in defiance. "It's not what *I* want."

Realising that I can stand on my own now, Gaspar removes his arm from under me. "What do *you* want then?" His voice is hard, full of violent promises depending on how badly this evening goes.

Dix takes a step back, clearly not his usual cocky self. "I want the same."

"The same as what?" If he doesn't want to deliver Petite Alix to GoPol like Sébastien, what else is there?

"Happiness," Dix says. "I want you to... I want a favour."

Many weeks ago, Dix cornered me at Sorbonne. Hungrily, he listened to my view of ghosts, and when I asked him if he needed a favour, he'd seemed tempted, but he hadn't been ready. Now he is. And I slowly realise that, despite their origin, Sébastien and Dix are no longer the same.

"You want a favour?" I ask carefully.

He nods urgently. "Please." Then he adds quickly, "I won't tell. Séb doesn't know you found her. He's... He believes you."

It shouldn't have any effect on me, but I suddenly feel guilty. As if my antipathy isn't fully justified.

"I'll keep your secret. I have no interest in tearing apart a happy little family, nor do I want you to stop helping ghosts. You're the only one who does." He's starting to sound more desperate with each word. "Please. I... I can't do this anymore."

His distress does something to me. I let go of all my reservations, bridge the distance between us, and pull him into a hug.

Like a typical teenager, Dix stiffens at first, but then he lets out a sigh and accepts the comfort, leaving me to wonder when the last time was anybody hugged him. Did it ever happen in death? Did it even happen when he and Sébastien were still one?

"What exactly do you need?" I ask when I feel him pulling back at last.

Dix takes a moment to sort his thoughts, looking as if he's overwhelmed by his own emotions. At last, he looks at me. "Are you really going to join GoPol?"

"That depends," I say, staying deliberately vague. Despite his heart-rendering admission, I don't quite trust him. I know too little of Dix and Sébastien to understand their bond in all its intricacies, and my situation is too delicate to trust too much of it to him just yet.

He bites his lip and nods with a bitter expression. "Well, let me give you a warning. GoPol isn't... I know that our work protects our country's interests," Dix says carefully, clearly quoting someone else. "It's important and it requires sacrifices. And sometimes we do things we're not proud of because they have to be done." He scoffs, irritated with himself. "My father is an asshole."

I keep quiet, not wanting my own opinion to colour what he decides to entrust me with.

"Like, first-grade asshole. When I was growing up, I was so proud of him. My father was the greatest. Sure, he rarely made it to one of my competitions, and he was always too busy to bring me to bed or read me stories, but that was because he was saving the world." Dix grimaces and laughs coldly. "I wanted to be like him. I wanted him to be proud. And I trusted his opinion in everything."

He swallows. "But I wasn't blind. Even if I understood *why* my father wouldn't have time for me or why he always expected so damn much of me, it hurt. Sometimes, I wanted… I guess I wanted Charles the father, but I always just got Charles the GoPol officer." He bites his lip again and scoffs.

The way he explains it makes a lot of sense. Charles Roubert is a busy man with great responsibility. But having him as a father—and only parent—sucks. I wonder if in hindsight Dix would've preferred staying with his mother or if that relationship has its own complications.

"Anyway, I rebelled a little when I hit fifteen. Not much, because I *wanted* to follow in his footsteps. I suppose I was just trying to get his attention or simply stop treading the same old path I'd always done. It was a regrettably short-lived phase," Dix says with a sigh. "I wish we'd done so much more. I mean, he was barely there anyway, but no, Séb is a good little boy who doesn't want to disappoint his Papa." From the tone of his voice, I can tell that he's since disassociated from that version of himself.

Dix shakes his head. "And good little boys trust their father. And that gets them killed."

"What?" Until now I'd assumed that Sébastien purposefully got himself killed to join his father's agency. That in his blind hero worship he ignored the red flags and betrayed himself to win his father's appreciation. "Dix, are you saying...?" I can't say it. The words don't even want to form in my mind.

Dix's face darkens. "My father decided it was time. That I was old enough to enter the next part of my training. I let him strap me to the bed. I—"

"Don't!" I whimper, closing my eyes as images assault me instantly. Sébastien on the ground, unable to move no matter how much he jerks around.

But Dix won't stop, not now. He needs me to know. Needs someone to know. "He stopped my heart, Alix. He *killed* me. And then he brought Séb back to life."

Sébastien, but not Dix.

It's so terrible, hot tears run down my cheeks. "How? How is that allowed?" My voice is a pathetic whimper.

Gaspar's arms wrap around me. He holds me and growls at Dix, "What kind of fucked-up agency is that? You discard the whisperers you don't like and murder teenagers so you can turn them into little soldiers?"

Dix looks at him sullenly. "Pretty much, though the latter only applies to us, as far as I know. The other agents are all natural whisperers. Only *he* is the perfect little soldier."

His words make me shudder and a strangled sob escapes my mouth. "Stop," I whisper, struggling for breath.

"Here's what I want you to do for me," he continues, despite my protests. "Get me out of GoPol, or failing that, bring down my father."

I gulp. That's by far the most intense favour I've ever been asked for. This is far removed from a quick clean-up of a grave or a little trespassing at night. This is a full-on commitment. One I'm definitely not ready for.

To buy myself time, I ask Dix, "You really want to leave GoPol?"

"Why would I want to stay at the place where my father murdered me?"

Good point. "Sébastien does."

Dix snorts. "Séb isn't disposable. Not in the same way I am."

"Disposable?"

"The elimination of whisper ghosts? You think my father will stop even a minute to eliminate me if he thinks I'm no longer useful to him? To him, I'm nothing." Dix scrunches up his nose in anger. "Sébastien is his son. I'm just a spectre, a tool. And broken tools get discarded. He'll just create a new one later."

The very thought of it makes me sick to the stomach. "That's horrible."

"That's the GoPol way. Ghosts are nothing to them. We don't actually exist to them. Our feelings don't matter. We're not even supposed to *have* feelings. After all, we're *dead*."

"But that's rubbish. Ghosts are still human. I've never once met a ghost who was truly dead inside. Those that are move on." At least that's what I think happens eventually.

Dix gives me a helpless little shrug. "See, that's why I've come to you. You're different. And that's why you can't join them. GoPol will destroy you. They don't believe in us like you do. They don't care."

"I'm so, so sorry, Dix."

Tears are shimmering in his eyes. He blinks them away furiously. Boys don't cry. Not boys like him, at least.

Angrily, he asks me, "So, will you help me?"

"Dude," Gaspar chimes in. "Do you even hear yourself? What you're asking her is dangerous. How is she supposed to help you?"

Dix looks dismayed, as if Gaspar told him that Christmas is can-celled—which it has been for him for the last eight years. "Please."

I can't commit to this favour. It's not one I even think I've got the power to grant. I mean, who am I to take it up with GoPol? To go against someone as powerful as Charles Roubert? Someone who'd even murder his son with his own two hands to get what he wants.

But that doesn't mean I can't try. I've been on the fence too long already. Joining GoPol is absolutely out of the question. At least, not for real. I don't want to become brainwashed, another tool in Charles' arsenal. And I don't want to deliver my beloved ghost friends to them to be used and discarded like everyone else.

I don't trust Dix, just as I don't trust the Chevalier, but in this impossible situation, they're my allies. And I need their help as much as they need mine.

"There might be a way to get you out of there," I say softly, trying to decide how much information I want to entrust to Dix. At last, I decide to take a page out of the Chevalier's book. "There's a file I need to get out of your father's office. Gaspar tried to get it on our visit—"

"Alix," he warns.

I shake my head, silently bidding him to trust me. "But he got caught by... C-Trente?"

Dix pulls a face. "Ugh, I hate that guy."

"Same," Gaspar adds.

"We'll have to try again. It's important if you really want to bring your father down. If you want things to *change*." After all, that's what the Résistance is all about. An alternative way. It's also the only place I can think of that Dix would be safe from GoPol.

Dix nods sharply. "I'll help you. I know where my father keeps the spare key, and I can distract C. He hates me even more than my father does." He shrugs. "See, I wasn't born yet when he came to be."

I understand. C-Trente is Charles' younger self. He died before he became a father.

"What happens after?" Dix asks eagerly. "When you have that file?"

If I've learned anything from Jean Moulin, it's that I need to keep my cards close to my chest. *Never pass on all your information to one source.* "I'll take it to someone who might be able to help both of us."

Dix stares at me for a moment, but then he nods. "Good. I trust you, History Girl."

I can't help myself. "Why?"

He waves up the hill. "Because you're one of us. Whatever it is you're planning, I know it's a good thing. A thing worthy of sacrifice."

Once again, I shudder. "No one's going to sacrifice themselves."

Dix rolls his eyes slightly. "If you insist."

"I do."

He smiles so suddenly it hits me by surprise. I missed that cheeky grin. "Thank you."

"Don't thank me yet." I'm completely in over my head. If there was a way to get out of this whole mess, I'd take it, but the only way I see is going through.

Dix takes his leave, promising once again to help me to the best of his abilities, and Gaspar and I slowly turn our feet towards the exit. I sort of wish Cédric was waiting at the gate because my legs are still a bit wobbly, but that only proves how messed up I am at the moment.

"Do you trust him?" Gaspar asks me.

I snort and instantly shake my head. "How could I? I want to. I mean, I feel terribly sorry for him. And I believe what he told us is true." No one can fake that much heartbreak. "But we can't forget that he's literally tied to Sébastien who, even by his whisper ghost's admission, is a loyal follower of his father's rules. What if Sébastien guesses Dix's intentions? What if he has a way of forcing him to cooperate?" In the end I *do* trust Dix, but he's not safe.

Gaspar nods grimly. "That is some fucked-up shit. I wish you could just turn your back on all of this. I hate to see you get dragged into everyone's mess."

Grateful, I lean into him. "And that's why I love you. You always have my back."

"Always." He sighs, losing a bit of tension. "I suppose I can't talk you out of this?"

"What would you have me do instead?" Honestly, if he's got a better solution, I'm eager to hear it.

But he doesn't. Gaspar drops his shoulders, looking absolutely miserable. "I just don't want you to get hurt."

Me and him both. "I'm sure it won't come to that." My voice wavers, though. So far, I've been shot at, and was nearly driven insane and cleaved in half by a mad ghost. I don't think messing with an agency that's not above murder does a lot for ensuring my safety.

"Alix, I'm worried."

I swallow heavily. "Me, too."

He closes his arms around me and holds me close to his chest. "If they come for you, I'll haunt the shit out of them."

Even if there's very little Gaspar can do against living people, I appreciate his declaration. It makes me feel a little better about the mess I got myself into when I followed Emily Durant down the rabbit hole.

Chapter 21

Christmas is celebrated in our apartment with my parents, Odile, Hélène, and Cédric. We have a delicious and hearty lunch with much laughter, and exchange presents in the late afternoon under the tree.

Hélène discovers the atrocity I picked for her. "What's this?" she asks in pure bewilderment. "A clown?" She turns the puppet around. "What am I even supposed to do with this?"

"Use as a trash gift for Trash Santa?" I suggest, asking myself why I even went along with Sébastien's stupid idea. Sure, the look on Hélène's face is worth gold, but it's a really ugly gift. "I got you something else."

"Thank god. Where?"

It takes me only a few seconds to find the gift in the small pile of unopened presents. "There. Something blue for your wedding."

Hélène throws the clown aside and eagerly unwraps the earrings I found for her. "They're beautiful! Thank you!" She leans over the pile and hugs me.

As soon as she lets go, Odile hands me Malou, who can't be left alone in a pile of paper. "Hold her, while I give her my present."

I know it's an outfit. Odile has made a tradition out of gifting little outfits to Malou ever since I got her. Still, I'm surprised when she unpacks a grey scarf and miniature fedora.

"The hat took me ages. I poked my fingers a million times," she tells Malou. "So you'd better appreciate it."

I hold Malou up so Odile can wrap the scarf around her and put the little hat on her spines.

"There, perfect. Malou Moulin."

I can see it. With the signature hat and scarf, Malou truly looks like the hedgehog version of Jean Moulin. "Aren't you a handsome little girl?" I nuzzle her nose with mine.

Malou rears her head, promptly upsetting her fedora.

Odile clicks her tongue. "You have to keep it on long enough for me to take a picture." She puts the hat on her again and looks for her phone in the pile of wrapping paper.

Meanwhile, Malou tries to nibble on her scarf, jogging my memory. As fashionable as Moulin looks in it, there's a sad story behind the scarf. He was arrested early during the war and attempted to slice his own throat so he wouldn't pass on any secrets. They found him before he bled out and he survived with scars on his neck, which he used to cover up with his scarf.

Despite the danger, he never stopped fighting for his country and the values he believed in. Even to his own detriment. And he never broke. They didn't get a single word out of him before they bashed his head in. A true hero of the Résistance.

"Alix?" Maman asks. "Are you okay?"

I blink, returning to the present day. Moulin's life story puts what I'm currently experiencing into perspective. When learning about World War II and the Résistance, I'd always believed I would've been on the right side. That I wouldn't have sat by or ducked my head to escape notice. I wanted to fight for my rights loud and proud. That's what I love so much about the French revolutions. We don't go down quietly. We scratch and fight and claw our way back up again and again, even if it takes a couple of tries.

In the grand scheme of things, my situation might not be as dire. After all, I'm still just a history student who's found herself between a rock and a hard place. It's highly unlikely someone will torture me or execute me. Yet, I can't shake the fear. I don't feel brave enough to stand up for my beliefs. And that hurts.

"I'm good, Maman," I say with a fake smile. "Do you like the painting I got you?"

"Yes. It's very beautiful." She strokes my hair, regarding me warmly. Softly, she says, "Whatever it is, you'll find a way through. You're nothing if not resourceful."

Parents. Always with the impossibly high expectations.

Who am I kidding? I lap her trust in me up like I used to lap up chocolate mousses. Which reminds me... "I'll check on the soufflés."

I drop Malou in Papa's hands and make my way into the kitchen, away from the festivities. A dark thought crosses my mind, that this could be the last time I have Christmas with my family. It's ridiculous and untrue. Next year, GoPol and the catacombs will be long forgotten. An adventure of the past.

The soufflés are rising wonderfully in the oven. I refrain from disturbing them and pour myself a glass of wine instead.

My peace doesn't last for long. Two sips later, Cédric joins me in the kitchen. He latches onto my idea and sighs softly after his first sip. "That's a good one."

Not knowing what he expects me to say, I simply smile.

Cédric leans against the kitchen counter and regards me thoughtfully. "Hey, thanks for suggesting GoPol as a venue. It took a bit of convincing, but my uncle agreed to let us have the hall downstairs."

"He did?" It was a ridiculous notion. And with everything I've heard about the Rouberts and their relationship with Cédric, I didn't think they'd indulge him.

"I was surprised too." Cédric laughs. "I guess I have you to thank."

"Me?"

He shrugs. "My uncle seems quite enamoured with you—so is my little cousin. He really wants you at GoPol, and that seems to have opened up a path for me as well."

According to Sébastien, Cédric has always wanted to join GoPol. His eagerness makes so much sense to me now. He grew up with that dysfunctional family, always measured up against his younger cousin, and always coming short. Knowing what I know about *how* Sébastien became a GoPol agent, though, I think Cédric should be glad for the lack of attention.

"You know what that requires?" I ask carefully.

Cédric nods softly. "I do now."

I sigh. "Cédric, you're set to marry my sister. If anything happens to you, she'll be heartbroken." Only a few weeks ago, I wouldn't have cared, but now I worry for him.

"Don't worry. I won't do anything stupid. There are plenty of other pathways. I don't need to become a ghost whisperer like you."

I exhale in relief. "Good."

Cédric raises his glass. "To being co-workers, soon."

Surprised, I clink glasses with him. I have no intention to work at GoPol for long, but I no longer abhor the idea of spending more time with Cédric. Perhaps he could be an ally as well.

CHAPTER 22

Three days after Christmas, I meet with Sébastien at GoPol. The last time I was here, it was Charles' show. This time it's just the two of us. Everyone else is off enjoying their holiday. I left Gaspar at home in case Charles' ghost recognises him, but Dix greets me when we enter Sébastien's office at the very back of a corridor on the second floor.

"History Girl!" he calls out with a wide grin, not a sign of the distraught teenager I met on Père Lachaise in sight. "Long time no see."

"Dix," Sébastien says with a little sigh. "Get out of my chair."

The office is quite small. There's only the one chair behind the desk, a computer, and a filing cabinet. I try to spot anything personal, but Sébastien seems to keep his office strictly work.

Instead of listening to his whisperer, Dix puts his feet up and leans back. "What? You're gonna sit down and make Alix stand there like some poor orphan girl?"

Sébastien doesn't appreciate the mocking. "I would've offered her the chair, but now that your dirty shoes have been—"

"What dirt? My shoes have been squeaky clean ever since we died. Just one of many advantages death brings." If Sébastien doesn't hear the sarcasm behind the wide grin, he must be deaf.

I chuckle softly before deciding to smooth the waves. "It's okay. I don't need to sit down."

"Happy?" Sébastien hisses at Dix, who folds his arms behind his back, looking pretty chuffed with himself. "God, you're such a child sometimes." Sébastien snorts, then turns to me, ignoring his whisper ghost. "Alright, let's talk about work."

I don't want to talk about work. "Why aren't you on leave like everyone else?"

He shrugs. "What for? So I can sit at home and watch TV?"

"Don't you have any hobbies? Passions? Friends to meet?" I shouldn't have asked the last one.

Sébastien's face tightens and, sure enough, Dix calls him out on it. "He's a loner, remember?"

"Shut up, Dix." He forces a smile for me. "Don't listen to him. I..." He starts biting his lip. "Fine, I guess I *am* a loner." With a sigh, he leans against his desk. "You probably know what it's like. When you're... different from anyone else. This ability... it's as much a curse as it is a boon. There aren't that many people who understand what it's like."

"What about your colleagues?" Against my will, I feel sorry for him. I know exactly what he's talking about. Before I met Gaby I didn't really have any living friends either. I wouldn't have called myself a loner, though, since I had all these wonderful ghost friends. Something Sébastien wouldn't even consider.

He shrugs. "Most are older than me, and I'm the son of the head of the agency. It... I guess, I'm not very good at building connections."

No kidding. "So, it's just you and Dix."

"Most of the time. Yes." Sébastien throws a look at Dix, daring him to make a stupid comment, but the ghost looks oddly fond of him. "Anyway..." Sébastien clears his throat. "Let's get started."

He reaches over the table and opens a case file. "My father wants the two of us to partner up. It probably won't surprise you I've been working on the Chevalier's case. I took over the case at the beginning of the year."

"What does that mean? Working on?"

"Remember when I told you we don't have much information on him?"

"A lie, I suppose?"

Sébastien frowns. "No, that wasn't a lie. Why would you think it was?"

I wince. The words slipped out against my better judgement. I'm still angry and disappointed with him. The betrayal runs deep, but after learning about his whisper origins, I feel sorry for him. Damn Dix for messing with my head.

"I just thought it was. Look, I don't know how intelligence agencies work, but it would've made sense if you…"

"Lied," he finishes for me when my voice tapers out. Then he swallows. "Well, I didn't. We don't know anything about the Chevalier other than that he's a prolific cataphile who turned up on the scene ten years ago. Ghosts don't want to spy on him, and when our whisper ghosts shadow him, they find nothing but endless catacombs crawling. We don't know what he's looking for or who he really is. Those pictures you took of Ossa Arida were the first true proof there's something sinister going on. And of course, now we know that he knows how to permanently destroy a ghost and perform weird rituals."

"Wait a minute. Are you saying you followed this man for a decade without reason?"

"Not without reason." Sébastian scoffs, as if he can't believe I'd ask that. "I'm sure he's done something to land himself on GoPol's radar. He has a reputation, and look, most intelligence work isn't some quick mission. We don't listen to one meeting and call it a day. Long-term observation isn't unusual, and we were right." He waves his hand at me. "The Chevalier's planning something. Normal people don't kill random strangers or perform occult rituals."

I cross my arms, not quite convinced. "So, what's next?"

"Well, with the recent developments, we might be close to cracking this case. Don't take this the wrong way, but I believe there's more than one reason as to why my father decided to recruit you. It's your obvious talent, but it's also because the Chevalier's interested in you."

"I'm the bait."

Sébastien sighs. "If you want to call it that. The thing is that you've got an in. We can use that to find out what he's planning. What are these places of power he mentioned? Why is he so obsessed with finding them? And why does he defend his operations with violence?"

"We don't know for sure that he murdered Emily."

"True."

Overwhelmed, I blow some raspberries. It would be funny if the whole thing wasn't so dangerous. The Chevalier wants me to spy on GoPol, and GoPol wants me to spy on the Chevalier. It's as if they want me to be a double agent.

The good thing is that it makes my job a lot easier. Neither of them will question it if they see me with the other. It buys me more time to figure out how I'm going to navigate this, I suppose.

"Okay."

"Okay?" Sébastien looks surprised.

"Well, yes. I'll do it." His stunned expression is freaking me out. "Isn't that what you want me to do?"

He manages to regain control over his features. "Yes, but... aren't you scared?"

"Of what?"

"Dealing with the Chevalier?"

"You just said it yourself. He likes me. Why would he hurt someone he hopes to recruit?"

Sébastien is starting to stare at me again, but this time he notices before he gets lost in it. "I can't decide whether you're incredibly naïve or incredibly brave."

"Should I give you two some time alone?" Dix chimes in. While his words are directed at Sébastien, his eyes are watching me. "I could pop out for ten minutes, haunt the empty halls, bore myself to another death."

"If only," Sébastien says, but I can see he doesn't mean it. "You already know the job, so sure. Go annoy C. We all know that's what you really want."

I wonder if Sébastien knows how right on the money he is.

Dix grins at me with all the charm of a naughty schoolboy and gets to his feet. "Ten minutes. Don't do anything I wouldn't do."

He walks straight through the closed door and leaves me alone with Sébastien, who massages the bridge of his nose. "I'm so sorry," he says when Dix is gone. "The trouble with him is that... well, he never grew up."

Because his own father murdered him.

I shake off the chilling thought and reach for a shy smile. "So, what do you want me to do exactly?"

"Go to the Chevalier, tell him you're interested, and try to get him to trust you. Do you have any plans for today?"

"You want me to go today?"

"If you're free?"

This guy really has no respect for the holiday season. "Sure. We can do it today. Am I going in alone?" I steal a glance at the clock. Ten minutes go by faster than you think, but I'm good for now.

"The Chevalier knows I work for GoPol. Plus, he knows that I'm my father's son. He'd never believe me if I suddenly showed interest in what he's doing down there. Dix will stand by, and I suppose you could bring your... is it your boyfriend?" He grimaces, as if he has any right to have an opinion about that.

"Gaspar? Yes, he's my boyfriend. You got a problem with that?"

The pained look only deepens. "He's a ghost."

"Very observant."

Sébastien gives me a flat stare, but then he raises his hands. "Fine, it's not my business what you do with ghosts. Since you don't have a whisper ghost of your own yet, Gaspar fills that niche quite nicely. I don't know if it's your special talent, but he seems to be more... present than the usual ghosts."

Under other circumstances, I would've fought him on that. Gaspar isn't the grand exception amongst ghosts. The only one who's almost a person. They're all like that. His father just never taught that to Sébastien.

However, there's no time for a discussion like this. I need to find an excuse and make my way upstairs to meet Dix. For a moment, I consider faking another toilet break, but that might get awkward if I stay away too long.

Instead, I pretend to pick up the buzzing of my cellphone. I pull it out of my purse and check the blank screen. "Oh, sorry, uhm, I need to make a call." I point to the door. "Is it okay if I step out for a minute?"

Sébastien immediately waves me away. "Go ahead. The catacombs aren't running away from us."

That was easy. I flash him a smile and leave the room, pretending to make the call. Once I close the door behind me, I hurry down the corridor, my heart beating like a hummingbird. This is it. *And what did you do over the holidays? Oh, I broke into the office of the CEO of the ghost police and stole a classified file.*

I'm gonna be in so much trouble if I get caught. Hopefully, Dix can pull this off for me.

Once I reach the top of the stairs, I listen closely. The third floor is just as deserted as the two below it. When I'm sure all is quiet, I dash into the fancy break room and go for the pool table. Dix let me know that the spare key is hiding under the right back pocket. He, of course, failed to mention which side he considers the back of the table.

I decide to go with my gut and try to get under the pocket. My fingernails aren't terribly long, which gives me a disadvantage. I attempt to pry the plastic off, but it won't budge.

Frustrated, I move to the next corner. And here I'm in luck. This one immediately allows my nails to go under the rim and pop it out. The key is right underneath. I grab it and put the pocket back in case someone walks into the room before I'm finished.

My heart is beating even faster now that I've already crossed a line. My hands are starting to feel a bit clammy, and it only gets worse as I near Charles' office.

The ten minutes are over. By now, Dix should've lured C-Trente away. I can't hear anything behind the door. Still, it takes me almost another minute to build up the courage to peek through the little window in the door.

The room seems empty. My hand is shaking and I nearly drop the key.

Why am I doing this again?

Moulin comes to mind. If he fearlessly parachuted into occupied France, I can break into an empty office.

I hold my breath as I slide the key in and turn it. Two clicks, then it opens.

No one's here. I keep thinking someone's going to jump scare me, but everything stays quiet.

If I was moving in slow motion until now, I suddenly speed up. I close the door behind me a bit louder than I'd have liked and rush over to the desk, quickly flicking through the piles of files.

Coullier. Coullier. Nothing in this pile. Nothing in the other either.

I try the drawers, but most of them are locked and my key won't let me in. Panicked, I look around the room. There's another drawer behind me, but again, everything's locked.

Why did it have to be a specific file? Why can't I just take pictures of one of the ones on the table to prove myself?

A whimper escapes me as I feel the urgency bite me. On a whim, I get out my student ID and slide it into the top drawer. I have no idea what I'm doing other than wriggling a plastic card across the lock. While I've heard about it working, I've never looked it up, much less tried it out before.

Either I'm the luckiest girl in the universe or these drawer locks aren't exactly the strongest. It opens suddenly, nearly falling into my hands. It's full of papers and I want to close it again, when I notice a brown folder peeking through the white.

I dig out the file and gasp in relief. "Romain Coullier" has been scrawled on top of the heavy folder.

Romain Coullier. *Romain.*

Something heavy crashes to the floor outside the office. Startled, I grab the file, hide it under my sweater, push the drawer closed, and dive under the desk.

The blood rushing through my ears is all I can hear as I desperately listen for more sounds from the corridor. I try to count my heartbeats to calm myself, but I skip two and get all messed up in my head.

Just then, I hear Dix exclaim. "Oh, come on, you can't just walk away from me."

"Go play somewhere else, little boy." *C-Trente.* "You'd better tidy up that mess you made."

"I can't. I'm a ghost."

I bite my lip so hard I draw blood. If C-Trente finds me here, it's all over. I wish I could come up with some kind of excuse, but my mind is riddled with high anxiety. I'll be thrown out. Arrested. Shot on the spot.

"You're a *whisper* ghost," C-Trente's cold voice hisses. "You threw them down, you can pick them up."

Dix sighs greatly. "I feel terribly weak, you know?"

"Are you asking for trouble?" Suddenly, I have no problem imagining this man killing his own son for his plans. He scares the heck out of me.

But Dix just laughs. "As if you could catch me."

Something like a gun-shot releases, followed by an angry grunt. "You little shit. I'm gonna make you pay for that!" Whatever he plans to do, it involves chasing after Dix first.

I'm shaking so much I need half a minute to move into action. My lip hurts, as do the sharp short breaths, which are all I'm capable off. But time is running out. I don't know how long C-Trente will chase Dix or if he realises he's being drawn away from the office.

Though I'd rather sit here and cry or breathe until I feel safe again, I need to move. I crawl out from under the desk, pressing the file against my stomach and stride to the door. Once again, I pause to listen and then peek first. But this time, I don't allow myself much time for it.

Dauntlessly, I grab the handle and open the door. The corridor is empty, though on my right, a bunch of framed certificates are lying on the floor, their frames split, glass splintered. Dix's warning to me.

I lock the door behind me and hurry back to the break room to deposit the key. My fingers are so sweaty I struggle with lifting the pocket, almost whimpering with the effort. In the end, however, I manage to put the key back and sneak down the stairs again.

It's not until I've gotten out my phone to return to my alibi call that I realise I took the file instead of taking pictures of it.

Now it's too late to go back upstairs to rectify my mistake. I'll have to smuggle the file out somehow and hope no one notices it's missing until I'm no longer the only possible suspect.

I make sure the file is secured by my trousers' waistband under my sweater, then I say loudly into my phone, "I'll call you later." The sound of my own voice makes me shudder. There's no way

I'll be able to hold a normal conversation with Sébastien while the adrenaline is still racing through my veins.

Nevertheless, I open the door and slip back in with a fake smile. "Sorry about that. Gaby had a little crisis. New relationship and all." Hopefully, Gaby will forgive me for using her as an alibi.

Sébastien has been working on something that looks like a big mess of cables. When he looks up, a frown appears. "You've got some—"

Suddenly Dix throws the door open again, nearly taking me out in the process. He looks a bit dazed but quickly recovers and hides behind Sébastien. "That ghost is crazy!"

Irritated, Sébastien looks at the door. I'm grateful for how the open door covers me from C-Trente's view. "What's this about, C?"

"Your whisper ghost is out of control," C-Trent informs him coldly.

"What did you do, Dix?" Sébastien asks annoyed.

"I just thought the old man could use a little distraction from his boring, boring job." Dix rolls his eyes in a funny grimace.

C-Trent growls in response. "You should put him on a leash. This isn't a playground."

"Thanks for the suggestion," Sébastien says, with a pained grimace.

"I told your father he made you too young. He should get rid of this idiot and make a new one."

The reaction on Sébastien's face is immediate. His features sharpen as every muscle on his body tenses. All colour has drained out of him, and his voice drops dramatically in temperature. "You can go back to your post now. I'll take care of Dix." It's not a suggestion but an order.

"If he plays one of his stupid tricks again, I'll wipe him from the afterlife." Judging by the thud of his steps, C-Trent is leaving.

Sébastien's face is still as rigid as a mask as he walks over to me and closes the door. He releases the breath he's been holding since C-Trent suggested another murder should be in order. Slowly, his face softens. "I'm sorry about that."

At least now my agitated state no longer raises any questions. "Are you okay?"

"Of course. Why wouldn't I be?"

I know it's a front and I don't have the mental capacity right now to keep mine up. Instead, my eyes widen pointedly, and I jerk my head towards the door. "He just threatened to *make* another whisper ghost. That means..."

"I know what it means. Don't worry about it." Sébastien comes up with a hurried smile. "C is just grumpy. Dix gets on his nerves a lot. Right, Dix?" His voice rises in the end.

"Yeah, grumpy old man. That's what he is." Dix gives me a thumbs-up and a grin, but the look in his eyes remains haunted.

Sébastien forces a laugh. "He's harmless."

Nothing about this was harmless. He knows that. Dix knows that. And I know that, too.

"I want to go home."

His face falls again. "What about the mission?"

"The..." Right. I can't just go home and leave this all behind me. I'm a double agent now with a stolen folder under my sweater. "Sorry, yes, do we have to leave immediately though? I'm not dressed for the catacombs and..."

Sébastien regards me warmly. "Of course not. You need a break. I get that. How about we get you set up quickly, and then you go home, have some lunch, maybe a nap and we'll meet at the Métro station at three."

"Set me up?"

He points to the cables on his desk. "This will record everything you hear while you're down in the catacombs."

Shocked, I realise what he means to do. And how that will lead him to discover that I'm hiding a file under my sweater. "Surely, we don't need that."

"It's an easy set-up."

"No!" Panicked, I look at Dix, but he has no idea why I'm acting so strange right now. I struggle to come up with a good reason for Sébastien. "I'm not taking my clothes off in your office."

Instantly, Sébastien blushes. "I wasn't suggesting... I... Look, I can get a female agent in to set you up and..."

His stammer gives me a little more confidence. "I'd rather do it without. Having those on me would make me far too self-conscious. I wouldn't move naturally, and if the Chevalier discovers it he might—"

"It's really quite subtle. Unless you plan to undress down there..." Sébastien swallows, blushing even harder.

I don't give him the chance to recover. "And if it gets wet? You know I'll need to cross the Banga, and there are more flooded channels. Look, I promise I'll report everything back to you."

"You could forget something. It's hard to know what details are important and which aren't."

It's exactly what Josephine said. Her method was to write down everything she could remember as soon as she left a party.

But I give Sébastien a cool look. "I'm a history student. It's literally my thing to remember half a million dates and details. I think I'm good." And here they say a history degree is useless.

Dix comes to my aid. "Let History Girl do it her way." He might not know *why* I'm so against the listening device, but he's realised that it's important.

Beleaguered from two sides, Sébastien gives in. "Very well. Let's go with your plan."

As soon as I'm out of the premises, I send an emergency text to Gaby. I only have to wait five minutes at home before she drops in. As soon as she's pulled off her shoes, I drag her into my room and do something I almost never do: lock the door.

As much as I appreciate Odile's enthusiasm, I won't be dragging her into this mess.

Gaby looks at me confused. "I'd just got back from my parents' place when I got your text. Marie and I are having a date later tonight and—... Alix, what happened?" she asks, slightly alarmed.

My experience at GoPol still has me breathless. I look back and forth between her and Gaspar, not knowing where to start. And then it suddenly all bursts out of me.

At some point in my retelling, Gaby plops down on my desk chair, her eyes wide, while Gaspar pulls me into a hug. "I thought I knew what fear was after my experience in the Boutique, but holy shit, I nearly peed myself hiding under that desk."

"Well, what were you doing breaking into Monsieur Roubert's desk?" Gaby asks with mild terror in her voice. "Alix," she whimpers.

"I know! Believe me, if I could turn back time and never take on Emily's stupid favour, I would."

"That woman has a lot to answer for," Gaspar growls.

The poor woman was killed for stumbling along the same paths as I do now. It doesn't look very good for me.

"I cannot align myself with GoPol's values."

Gaby shakes her head. "Oh, absolutely not. I mean, Sébastien was murdered by his own father just so he'd become a whisperer? And he still works there?"

"He's obviously been brainwashed since childhood. He'd probably agree that it was needed." I'm not quite so sure of that after C-Trente's warning, though—and the memory of how he folded in the Boutique. And then I remember that he's a loner. He's got no one else in his life to tell him he needs to get the hell away from his father.

"You'd think it couldn't get any messier, but now we've got this." I pick up the Coullier file and drop it on my desk.

Gaby immediately swivels around and checks it out. "What am I looking at?"

"That name?"

"Romain Coullier? Who's that?"

I flip the file open. A picture from at least ten years ago has been attached to the first page. Gaby gasps.

"Is that?" She looks up at me. "Wait, he... The Chevalier sent you to steal his file?"

I sit on my desk. "Well, no. He sent me to take pictures of the file to prove I'm on his side. And to make sure I'd really be on his side as soon as I had a look at this."

"You've read it?"

During my trip home I'd only stolen a few peeks at it from inside my bag. "No, but..." I swallow and turn my eyes to the page. "He used to work for GoPol. That's how he knows them all. Worse: he used to be Charles Roubert's partner."

CHAPTER 23

I wish we had Gaby's big poster that she made of the ghost politics I'm getting tangled up in. Then again, the information from this file would probably fill every last bit of the poster. It's like every page holds another shocking revelation.

The Chevalier died at a similar age as Sébastien. According to the file, he got caught up in a street fight and was beaten pretty badly. He died on the way to the hospital and had to be brought back from the brink, once in the ambulance and then again at the hospital, which left him with two whisper ghosts.

Yes, two.

At that point, Romain was already well-known to the police. He had a catalogue of small misdemeanours and was on his last warning, but instead he was recruited into GoPol by Charles Roubert.

The file doesn't include how that came to be or why. It's strictly factual, but judging by the lengthy report on how the Chevalier's two ghosts behaved, I'd wager the opportunity to study this phenomenon was the only reason the Chevalier's powers weren't immediately taken away.

From what Gaby, Gaspar, and I gather from a quick read through, having more than one whisper ghost at the same time led to all kinds of problems, such as a weaker physical condition and disharmony between the three of them. It also left the Chevalier with a keen interest in the occult. I can't quite tell whether his unique ability gave him access to more than just whisper power or whether it just nurtured the interest and led him to it. The only thing we can be sure of is that Charles documented all of it. They worked together, experimenting with the boundary between life and death.

At one point, the Chevalier even agreed to die a third time. The document is a bit sketchy here. As if someone covered up an earlier entry. Now it just says: "In his vanity, Coullier risked his life for the creation of a third whisper ghost."

It was an immediate disaster. The Chevalier was in a coma for three months. The whisper ghost went amok and had to be eliminated. Apparently, he almost killed Charles, and severely injured two other agents. A woman lost her eyesight because of it.

While the Chevalier was still in a coma, Charles made the regrettable decision to eliminate the other two ghosts as well. The Chevalier woke up cut off from the ghost world and fired from GoPol for "immoral experiments on the dead". He was charged with attempted murder and a bunch of other stuff that he hadn't actually done, judging only by what's in the file—no mention of the ghosts of course.

He went to prison for five years but was released early for good behaviour. And that's when he vanished.

The rest of the file is comparably thin. Whispers of the Chevalier d'Os and Nexus, a grainy picture, but no information on how he finances his endeavours, where he lives, or what he's truly been up to since then.

"Phew." Gaby leans back and rubs her forehead. "I feel like I just read a horror story. You can absolutely not work for GoPol."

"I won't."

"No, I mean, you need to get out of there. Like, now." Her voice is near the breaking point. She suddenly spreads her arms, tears shimmering in her eyes. "Come here."

I flee into her arms only too gladly. Gaby holds me tight, sniffling into my shoulder as she tries to come to terms with what we just read. "This is all fucked up."

"You need to go to the Chevalier," Gaspar says, sounding horrified as well. "He's the only one who can protect you."

"He's not an innocent," I say, sighing heavily. The file is only half the truth, but if even a third of what's in there isn't a lie, then the Chevalier *has* conducted highly immoral experiments, even if in the end he was thrown under the bus.

"Maybe not, but I'm more inclined to trust him than that creepy agency."

I look up at him. "Why?"

"Because I met that whisper ghost of Charles'. He's a total psycho. And if Charles was already a psycho at thirty, I don't want you anywhere near him."

"What's Gaspar saying?" Gaby whispers, correctly assuming that he's talking.

I sigh. "He wants me to go with the Chevalier. Ask for his protection."

Gaby closes her eyes for a moment. When she opens them again, she nods. "I agree."

"You do?"

"He seems to know how to vanish."

But that's the big thing. The Chevalier has completely vanished. He has no connections in the upper world. On the opposite hand, GoPol knows all about me. They know my family, where I live, and what I study. Vanishing like the Chevalier means giving up on all of that. I might as well leave the country and hope Charles' powerful arm doesn't reach that far.

"Vanishing is not the solution. I'm not going to let the Rouberts ruin my life." Tears are burning in my eyes. What can someone like *me* do against an organisation as powerful as GoPol? "I'll go to the Chevalier and join the Résistance. And then, we'll bring that murderer down."

Gaby pulls me close, squeezing me so tight I can barely breathe. "You're right. We need to expose him. We need to... I feel like I should come with you."

Instantly, I shake my head. "No, Gaby. You'd go crazy in the catacombs." I gently wipe the tears from her cheeks. "Look, for now, I'm safe. GoPol believes I'm working for them, and the Chevalier wants me on his side. As long as I can keep up the pretence, I'll be safe."

She hugs me again. "I still hate it." Then she lets go of me and directs her words to the thin air. "Gaspar, you need to take good care of our girl. Don't let anything happen to her."

"I'd give my existence for her."

Hopefully it will never come to that.

With a shuddering breath, I stand up and pull out my phone. Though he has my sympathies, I can't quite trust the Chevalier yet. I don't want him to know that I accidentally stole the file, so I take pictures instead, then hide it in my drawer under my lecture notes. At some point, I'll have to figure out how to deposit it back at GoPol, but that's a problem for another day.

For now, I have to get ready to fool Sébastien and hold my own against the Chevalier. It's time to see if I've got what it takes to join the Résistance.

Chapter 24

We meet Sébastien and Dix at the abandoned Métro station. Though it isn't that late, it's already dark outside. Underground, only a single working bulb emits a flickering light.

Sébastien gives me a short wave and an encouraging smile. "Feeling better?"

My hands are clammy, and my heart is beating a little too fast, but I nod enthusiastically. "Are you coming along?" It'd be a lot more complicated to keep up my act with him there.

"I wish I could. It doesn't feel right to let you walk into this alone." I can't quite tell if he's concerned about my well-being or my chance of success. "Dix will go with you as far as he can, but he'll have to stay out of sight if there are any other ghost whisperers. If anything goes wrong, he'll come and get me. Just..." Sébastien regards me, looking a little helpless. "Be careful, okay? Don't take any risks. If the Chevalier tries to pull some creepy stuff, just come back.”

“Stop worrying so much.” Dix puts an arm around Sébastien’s shoulder and grins. “History Girl is tougher than you think. She’s got this.” He proceeds to ruffle his short hair and laughs.

Sébastien might roll his eyes, but he looks a bit relieved, too. As embarrassed as he often is, I think Dix is good for him. His only true friend. The one who knows exactly what he’s been through.

I shake my head to get rid of the thoughts and concentrate on my mission ahead. “It’s going to be okay. The Chevalier doesn’t know I work for you guys now. I’m just gonna meet with him and see what it is he wants me for. And hopefully that will give you the information you need.”

“Good.” Sébastien nods sharply. “Take care.” His gaze crosses Gaspar’s. “Do your best to keep her safe, okay?” It doesn’t sound like he has much confidence in the ghost’s ability to do so.

“Don’t worry. We’ve got this,” Gaspar replies coldly.

And with that, we finally enter the catacombs.

“You’re awfully quiet today, History Girl,” Dix teases as we climb from the lower floor to the upper one. “Did your plan not work out?”

“What happened with C-Trente?” I ask him instead.

Dix snorts. "I just made him mad. He's used to it."

"That ghost's a psycho," Gaspar mutters. "He threw me out the window when I tried to scout out the office."

"Yeah, that's kind of his signature move. Only hurts when you're fresh, though. Once you forget what pain feels like it's just a fun—"

"Stop."

Dix looks at me curiously. "Did you hear something?"

"No, I need you to stop making light of the abuse you've experienced."

I shouldn't have said anything. Dix's grin slips and he swallows. "It's just a ghost thing. We can't die, remember?"

That's not entirely true. The Chevalier's ghosts all "died" in the end. And Jacques de Molay vanished as well. And C-Trente threatened to end Dix. "Just…" I don't know what I want from him. Probably just a break from all the awful stuff I've learned recently. "Never mind."

"You do realise that it *is* abuse, right?" Gaspar asks softly. "What you and Sébastien experienced?"

"I think the courts would call it murder," Dix quips.

It hurts me physically the way he jokes about such a horrifying thing. "Why… why are you still going along with it?"

"You mean Sébastien? Because if it was up to me, I would've been out of there in an instant." Dix shrugs and then his face grows a little more serious. "He knew he had to die if he wanted to join GoPol. Somehow it would've had to happen. Technically, he consented to it."

"At seventeen?"

"Yeah, there's that."

I take a deep breath, trying not to lose my mind over this. Even if Sébastien thought he was okay with it, he wasn't old enough to make that decision. Besides, it wasn't the first time Charles had done something like that. Which reminds me...

"Dix. Did Sébastien lie to me when he said he didn't know anything about the Chevalier?" Is this whole mission just a test as well?

"What do you mean?" Dix looks confused.

"How much does he really know?"

The groan he emits doesn't bode well. "Very little. He and his partner have only been on the case for the last year or so."

"His partner?"

"Yeah, about two months before he met you they got into a little altercation down here with the Chevalier's men. She fell through a hole into the deeper floors, and well... When Sébastien came back for her, Samara was gone. She's been missing ever since."

"Samara?" I cough. To hide my blunder, I quickly ask, "Is she dead?" Sébastien never mentioned his partner's name. It's quite the shock to realise I know her.

Dix shakes his head. "No, if she were dead, she'd just go to GoPol to debrief. You don't think agents stop working just because they die?" He chuckles softly, but when neither Gaspar nor I join in, he sighs instead. "We don't know what happened to her. Maybe the Chevalier locked her up somewhere. Or she decided to get out when she could." The last words are tinged with bitterness. "Either way, don't mention it to Sébastien. He blames himself, because he ran and hid—injured, mind you."

I almost feel bad for him. While he's still grappling with his failure, Samara has happily switched sides and works for the target now. Did she find out what GoPol did to him? What horrors has she gone through that made her seize her chance at freedom?

"It didn't help that Papa was pretty angry with him."

The more I hear about Charles Roubert the more I want to strangle him. "So, does Sébastien know who the Chevalier is then?"

"No. That's the thing. The closest we came to anything of substance was when you showed us to Ossa Arida. That's why he wants you to infiltrate them."

I suppose Dix could be lying, but he's been pretty open with me—despite all the misplaced jokes. I don't want to compromise Samara, but I don't leave him with nothing either. "His name is Romain Coullier."

"Huh?" Dix stops cold. "Say that again."

"His name is Romain Coullier."

"That can't be right."

"Why not?"

"Because Papa's old partner's name was Coullier. He used to talk about him all the time when we were kids." Dix is sounding more and more confused. "The Chevalier is ex-GoPol?"

So, Charles sent his son on a reconnaissance mission but held back all the important information from him. I wonder what he was trying to achieve. At least that makes me feel better about Sébastien. All of that went down long before his time.

I nod at Dix. "The thing I had to get out of your father's office? It was the Chevalier's file. I didn't know it was going to be that, but GoPol actually knows a lot about him." I tell him the main points in broad strokes. By the end of it, even Dix is speechless.

"Your father needs to be behind bars," Gaspar says.

Dix swallows, staring straight ahead. "It doesn't work that way." His voice drops. "Don't you think his superiors know? When you're this high up in the ranks, normal rules no longer apply. It's all for the good of the country, after all."

Tears of frustration are stinging in my eyes. "How is it good for the country to murder your own son? How could you possibly justify that?"

"Easy," he says, to my horror. "Sébastien is a highly qualified, trained, and loyal agent. He knows what the job demands and does it well. Why go with a random stranger if you can create the perfect man for the job? Look how hard it is to convince you of doing this job."

His bitter irony chases the tears away, leaving me grimacing. "Right, raise the psychos you want."

"Now that's just mean," Dix quips. "Séb's actually really nice. Just had a shit upbringing."

"Well, so did Gaspar, and I don't see him joining any murderous organisations."

Gaspar snorts softly. "To be fair, my parents never killed anyone." He takes my hand and squeezes it softly. "It's going to be okay, Alix. We'll figure something out."

I'm glad he's here with me. I would lose my mind if I didn't have people like Gaspar and Gaby firmly in my corner.

Dix beats it once we make it to the Crossroad of the Dead. He says he'll be close, but I have no idea how he attempts to do that. Instead, I meet up with the Chevalier in his usual spot.

"Alix." Apparently, we're at the stage of cheek kisses now. "How were your holidays?"

Christmas is already a blur, and I don't really feel like chitchatting. "I had my first day at GoPol and got your file."

"Did you now? That was quick."

I'm not being bought by his flippant attitude. "No, I meant, I got *your* file. The file about you. I read it too."

The smile only starts to widen. "I expected you would. So, do they know anything new about me?"

"So, it's true?" I expected him to deny his connection and try to gaslight me, not admit it. "You worked for GoPol? You were Charles Roubert's partner?"

"Junior partner, yes. Didn't quite work out, though. He threw me under the bus for a promotion." The Chevalier shrugs in a way that reminds me an awful lot of Dix. His features harden. "I don't know how much you've read, but yes, I worked for GoPol for six years before things went south."

"Because you created a third ghost."

"Ah." The Chevalier raises a finger and wriggles it. "See, that wasn't just me. Charles was in it too. In fact, it was his idea. He kept bringing it up for a year before I agreed. But let's not dwell on the past. Show me what you've got."

I get out my phone to show him the pictures I took from his file. The Chevalier flips through the first couple of photos, the ones about his *past,* and only studies the recent ones. At last, he gives them back to me.

"Very good. You've proven yourself. Just as I knew you would." He cocks his head, looking compassionately at me. "I suppose you're no longer interested in working with GoPol?"

"Is there a way to get out of it? I don't want them to take my powers away or do... do that kind of stuff to me." It all bursts out of me like a waterfall. "They're insane. They… Please, I just want to return to my studies, talk to my ghosts, and have a normal life."

The Chevalier puts a hand on my shoulder, regarding me somewhat fatherly. "That would be a waste of your talents. Believe me. You don't want to return to that mundane life. You're a ghost whisperer. We don't belong in the mortal world."

I swallow hard. "Where do we belong then?"

He grins suddenly. "Right here, with one foot in either world. That will never change, but I promise to protect you with everything I have. You're important to me. And now, come, we have to celebrate."

The Chevalier leads me back to the Monastery of the Bears where the rest of the Résistance has gathered. Pierre waves at me, but not all the ghosts and living people from last time are there. Instead, there are some new faces, which makes me think it's not a stationary crew but a team constantly in flux.

There's only one other face I recognise: Samara. And she looks mighty annoyed seeing me return.

"Did she give up already?" is the lovely greeting I receive from her. Or rather the Chevalier, since she doesn't even look at me.

I wonder if her animosity has to do with my connection to Sébastien. She's probably afraid I could blow her secret.

"Quite the opposite." The Chevalier puts a heavy hand on my shoulder. "Alix is a bit of an overachiever and has completed her task already."

"I told you you'd be an excellent fit," Pierre says, grinning.

Samara doesn't seem to think so, rolling her eyes heavily.

One of the guys at the listening station doesn't look too impressed, either. I can't tell whether he's a ghost or not, though judging by the amount of pomade in his hair, I assume it's the former. "Isn't that suspicious? Breaking into Roubert's office takes skill. To have done it so quickly probably means they handed it to her. She's running with Roubert's kid, right?" He crosses his arms. "I don't trust her."

"I'll vouch for her," a familiar voice says behind me.

I whirl around, relieved to see a familiar face. "Jean!"

Moulin tips his fedora toward me. "I had to see what you guys have got here for myself. My name is…"

"You're Jean Moulin," Pierre says, completely awestruck.

The guy at the console is equally impressed. "I… We talked briefly in London." He jumps up, eager to shake Moulin's hand. "I didn't know who you were then, but I heard about your mission. It was a shame. A goddamn shame." He must be a ghost, then.

"I think I remember you—Clément, was it?"

The man's face lights up like a Christmas tree. "Yes. Clément Beaufort. It's an honour, such an honour."

"What's happening?" the Chevalier asks. "I can sense ghost activity."

I'd almost forgotten that the Chevalier can't actually see ghosts anymore. He's been cut off from this world, despite trying to bridge it.

"Jean Moulin has just appeared," Samara answers him, sounding a little impressed herself. "*The* Jean Moulin. He said he'll vouch for Alix." Her eyes hit mine. "How do you know Jean Moulin?"

Despite not seeing ghosts, the Chevalier recovers remarkably fast. With a wide grin, he puts both his hands on my shoulder and presents me to the room. "This is exactly why we want her with us. Alix is so much more than a simple résistante. She's the key to our future."

CHAPTER 25

Now that I've proved myself—or more importantly because I'm acquainted with *the* Jean Moulin—the group has become a lot more friendly. They break out a surprising number of delicacies for the living, including soft cheese, fresh bread, and champagne, and we have a picnic in the Monastery of the Bears.

I get to know everyone, though most are introducing themselves to Jean, not me. There's Pierre Roche, who still can't get over the fact that I brought such a legend to the new Résistance, and Clément Beaufort, who soon acts as if he was much more than an acquaintance. He was killed in a conflict with the Milice in 1943, surviving Moulin only by a few months.

Margot Fleury, a small but confident woman with beautiful red lipstick and coiffed hair, is from the same period. She tells me she used to spy on the Germans by having sex with the officers. Clément sneers and calls it the "collaboration horizontale". Like so many of his time, he doesn't understand that women often slept with the oppressors to protect their family. Margot had two young children to support, and she's long since satisfied her conscience with the fact that she passed those secrets on to the Résistance. She died when a jealous "friend" betrayed her.

Not all the ghosts are from the 40s. Or died then. Louis Gagnon is an older gentleman who saw France liberated and died in his late sixties in 1987. During World War II he fought with the Maquis, though he's not willing to go into much detail. "It was such a long time ago. The world's a different place now." I take it he's not too proud of his actions. After all, the conflict between the Maquis and the Milice got more and more savage towards the end of the war, and not all guerrilla warfare was held against military targets.

On the other hand, Celine de Guerineau has no living experience with rebelling. She lived through the Belle Époque in the late 19th century, dying of tuberculosis before she hit thirty-five. Her reason for joining the Résistance is pure boredom. "It's such a long existence. You want to do something with meaning."

"And the Résistance gives you meaning?"

"If we succeed."

Before I can ask what she means by that, she rushes off to catch the opera. The only good thing about being dead is being able to go to the opera for free, according to her. A valid point.

Not every member of the Résistance is dead. Gabriel Allard, a thirty something of Nigerian heritage, appears to be something like the right-hand of the Chevalier, pulling him aside to discuss some problem in the lower tunnels, while twenty-eight-year-old Alain Hasbrouck tinkers with the equipment in the Monastery. He's the one who shows me why they call it the Monastery of the Bears.

In a room next to the monitors, scratch marks cover the walls. "Bears," he declares.

"Bears?" How did bears get down in the catacombs? "I'm afraid I don't understand."

"In 1870, when Paris was besieged, the people were starving. Around Christmas it got so bad they pilfered the zoo. Armand de Crecy loved the bears so much he decided to save them. He and a group of like-minded people stole the bears before they could land on the menu and brought them here. Problem was they couldn't feed the bears, and once they were dead, they ate them just like everyone else."

It's a gruesome story but I remember Victor telling me about eating elephant steak at some point during the siege. He doesn't recommend it.

We return to the main room, and I have some more cheese, when Samara sits down next to me. "You've got him all wrapped around your finger, don't you?"

"Who?" Gaspar is currently talking to Louis and a woman I haven't got to know yet.

"The Chevalier." She redirects my look to the Chevalier, who gives some directions to Allard and sends him off with a shoulder clap.

I shrug, uncomfortable. "What do you mean?"

"Oh, it's all, Alix this, Alix that. We need to convince Alix to join us. She's the key to our future," Samara repeats and rolls her eyes. "He's obsessed with you."

"Hey, Alix," the Chevalier calls out that minute. "Want to join me for a little walk? I want to test something."

"See?" Samara doesn't even disguise her contempt. "He guards his secrets jealously. Not from you, apparently."

There's no time to ask what she means, since the Chevalier comes over. "Shall we?"

With a frown, I get to my feet. Samara seems to be harbouring inexplicable resentment towards me. The Chevalier is almost twenty years older than me, so I hope she doesn't think we're having an affair or something. I decide that she was likely traumatised by GoPol and that her feelings have little to do with me. With time she might come to see that for herself, but until then, I'll just have to keep my distance.

I get up and join the Chevalier. Gaspar notices us leaving and excuses himself to tag along. The rest are too engrossed with Jean Moulin's tales or working on their own projects to care.

"Where are we going?" Gaspar asks. Since I don't know, I relay the question to the Chevalier.

"Just somewhere quieter."

It's another chamber not too far from the Monastery of Bears. The first thing I notice is the circle of arcane symbols drawn on the ground with chalk. The Chevalier lights a couple of candles before taking out some chalk to fix symbols that have been smudged by feet and time.

"What is this?"

"A meditation circle." The Chevalier sounds amused. "I know you don't believe in magic and fair enough, it's not as tangible as ghosts when you're a ghost whisperer. But I wanted to show you that I'm not a madman. There are things in this world beyond sense and logic."

I stand awkwardly at the edge of the circle as the Chevalier settles in the middle. "Isn't magic just stuff unexplained yet by science?" I remember having this discussion with Sébastien. He'd struggle with this.

"That's one way to put it." The Chevalier grins. "Call me a researcher then, because I intend to figure it all out. Now watch. Gaspar's here with us, right?"

"Yes."

"Good. Let's play a game. Gaspar, pick a spot. I'll have to guess where you are." He closes his eyes and takes calm, measured breaths.

As he starts to meditate, the symbols around him seem to shimmer slightly. Gaspar and I exchange a glance, then he shrugs and heads down the left side of the circle. I try not to look at him and study the Chevalier instead.

He raises his arm and points straight at Gaspar. They go for a couple more rounds. Every time, the Chevalier manages to pinpoint Gaspar's location with frightening accuracy.

"Are you sure you can't see him?"

The Chevalier lowers his arm. "A hundred per cent sure. I feel the ghosts' presence when they're near, and with the help of this, that ability strengthens. But it's not enough to be of use. I still can't *see* him, much less talk to him." He gives me a sad little smile.

It must be frustrating to know ghosts are out there, yet outside your reach. I want to ask him if he's ever considered creating another ghost, but I don't dare. The thought alone is horribly wrong. Besides, he obviously made his decision. Coming close to dying three times is bad enough.

"So, is that what you do? Find ways to talk to ghosts without having to die?"

"Wouldn't that be grand?" The Chevalier gets to his feet and dusts down his backside. "I have a lot of ideas. And if you want, I'll show you more. How much time do you have?"

I shrug. Sébastien and I never discussed how long I'd be staying in the catacombs. "Not too much. GoPol wants a report."

"Ah, yes. Let's figure out what you'll tell them instead. I can show you my workshop another day. We'll have to go to the ruins of Lutetia instead."

Great. Now I *want* to go there. Why did I have to mention Sébastien? I could've explored my cities' beginnings instead. "I'll come back tomorrow."

The Chevalier grins again. "I knew I'd get you."

Chapter 26

The next day, I report to Sébastien. I keep all the details about the Résistance and who's in it to myself. Instead, I call them a group of cataphiles who seem interested in charting and mapping the underground maze. It *is* one of the Chevalier's interests, after all.

There are a couple of things the Chevalier instructed me to say to keep my act up, which I relay almost verbatim. "I haven't seen much yet, but he showed me his maps. You know about the places of power, right? He briefly talked about them when we went up against Jacques de Molay."

Sébastien nods, hanging on to every word. "Yes, what's up with those? Why is he so interested in them?"

"He's like half a ghost whisperer," I say, keeping the reason for that to myself. "He can't see or hear them, but he knows when ghosts are near. A little bit like Malou."

"Who's Malou?"

It baffles me for a moment that he doesn't know her, but then I remember I never introduced the two. "My pet hedgehog. She can sniff out ghosts."

Sébastien did not expect that answer. He blinks rapidly, then clears his throat. "You've got a pet hedgehog that can see ghosts?"

"Yes, she even has her own Instagram." I pull out my phone to show him. Odile has posted Malou's Moulin costume, putting up a series of Noir shots. It's ridiculously adorable.

I glance at him, noticing the pained expression. It's safe to say he's not a hedgehog boy. "It's cute," I admonish him.

"Very," Dix says with a cheesy smile, nudging Sébastien. "Why did we never get a hedgehog pet?"

Desperately, he defends himself. "I didn't even know you could have hedgehogs as pets. Or that they could be ghost whisperers. Did it die or something?"

"No." I shake my head, taking my phone back. "Not that I know of. It's probably an animal thing. You know how some pets can sense ghosts. Malou is one of them. And she's a true ghost sniffer. Gaspar can pick her up."

The poor guy looks like he's about to lose his mind.

Meanwhile, Dix's enjoying Sébastien's discomfort a little too much. "Please let us get a hedgehog pet. We need one. Ghost sniffers." He starts laughing.

"This is real?" Sébastien asks, not even close to laughing. "You're not messing with me?"

"Do you want me to bring her in? Have Dix give her a belly rub?"

Dix's eyes light up. "Yes, please."

It's too much. Sébastien leans forward and massages the bridge of his nose. "Can we get back to the Chevalier, please?"

"The other ghost sniffer," Dix jokes.

Now *that* gets a snort from Sébastien.

"Yeah, I don't think he'd appreciate the term." I'm glad for the distraction Malou has provided without even being here. It's taken the tension out of the meeting. "Well, as I said, he searches for these places of power because that's where his powers are the strongest. He sees himself as an occult researcher. Well, a ritualist, really. He's testing what's possible and what not."

"Doing what exactly?"

"I don't know yet. He showed me one thing which is basically a meditation circle or something. It's an array of complicated symbols that help him centre himself and stretch out his senses. When he showed me, he was able to point to Gaspar, but he never heard a word."

Sébastien leans back, his arms crossed. "Did he say anything about his life outside the catacombs? Like how he finances that 'research'? Anything like that?"

"No." And that's the truth. We had little opportunity to talk about much more with the whole introduction of the Résistance. "I'll try to bring it up next time."

He loosens his arms and smiles. "Don't rush it. Just probe gently when you feel like it's natural. This is a long game, and by the sounds of it, you did incredibly well. Great job, History Girl."

It's the first time I've heard him use Dix's nickname for me. I'm not sure he even noticed, but it's one of those rare moments where I can really see the connection between the two.

"Thanks. So, do you want me to go back? The Chevalier offered to show me the Ruins of Lutetia. Apparently, they're a place of power as well." If I'm being honest, I couldn't care less about the occult power in them. It's history! And unlike the tiny part preserved inside the Louvre, these ruins are supposedly more extensive.

"Yeah, if it's not too much of a burden? Obviously you can't go every day—"

"I'm on holidays." Sure, I should probably spend some of my recent criminal energy on prepping for exams, and there's also two essays I still need to write, but who *actually* works between Christmas and New Year's?

Sébastien chuckles. "Then, sure. It can only be to our advantage. The history angle is a great cover."

"Cover?" Last time I checked I was still a real history student.

"It gives you a genuine reason to be interested in the catacombs. You don't have to come up with some flimsy excuse. You can just be yourself and build this relationship. Eventually he'll slip you something we can use." He gets up. "Do you want a coffee? We can also raid the cookie jar. I think there's still loads left downstairs."

The unexpected cheekiness is another glimpse at the Dix inside him. Am I only noticing it more or are we becoming closer? Are we accidentally building a relationship?

Downstairs, Sébastien puts the coffee on and hands me three tins of cookies to choose from. He was right, there are still a lot of cookies leftover.

"What did you get for your Secret Santa?" I ask as I make my pick. The Christmas tree is still there, but the presents have all been collected.

"I didn't take part."

"Why not?" I decide on a round cookie that looks rather plain but sports half a walnut and a bit of chocolate on it. The first bite is promising: sugary and nutty at the same time.

Sébastien shrugs. "It's not really for me."

"Why?"

Another shrug. "It seems to be a downstairs thing."

"Were other agents part of it?"

"I guess."

I roll my eyes. "You're hopeless."

"Exactly what I always say," Dix adds. "Hey, maybe you could take Séb here to a student party or something."

The pained expression on Sébastien's face is hilarious. Though in this case, I almost mirror it. "I'm not really a party girl."

Sébastien sighs in relief. "You didn't seem like one."

"Boring," is Dix's incredibly mature assessment.

"So, do you ever do anything for fun?" I ask, nibbling on my cookie. "And you can't say work."

"I like the theatre. The opera if I can afford it."

My mouth falls open. "No way. You go to the opera?"

A shimmer of red graces Sébastien's cheeks. "Is that wrong?" Judging by his intonation it seems as if he's asking whether guys his age are allowed to go.

"No, why would it be? I'm glad you like something other than work."

He snorts. "I'm just very busy."

I almost invite him to come walk Père Lachaise with me and meet the ghosts, but luckily remember that I can't bring him to the cemetery under any circumstances. Before my lapse becomes evident, we hear the front door buzzing. Someone else is coming to work.

It's two people I know: Sébastien's father and Cédric. They spot us immediately.

"Alix!" Cédric calls out. He comes over and kisses me on the cheeks. "I didn't expect you to be working over the holidays."

"What are you doing here?" I ask, because *I* didn't expect to see *him* here either. He's not going to try and become a ghost whisperer, is he?

"Oh, I'm just taking a look at the space." When I don't react immediately, he adds, "For the party."

Relieved, I gasp. "Oh. The party, yes. When is it?"

"On the thirty-first?" Cédric laughs at my slowness. "Are you okay?"

"Yes, yes, I'm good. It just slipped my mind for a moment." It seems ages ago that we talked about the engagement party.

Charles joins us, taking a cup of coffee from Sébastien without asking for it. "My, this is becoming quite the family affair." He claps Cédric's back. "I love it."

Behind his shoulder I see Dix indicating a gag reflex. I quickly pick another cookie to avoid giving him away.

"How's it going?" Charles asks Sébastien. "Did you manage to make contact yet?"

"Yes." Sébastien perks right up. "Alix did an amazing job. She has a perfect in, the"—he looks at Cédric and pivots flawlessly—"subject likes and trusts her."

"Trust is probably a bit much," I mutter.

Sébastien shrugs. "He will. She already knows more about him than I managed to find out in the last year."

Oh, how absolutely right he is in that regard. If I'm honest, I wish I didn't know quite as much.

"That's not quite the boast you think it is," Charles says, instantly killing Sébastien's enthusiasm. But then he laughs. "Just kidding. That's great." He nods to me. "Good job, Alix. You seem to be taking to this job incredibly well." He clasps Cédric's shoulder. "Shall we go upstairs?"

"Yes, of course." He looks at me. "Listen, if you're still here in an hour, I can take you home."

"Thanks, but I have to get back to the mission."

A shadow passes over Cédric's face as I reject his kind offer. He catches himself quickly, though. "Of course. How long will you be gone?"

"I'll probably stay the night. You really don't need to drive me all the time."

Cédric laughs. "It's not a burden." He waves to the two of us and accompanies his uncle upstairs.

It's then I notice Charles never once acknowledged Dix. "Does he usually ignore you?" I ask him.

"Papa?" Dix asks. "Or Cédric? Because that one's blind as a bat."

"Your father. He's a ghost whisperer, right?"

"He can see Dix alright," Sébastien says softly.

"I'm just a ghost," Dix says, sounding awfully upbeat. "What could he possibly talk to me about?"

I grimace. "You're his son. The least he could do is look at you."

"And be reminded of his deed? I don't think so."

"Dix!" Horrified, Sébastien looks at him. With a nervous laugh, he turns to me. "The two of them don't get along very well. Dix can't stop teasing him and Papa can be... grumpy about it. It's childish, really."

He's rambling, trying to cover up Dix's blunder so I don't get all scared about the fact that GoPol is led by a child murderer. Since I don't want him to know that Dix and I have been talking behind his back, I let myself be distracted, dutifully nodding along at his long-winded explanation.

When he appears happy to have averted the crisis, I check my watch. "Time for me to go."

"Good luck. Stay vigilant, okay?"

I give him a bright smile. "Always."

CHAPTER 27

This afternoon, the Chevalier doesn't bother with the Monastery and takes me straight down to the ruins of Lutetia. I assume I'm not the first historian to wander amongst them, and even if I am, I don't have the right tools with me to do anything but marvel over being in the presence of a piece of ancient history.

The ruins themselves aren't very spectacular. It's mostly an array of broken wall fragments that hint to the houses that once stood in this place, but there's a lot of them, and as I walk through, I imagine what it must've been like when the sunlight still hit these walls two thousand years ago.

"Do you feel it?" the Chevalier asks, running his hands lightly across a stone wall. "The power in this place?"

I try to push past the awe history itself inspires in me and look deeper. There are no ghosts apart from Gaspar down here. No one remembers the particular people who once lived here, though I'm sure their bones are buried beneath our feet. Still, there's something about this place, a hum in the walls, a tension in the air. "What is it?"

"The power of life itself."

"Life?"

"So many lives that passed through here, century after century. They all left a trace that can't be washed away but is only added to by each generation." The Chevalier stops and turns to me. "Are you ready to find out what I'm really working on?"

My heart beats faster. Could it be? Would he truly reveal his secrets so easily to me? "Why are you showing me this?"

"Because I believe you'd have a particular interest in continuing this work with me." He looks in the general direction of Gaspar. "Your boyfriend surely will."

Gaspar and I exchange a look. He shrugs. "Let's just see what it is, right?"

"Okay."

"Follow me." The Chevalier picks his path through the ruins until he arrives at a pile of rubble, not much different than any of the others. Though, on second thoughts, it doesn't look as dusty.

With the tip of his shoe, the Chevalier shoves the rubble aside and exposes a trapdoor. "It took me nearly six years to build this place. Few others know of its existence. You have to promise not to let on any of this to GoPol."

I don't see myself trusting anything to GoPol at this moment. "I promise."

"Good. Now, behold. My workshop." He opens the door and shines his light into the darkness below. "Ladies first."

"Let me," Gaspar says instead. He sits on the rim of the trapdoor, feeling with his feet. "There's a staircase." Slowly, he goes in.

"Alix?" the Chevalier asks.

I wait until Gaspar's hollow voice rings out, "You've got to see this."

"You're not gonna lock me in, right?"

The Chevalier laughs. "Why would I do that? Oh well. Close up behind us, would you?"

He goes in first. By the time I make my way down there and close the trapdoor above my head, the Chevalier has lit a row of torches along the round walls of his workshop. They illuminate two tables surrounded by occult symbols, a row of boxes at one wall, and bones. So many bones.

I'm strongly reminded of what Ossa Arida looked like and wonder if this is where all the bones have gone.

"There's no electricity down here, so we have to do it the old-fashioned way," the Chevalier says as he sticks the torch he used to light all the others in its place along the wall.

"What are we doing down here?" I hold my breath, waiting for the answer.

"Something's alive in here," Gaspar hisses suddenly, taking a step away from the boxes.

And truly, I hear the scuffle of small feet. "Is that a rat?" I don't usually mind rats, unless I'm stuck in a dark hole surrounded by creepy bones.

The Chevalier's toothy smile is more ghostly than Gaspar's in the flickering light of the torches. "Not quite. Come." He walks over to the wall, niftily evading Gaspar, and picks up the top box to carry it over to the table. Then he lifts the top, waving me towards him.

My feet appear stuck to the floor. The scratching is definitely coming from the box. It feels frantic, desperate to get out, and... I don't know what it would do. Something terrible.

"Just have a look. It's not gonna bite you. I didn't find the teeth."

That nearly pulls the floor out from under my feet. "Teeth?"

Suddenly, Gaspar is at my side. He takes my hand and squeezes it, his face unreadable, eyes looking straight ahead. "Let's do this together."

Borrowing from his courage, we step closer. My heart is beating in my throat as I stretch my neck to throw a cautious glance inside the box.

Something scuttles across the floor, startling me. A second glance reveals white bones. Moving white bones. It's a little creature I can't quite identify. Something with four legs, a bent back, a long tail, and an elongated skull. Without teeth.

"What is this?" My voice is shaking so much I don't think the Chevalier can even understand me.

"A squirrel."

A squirrel. I can see it now, the bent back, the hunched over movements when it sits still. But there's no fat to it, no fur, nothing that makes it remotely recognisable as the cute critter you sometimes see in parks. "Why... How...?"

The Chevalier grins at me. "Two excellent questions. The questions we all have to ask ourselves. How? Well, that requires a complex understanding of occultism, necromancy, and biology, of course. As for the why... to bring back the dead."

I swallow heavily. *Necromancy.* The art of raising the dead. How is that possible?

"You can bring back the dead?" Gaspar asks.

Oh no.

I believe you'd have a particular interest... Your boyfriend surely will.

"But these are just animated bones. It's not really alive. Not like before." This is not good. Not good at all.

"True." The Chevalier puts the lid back on and carries the box back. He grabs another one. "But I'm getting closer."

I recognise the creature in this box immediately. A hedgehog. Not an African Pygmy like Malou, but a standard European brown hedgehog. Contrary to the previous creature, it looks almost correct. It still has most of its spikes and there's even fur. The only trouble is it's been run over by a car. It's not much, but the back of its body is squished in, and there's blood all over it.

The Chevalier reaches into the box and pulls out the poor baby, turning it over. "I put the entrails back and sewed it shut, but I couldn't fix the damage to its skeleton."

Next to me, Gaspar stumbles back. "I do not want to come back as roadkill." I haven't seen the damage Gaspar endured after he was hit by a van, but since it killed him, I don't want him to come back like that either.

I'm not sure I want him to come back at all if that means diving into necromancy. It's just wrong.

Swallowing, I watch the little hedgehog squirm in the Chevalier's hands. It's trying to escape the grip of a predator. "Let it go."

The Chevalier puts the hedgehog back into the box where it rolls itself into a ball, shivering. Tears burn in my eyes.

"This... this..."

"Is a natural progression," the Chevalier says. "They're dead, Alix. At least, they were dead. But I'm getting better at bringing them back alive. I'm close. In fact, I succeeded with this one."

I don't even want to look, but the next box holds a perfectly well-looking white mouse. It scurries along the edges of the box, pausing to brush its nose before continuing its journey. "It's alive in all the ways that matter. It's only missing a functioning metabolism, but that's not necessarily a bad thing. It doesn't eat, drink, nor excrete."

"This mouse was dead?"

"Brought it back from its mere bones. I think it died years ago. Of course, there's no way to know if its brain made it, but it acts like a mouse, so I count that as success. We'll do a couple more trials before I move on to human ghosts."

"You're going to experiment on humans?" My knees feel weak.

"Only those who are willing. I believe the success will be greater with humans because their ghosts are still here. They're not just animated bones or weak-minded critters. As I told you, I'm close." He looks me straight in the eyes. "I'm happy to give your boyfriend first dibs. You don't need to do anything. I'll get his bones, prepare the ritual, and make him recall his body."

A whimper escapes my mouth. I look at Gaspar, but he seems too horrified to even move.

"You don't have to decide now. It's not like he's running away, right? But if you do decide you want more from this relationship than just a memory, let me know."

The Chevalier closes the box and puts it away. "It's not all I do, of course," he says, sounding completely unfazed by my sheer terror. "But it's been a dream of mine to revert death. To give all those who died prematurely another chance. To ease the pain of losing ones we hold dear, and ease the pain the ghosts feel just watching life passing them by."

I think of my ghosts at the Panthéon. All these great minds that are still churning but will never leave another mark on the world.

And still, I'm one hundred percent sure that they prefer it like this. They would never agree to being brought back into a world they simply no longer belong to.

"What else do you do?" I ask, eager to move on from this topic, while simultaneously fearing what other immoral experiments he has been conducting down here.

And I'm beginning to doubt. Was his firing from GoPol necessary? Were he and Charles both horrible? Or am I just squeamish because I've never experienced something like this? Are there some ghosts—less revered ones—that want to come back?

I look at Gaspar, who's still caught in this weird struggle of horror and longing. Now that there is a possibility, will it change anything? Has the Chevalier lit a fire in him that I won't be able to quench?

"What else?" The Chevalier takes some time to think about it. "Well, I work with ghosts, of course. Seeing if I can make them more corporal. So I may see and hear them again."

My heart eases a little. "You must miss being a ghost whisperer."

"Dearly."

"Have you ever...?"

"Considered suicide?" The Chevalier snorts. "No, after the last time, my heart is too weak to risk another arrest. It's too much of a gamble, and I'm not ready to be just a ghost yet. I never even got to meet my third ghost."

It was a part of him. According to GoPol's file, it was a deadly, insane ghost, but if I was murdered by my partner, I'd probably be deadly and insane, too. An idea crosses my mind. "Have you ever... split a whisper ghost and its partner?"

"Split?" The Chevalier cocks his head. "Is that how you want to protect yourself? By severing the connection between you and your little ghost, turning you into two separate entities?"

"Is it possible?"

"It's worth a try." I can see his mind churning. "Yes, I can see that working."

"Without losing my ability?" I wasn't even asking about Petite Alix, but now that he's mentioned it, it would remove the Sword of Damocles over my head as well.

The Chevalier frowns heavily. "That's the question. I suppose it's all in how well we can stabilise the whisper ghost. As you know, severing the bond is easy, but that usually eliminates the ghost. But yes, I could start from there." He smiles. "See, I knew we two would work well together."

I don't know about that, but I can't quite claim I'm not a little bit intrigued either. Suddenly, there are new possibilities. The question is only do I dare entertain them?

CHAPTER 28

After the horrors of the Chevalier's workshop, I can't stay the night with the Résistance. Instead, I take Gaspar—and Dix, who stayed close throughout our trip—to the cave of lights. Someone has added to the art installation and now there's some colourful lights in between, making it seem as if we're staring into some far away galaxy.

I'm lying on my back between the two, just soaking in the soothing sight of the lights, letting its beauty take away the memories of animated bones and ought-to-be-dead critters. For a few precious moments, I can find peace.

After a while, I feel Gaspar shift. "I'm not gonna do it."

A sense of relief washes over me. The temptation was there. Suddenly, a deep longing for more than we have filled me, but I know it's wrong. More wrong than dating a ghost. People don't come back from the dead.

"Not gonna do what?" Dix asks, slightly annoyed. He's been constantly changing position, clearly getting bored. Teenagers.

I check with Gaspar, and he shrugs. If Dix is keeping tabs on me for Sébastien, then I shouldn't tell him any of this. But in my heart, I know he's not doing that. He's too desperate for me to help him.

"There might be a way for Gaspar to come back alive," I say softly, testing the words on my tongue for the first time. "It's not a good way."

Gaspar squeezes my hand. "I'm happy with how things are. I don't need more than this."

That's a lie, of course. We both wish we could be a normal couple who nobody would bat an eye at. But it beats the alternative.

"It's not something that should be messed with," I say softly. I don't know enough about the occult ways the Chevalier travels on to fully grasp their monstrosity. At what point does magic become science? Is my understanding just not large enough to recognise the good in it? Is fear keeping me from someone I love? Or are my morals still intact?

I've experienced so many monstrous things in the past few days that the line between good and evil has become blurred. I'm not used to thinking so hard about my own morals. On the whole, I feel like I'm a good person. Sure, I've trespassed before and I've bent the rules a little, but always with good intentions, like when the rules didn't seem to fit my unique situation. This is different. This rule is not to be bent.

The living are alive and the dead are dead. You only cross that line once. There's no going back.

"I'm with you there," Gaspar whispers. "It's too risky. What if it goes wrong? I know what we have isn't ideal, but it's the best thing in my ... afterlife. I'm not going to risk it for a dream I shouldn't have."

"Yeah, that's fucked up," is Dix's concise assessment.

It serves me well to dash all irrational hope. "Right."

The lights have dimmed and I've yet to turn on my torch again to reactivate them. In the darkness, it becomes evident that I'm the only one breathing here. What a messed-up little world I live in. And yet, this is one of the moments to savour.

"Do you think the Chevalier will hold it against us, though?" Gaspar asks after a while. "He was clearly hoping you'd join him."

I shudder. Necromancy is not going on my New Year's resolutions. "He didn't sound like he was going to force me. I think he just hoped I'd be interested because of our unique situation, but you heard him. Most people in the Résistance don't even know about his workshop. So it doesn't seem like he's forcing them."

"Did you ask him about my case?" Dix asks. "Can he help?"

"He said he'd look into it. Are you sure you want to separate from Sébastien, though?" I can't help it but I feel sorry for the GoPol agent. He's already isolated from everyone else. He lost his partner—one way or the other—and now he stands to lose Dix as well.

Dix groans softly, clearly unhappy. "If that's what it takes." After a while, he says so softly that I need to strain my ears to pick up the words, "I dreamed about running once. When I... When we were still one, I had this plan. I'd get a motorbike and pack a few things, and then just ride off and never look back." He scoffs slightly. "It was stupid, of course. As if a bike makes you invisible, when we all know only death can do that." Bitterness has entered his voice, and he sighs. "In the end I convinced myself that I was just acting out. That a lifetime of training for this one thing had turned me off it, giving me this sudden thirst for freedom. But it'd be stupid to throw it away after all the work I'd already put into it. Like an athlete who stops just as they're at the height of their ability. I wasn't going to be stupid. And I wasn't going to be a quitter. That's when I told my father I was ready."

My heart aches for the teenager who dreamed of getting away from all expectations. Who only knew training and competition, purpose and responsibility. I understand the separation of Dix and Sébastien a little better now. And what Sébastien lost when he decided to follow the path his father had set out for him.

"I should have run," Dix says. Then suddenly, he gets up. "Let's head out of here. I've had enough of this whole navel gazing. If the Chevalier doesn't come through on this, we need to start building a case against my father."

With a sigh, I turn on my light and sit up. "It will take a lot to bring him down." As Sébastien once said: a ghost's testimony isn't worth shit in our court system. What we need is actual proof. Such as the file in my bedroom.

"Are you going to give up on my favour?" Dix asks, blinking a little too fast.

Gaspar stands up beside me. "Don't be silly. Alix is on your side."

"She's a bit on everyone's side at the moment."

And whose fault is that? Probably my own. "I don't care about GoPol or the Chevalier. The only side I'm truly on is the ghosts' and that won't ever change."

Dix smiles with sudden relief. It's an expression that doesn't last too long, as he switches into his blasé brat attitude. "Good, because I'm counting on you, History Girl."

I roll my eyes at him and start climbing through the window that drops into the tunnel leading us out of here.

We've almost reached the old drainage channel when Jean Moulin suddenly appears next to me. "Incoming," he says in a tight voice that makes me tense up instantly. "The secret has been compromised. You're under attack."

CHAPTER 29

It's four o'clock in the morning and snowing quite heavily when I reach Père Lachaise. I can immediately sense something's wrong. Usually, the ghosts here are a beautiful motley crew with everyone going on their way. Jim Morrison shreds his guitar, Chopin composes hauntingly beautiful melodies, Oscar Wilde holds a literature circle, and ghosts gather around or stroll across the premises, unhurried, relaxed.

Now every ghost is heading towards Abelard and Héloïse's hill. The closer we get, the more horrified faces we encounter. Ghosts. Horrified.

"What's happening?" It's good that Gaspar's dead and can't feel any pain, because I'm squeezing the hell out of his hand. "Grandma!"

I let go of Gaspar to run towards the familiar headstones where my grandmother and Beatrice usually hang out. What I find there makes my stomach turn.

My grandmother is on the ground, flickering as if she has a bad connection, countless holes in her body. Beatrice looks a little more stable, but she's suffered, too. Despite her own injuries—I can't see them as anything else—she holds my grandmother in her arms and is crying silently.

"Grandma!" I fall to my knees and stretch out a hand, but it shakes so heavily it never makes it to her. "What happened?"

"A police raid," Beatrice says bitterly and spits out in disgust. "They came to get your girl."

I knew that's what happened the moment Moulin warned me of an attack. Still, I squeeze my eyes shut and nearly choke on the sob. "Did they... did they get her?"

"I'm so sorry, darling."

No, I can't lose hope just yet. I pat my face dry and regard my grandmother. "Will she be okay?" They must have attacked the ghosts with salt. In the fresh-falling snow it's hard to see, but a few grains stick to the headstone.

"I don't know. We've never seen anything like this."

My grandmother and Beatrice aren't the only one who were hurt. All around us, ghosts are flickering, surrounded by moaning friends and family. Every breath hurts in my chest like a thousand needles as I take in the horror around me.

Ghosts shouldn't suffer like this. They're already dead. Rest in peace isn't just some empty phrase. But that didn't seem to matter to GoPol.

Bile rises in my throat. This is all my fault. I brought this doom to my ghost communities. I brought Petite Alix here.

Slowly, I rise, my gaze hefted on the top of the hill where I thought Petite Alix would be safe. Where I thought *I* would be safe. I can't quite comprehend what's happened yet. Or rather *why* it has happened. Was the mission GoPol gave me just a ruse? Did they want me busy and far away from the ghosts to go after my whisper ghost? And what will happen now that they've got her? Is my time as a ghost whisperer coming to an end or is Petite Alix going to be held hostage to keep me in line?

The thought makes my stomach turn. Faced with all the horror around me, I bend over and throw up into the snow. How could anyone possibly think this was okay? That you could do this to people? To ghosts?

I feel a hand on my back, stroking slowly. "We need to check," Gaspar says softly.

Even though I already know the answer, he's right. At the very least, we need to check on Abelard and Héloïse. And so, we slowly make the ascent, Dix in tow.

He's been quiet ever since we arrived at the cemetery. Whenever I steal a glance at him, his eyes are wide. He stares at the brutalised ghosts as if he can't believe what he's seeing.

But there are hisses, evil glares. At first, I think they're directed at me, since all this is my fault, but every ghost who meets my eyes just looks terribly sorry. No, they're not happy seeing Dix here, which means I know at least one agent responsible for this massacre.

Anger fills the empty pores of my body, pushing away the helplessness and shock I first felt. A deep sense of betrayal colours all my thoughts. You thought I'd have learnt the first time Sébastien betrayed me, when he sold out my father. Somehow I'd forgiven him the transgression, because in retrospect, it seemed as if it actually helped my father; but that's not why he did it. He couldn't care less about that. All he's interested in is being a good little soldier and gathering up whisper ghosts for his Papa to control.

My anger only grows when we reach the top of the hill. Before I can even see the mausoleum, I can hear Héloïse's heart-rendering wails. Her distress spurs me on and I quicken my steps to reach her faster.

A big group of ghosts has gathered around her, trying to offer comfort or find out what happened. They all part when they hear me approach, averting their eyes quickly.

Héloïse is on the ground, holes peppering her body. But it's her eyes, when she looks up at me, that are the most horrifying. I've never seen such deep despair. "He's gone. He's gone!"

Immediately, I search for Abelard, but the old monk is nowhere to be found. And neither is my little self. "Did they take him too?" My voice sounds unfamiliar to me, all squeaky and brittle.

Héloïse sobs uncontrollably. She holds her injured stomach and sways back and forth in an effort to regain her composure. Several times I see her pause to swallow and blink, but it takes her five minutes before she can speak again.

"He wouldn't let them take me. No, her... the girl." She's struggling to remember the details because she was salted. I tear up at the thought of all those many centuries wiped from her memory. "He... he..." Her voice breaks and she whimpers again. "They attacked him gruesomely. They cut off his—... No, they destroyed him. And then they took the child. Tore her out of my arms like the cruel demons they are."

I glance at the lying statues of Héloïse and Abelard and swallow hard. According to the Chevalier, a ghost can only be destroyed if their bones are scattered. As far as I can see they didn't violate the grave, but that doesn't change the fact that not a wisp of Abelard has remained. And if he ever reappears, he'll have forgotten everything. A thousand years. Gone.

"Monsters, that's what they are. Living monsters," the ghosts around us mutter. "She was a child. A baby."

I can't even imagine the kind of terror Petite Alix must've felt when GoPol came for her, when her adoptive Papa was extinguished in front of her. I can sense it. Like a faint whisper deep inside me, I sense her fear.

Gaspar puts his arms around me, but I'm too shocked to return the embrace. I can't stop staring at the mausoleum and attempting to grasp the terror of what's happened here.

He puts his hand on my head, holding me even tighter. "I love you," Gaspar whispers, and that's when I recognise it for what it is. A goodbye.

My clock has started ticking. We're on borrowed time now.

Chapter 30

As it turns out, I'm not supposed to lose my abilities right away. At least, when I arrive at the Panthéon at five in the morning, all my ghosts are there. I can still see everyone. News has travelled fast, though, and the first thing I hear is Voltaire raging.

"This is an atrocity. Under no circumstances can we sit still and let the living stomp all over us. I call for a revolution." He takes one look at me and shakes his head with barely contained anger. "Whatever you need, we stand behind you."

Our silly spat is completely forgotten. I tear up upon hearing his words and throw my arms around him. "Oh, Voltaire!"

I can hear him gulp as he awkwardly pats my shoulder. "Now, now, Mademoiselle, let's not get too sentimental here." His voice breaks a little, though, and I let go of him.

All around me, the ghosts have gathered. Their looks range from horror plastered over disbelief to sadness. Jean-Jacques Rousseau sits on the steps, resting his chin on his fist and mumbling, "There is such a thing as the dignity of death. Our afterlife matters."

"It does," I say, slinging my arms around him from behind. "Don't ever believe you no longer matter just because you're already dead. What they're doing is wrong."

My phone buzzes and a message appears on the lock screen: *"I'm outside."*

I let go of Rousseau and hurry back to the side door to open it for a very tired Gaby. She hasn't even put make-up on, her blond hair bound in a very messy bun. I instantly feel bad for getting her out of bed, but I need her. I can't face this without my best friend.

"Oh, Gaby! It's horrible!" I hug her tight, instantly starting to sob.

Gaby wraps her arms around me and pulls me closer. "What's happened?"

I tell her in quick hurried bursts broken by sobs as she closes the door behind us and walks with me to the crypt, where once again, we're surrounded by my ghosts. My head hurts because of all the crying and fretting, and because I haven't slept yet. But I'm too anxious to even think about taking a rest right now.

"Alix, I'm so sorry," Gaby says when I finally finish my tale, it's length more due to my inability to string sensible words together than the amount of detail.

"What am I supposed to do?" I ask her. "Why would they just take her?" I thought Petite Alix was safe. That even *if* Sébastien found out about her, he'd talk to me first, that he'd try to convince me of giving her up, not brutally rip her from her guardians' hands and terrorise an entire necropolis in the process.

Gaby keeps an arm around my shoulders and gives me yet another hug. "I don't know. I don't know why GoPol is such a shitty organisation. As far as I know, it's not illegal to be a ghost whisperer."

Neither is brutalising a bunch of ghosts. The law is of no help to me here. "What if they take it from me? I can't... I can't lose all this."

I raise my head, looking each and every ghost in the eye. Dix evades my gaze, leaning against the wall as far away as he can. With everything going on, none of the ghosts have objected to his presence. Nor have they kicked out Gaspar, who sits behind me, unable to speak. My gaze lands on Victor at last, and I whimper.

He looks so lost, so devastated. Every doubt I ever had about these ghosts not valuing me as much as I value them has been wiped away by this tragedy. Even if soon I won't be able to see them anymore, I'll know that they're here, watching over me.

It's not nearly as comforting a thought as it should be. I squeeze my eyes shut and take a deep, but very shaky, breath.

"They haven't won yet," a surprisingly firm voice says. "I know it looks bleak, but we can't give up. Now is the time to stand up and resist."

I open my eyes to see Jean Moulin has stepped into the circle of ghosts. He looks even more dashing than usual now that his eyes are glinting with fervour. Slowly, he turns around, his voice rising. "What we need is a plan. Our topmost mission has to be to free Petite Alix."

"How?" Voltaire asks, his eyes narrowing. "She's held in a living prison. We can't affect the world of the living."

"You!" Moulin points at Dix, who startles. "You know where they hold the whisper ghosts."

Dix swallows heavily. "I actually don't." Doubtful looks hit him. He quickly raises his hands. "I've never been down there. Why would I?"

"Down there," Moulin repeats. "That's a start. Down where?"

Dix shrugs, but slowly, he recovers from the surprise attention. "There's a lower floor at GoPol. Or maybe more. They always bring them down there. It's Restricted Access. I never tried going in."

"Are there measures against ghosts?" Moulin asks.

"On the door?" Dix looks baffled. "I don't think so."

"Perfect." The word is like a bullet. "Then your task is to find out exactly where they keep Petite Alix and report to Alix as soon as you know."

Dix gulps. "I…" His eyes meet mine and his shoulders deflate. "I'll do it, but I won't be able to get her out if I find her. If ghosts could walk through the boundaries, they'd just leave on their own."

Moulin nods sharply. "We need a distraction. Something that binds GoPol's powers at large, while Alix goes in and frees her ghost."

I'm starting to feel sick again. Breaking into Charles' office was hard enough. And that was when they didn't have a reason to mistrust me. Now they know I'll be coming for my ghost. I don't believe I can even show my face there.

Gaby nudges me softly. "The ghosts are doing something, right? What is it?"

I swallow. "Jean Moulin thinks we should try and free Petite Alix. Dix has agreed to gather information on her whereabouts, but I won't be able to free her without a distraction." How do you distract an entire agency? With a terrorist threat? Surely, that'd go well for me.

"I know it's two days away, but what about Hélène's party?"

"Hélène's party?" What has my sister's party got to do with all this? As if I could think of it right now.

"Her engagement-slash-New-Year's party. She and Cédric have booked GoPol's ground floor, haven't they? And you're invited."

Moulin snaps his fingers. "That's it. Now we're talking. Operation Petite Alix will start on the thirty-first, twenty-four hours."

My brain can't keep up with this. Dumbly, I stare at Gaby, then Jean Moulin, and then Gaby again. "We're going to do this at my sister's party?" Hélène will so kill me if I mess up her precious engagement party.

Gaby nods. "Yes, and you won't be alone. Marie and I will be there. Odile, too. They won't dare do anything to you in front of your entire family. We're going to cover for you."

"Yes, we need more people on the ground." Moulin nods, determined. "I'll prepare the Résistance to take you in."

Take me in like a fugitive. I close my eyes, breathing through my nose to keep from passing out.

"I'll come with you," Josephine Baker says, her deep voice suddenly right next to my ear. "It is important that you keep your act up during the party. You don't have to pretend nothing's wrong. That'll only make them suspicious. In fact, own your distress. You can't let on that you haven't given up yet."

"So I act all depressed?" I ask.

Everyone has gotten so hyped up, while I still feel like throwing up. Could it be? Could it really not be game over yet?

Gaspar is still massaging my shoulders. With a sigh, he leans in. "We've got to try."

A single tear runs down my cheek. "How?"

"Not how, why," Gaspar says softly. "Because giving up is not an option. Just think of Petite Alix. She must be scared out of her mind. And us. Think of us."

I whimper, but Gaspar is right. I can't let GoPol win. Even if it all gets worse, I can't not give it a try. I don't know what I'd do if I lost all the wonderful people in this room. Least of all Gaspar.

"Let's do this, then."

"That's our girl," Jean Moulin says with a wide grin.

The ghosts break into groups to discuss the intricacies of the plan and how I should act at the party, leaving me with Gaby, Gaspar, and Victor.

It's only then that I notice Victor hasn't added anything to the plan. He hasn't even warned me off.

"We're gonna get her back. I'm gonna have some serious words with them if they don't give her back," Gaby says, not even considering how detrimental that might be to her.

"Thanks," I say, but then I get up and walk down the stairs until I stand right in front of Victor. "I'm gonna miss you."

He blinks and swallows heavily, but then he jerks his chin. "No. This is not the end, Alix. One way or another, we *will* see each other again."

I appreciate that he doesn't lie to me. Our chances for success are incredibly low, and I'd kick myself if I'd failed and hadn't said goodbye to him. He doesn't take that from me. Instead, he gives me hope that we'll meet again. Hopefully, sooner rather than later.

With an awkward little sniffle that doesn't even come close to hiding his feelings, Victor pulls me close and hugs me tight. "I believe in you, kid."

CHAPTER 31

The hardest bit was waiting two days until the party. I spent every minute with either Gaby or my ghosts. I told Alexandre de Beauharnais about the attack on Père Lachaise, and together, we visited my grandmother. While still severely hurt, it looks like she'll recover in time. I can only hope the same goes for Abelard, even if it might take a couple of years. Whether their memories will recover, however, is another matter.

Josephine coached me for the party, but if I'm being honest, I was in too much of a daze to retain much of it. Gaspar stuck to my side, not leaving me for even a minute. He doesn't say much and neither do I, because facing the inevitable is just too hard. But we'll face it together.

When it's finally New Year's, I feel a strange fake calm settle over me. The plans have been made and there's nothing I can do but roll with it.

As promised, I'm not attending the party alone. Not only is my entire family there to celebrate Hélène, but so are Gaspar and Josephine—looking like the old movie star she is—Gaby, and Marie, who was briefed by Gaby and instantly assured me of her help.

Hélène has done an outstanding job at transforming the lower floor of GoPol. Silver streamers decorate the ceiling and walls, while fake greenery distracts from the work atmosphere. The kitchen has been taken over by a temporary bar, serving alcohol and finger food. She's even hired a DJ, who's currently still setting up.

"There you are," Hélène greets me, laughing nervously. "I thought you were going to skip when I didn't see you with Maman and Papa." We kiss and she moves on to greet Gaby, who introduces Marie as her girlfriend.

Gaspar rubs my arm. "It's a good sign, you can still see us." I suppose that means GoPol isn't finished with me just yet. And while I'm most definitely finished with them, I'm glad we get the opportunity to free Petite Alix. *If* today doesn't end in a big disaster.

"You haven't prepared a speech or anything, have you?" Hélène asks me.

"A speech?"

She puts a hand on her heart and breathes in relief. "Good. Because I haven't planned for one yet." Then she frowns a little. "I do want one at my wedding, though."

"Sure." I can't even think about her wedding right now, much less plan a speech.

More guests arrive, colleagues of Hélène's and Cédric's, old school friends, and family friends. The DJ starts playing his music, though at the moment he's keeping it quiet to help foster conversations.

"I've never been to a fancy party like this," Marie says. She and Gaby are both wearing glitter on their temples, looking absolutely radiant. I didn't even bother with make-up.

"Hey." Gaby nudges me. "Any news yet?"

I'm still waiting on Dix's report, hoping he hasn't betrayed me. Speaking of betrayal, an hour after the beginning of the party, Sébastien and his father finally appear, coming down from their offices. While Charles smiles broadly and immediately engages in conversations, Sébastien looks as if he's been forced to show his face for a few minutes.

Anger bubbles up inside me at the sight of his pathetic face. I down the flute of champagne in my hand in one big gulp. "Excuse me."

Sure, Josephine said to act all sad and distressed, but all her advice seems terribly out-of-date all of a sudden. I'm not trying to glean information from Sébastien. I want to give him a piece of mind.

His eyes light up at the sight of me, while all I want to do is punch his face. Instead, I grab his wrist with a short, "We need to talk," and drag him into one of the corridors.

"Alix, I—"

I jerk my hand away and snap at him, "I don't give a fuck about your excuses!"

Sébastien swallows. "I wasn't—"

"Going to apologise? No, because that wouldn't be your style. After all, you just did your job, right?" If my voice were acid, it would start burning little holes into his dress shirt now.

"I did, but—"

"I *trusted* you!" It's not my usual style, but I find myself pushing Sébastien against the wall. "All that talk about partnership was just a trick to lull me into safety. Oh Alix," I say, with a fake high voice, "we're so impressed by your talent, we really want you."

Sébastien swallows. "We do. *I* do." He has taken my physical assault without so much as a twitch.

"Bullshit!" Spittle hits his chin, but he's too stunned to wipe it off. "You played me. You gave me this mission so I'd be out of the way. What you did at Père Lachaise was atrocious. All those ghosts you hurt."

"They're just ghosts," he says, though his voice is shaking.

I grunt at him, too angry to articulate my frustration. "Just ghosts? Those ghosts are more human than you've ever been. Contrary to you, they have real feelings and morals. I know you only see ghosts as tools, but you're the only tool around here."

That hits him harder than the push did earlier. "Alix, you don't understand—"

"Oh, I understand perfectly. I know all about your so-called 'training' and what your father did to you."

His eyes widen.

"How did that work out for you?" I cross my arms before I start hitting him again. "Are you happy how you traded in your life so you can be your father's tool?" I scrunch up my nose in disgust. "Honestly, you deserve all the shit that's ever happened to you."

The worst thing is he doesn't even get angry. Instead, he keeps looking at me like a lost puppy, his eyes begging me to take it back. But I won't. I can't believe I ever let myself pity a spineless guy like him. "It's no surprise you don't have a single friend. Don't *ever* call me again."

Sébastien doesn't return my blazing gaze. He looks into empty space and swallows. With a disgusted snort, I turn around and stalk away. Only then does he find his voice again. "Alix!"

But I said my piece. Head held high, I march away from him and back into the party. Eagerly, I look for the first person I know, so he won't be able to catch up with me and continue the conversation. My Papa is standing close by, looking at me in confusion.

He nods over my shoulder. "That looked intense. You okay?"

"I'm better now." It's true. The things I said might have been hurtful, but they can't hurt nearly as much as the salt that tore through a whole community; as the loss of a millennium-long partner or the pain of the betrayal Sébastien put me through, not once, but twice.

"What was it about? That's Cédric's cousin, right? What was his name?"

Annoyed, I suck in my breath. "You don't need to learn his name. He doesn't care about people anyway."

My Papa grimaces, not ready to let me brush it off. "Alix. What's going on?"

"Shouldn't you know his name? It's Sébastien Roubert. He's the one who took your ghost away. I told him about your struggles, asking for help, and the moment I turn my back, he runs to you and sweet-talks you into giving Antoine up. Bet he sounded all reasonable and mature." I shudder just thinking of it.

Papa frowns. "That wasn't Sébastien."

I stop short. "What do you mean?"

"My ghost. Your sister and Cédric told me about it. Cédric was kind enough to drive me here and have GoPol take care of the whole affair." My father cocks his head. "Are you okay?"

My head is reeling all of a sudden. Cédric took him?

"Excuse me." I leave my father standing and hurry to Odile, who's attacking a plate of finger food, looking fed up with the party already. "Odi." My voice is shaking. "Uhm, can I ask you something?"

Odile turns to me, her eyes lighting up. "Alix, thank god you're—... What's happened?"

I probably look slightly deranged or something. "Did you talk to Cédric about Petite Alix?"

She frowns slightly. "Cédric and I don't talk. Least of all about ghosts. Why?"

"I..." Cédric dropped me off at Père Lachaise. I told him I was visiting my grandmother, but what if he'd parked the car and checked where I was really going? My head is reeling. I need to talk to him, find out...

Odile grabs my arm. "There's something you should know."

"What?"

"Yesterday, I caught Cédric in your room."

"What?"

"He said something about grabbing something for Hélène."

The floor is swaying under me. "Did he? Grab something, I mean."

"Some kind of folder?" Odile watches me worriedly. "Was that bad? Should I have stopped him?"

I feel like throwing up. My gaze wanders through the room until it hits my future brother-in-law. He's talking to his uncle near the bar. As I watch, they lean in for a manly shoulder clap.

My mind flashes back to all the times Cédric tried to recruit me and how he wanted to work for GoPol. How Sébastien said his father would never recruit him. That didn't stop him, though. And by the looks of it, he's finally managed to impress that elusive uncle of his enough to win his affection.

Guilt hits me. All those awful things I said to Sébastien when it was never him. My stomach feels like a big empty hole as I continue watching Charles and Cédric laughing together. Maybe they're laughing about the stupid little girl who had no idea what forces she was playing with.

"Alix?" Odile whispers fearfully. "Did Cédric take your whisper ghost?"

I can't look at her. "Apparently he bought himself a nice promotion with it."

CHAPTER 32

It's starting to get late, and I still haven't heard from Dix. I've updated Gaby, Marie, Josephine, and Gaspar on what I just learned, and it takes Marie, Odile, and me to keep Gaby from murdering Cédric at his engagement party.

"That bastard can go and die," Gaby spits out, when she finally agrees to keep her fingers off him. "What a slimy shithead."

Marie looks slightly overwhelmed, but she does a great job keeping Gaby calm. "You don't know for sure it was him, right?" She shrugs quickly when Gaby and I look at her. "I mean, I don't know the guy."

"Be grateful for that."

My gaze falls on Cédric and Hélène who have taken to the dance floor, drinking champagne and laughing. Does my sister know? She obviously helped him convince my father to give up his ghost, but that doesn't surprise me. She'd been pretty open about her intentions. I try not to tarnish her with the same brushstroke. Then again, I know exactly what she'd say to me if I tried to complain about Cédric's interference.

He's just looking out for you. This whole ghost whisperer business is far too dangerous for you. I wonder how she'll feel about it when Cédric puts his life on the line to gain my ability.

"I think you should talk to him," Josephine says softly.

"Who?" There are too many men who've pissed me off recently.

"The commander. Charles Roubert."

I freeze. Talking to Charles is the very last thing I want to do. Uncertain, I ask, "Why?"

"Something might have happened to that teenage ghost. He might have got caught or couldn't complete his mission. You need to find out where they keep Petite Alix."

"By confronting Charles Roubert?" I ask hoarsely. Just the thought of it makes me queasy.

"No way," Gaspar says, protectively holding his arm in front of me. "That's way too risky."

Josephine sighs softly. "Time is running out. You need to know what's going to happen. He might have other plans for you. If so, the sooner you learn of them, the sooner you can make a decision. Remember, information is gold."

Gaby has noticed me spacing out. "What's is happening?" she asks softly.

"I'm going to have a chat with Charles."

Her eyes widen. "You can't." When she notices my determination, she switches course instantly. "Not alone." And before I can protest, Gaby has hooked her arm into mine and told Marie that she'll be back soon.

Having Gaby with me makes me both more nervous and more confident. It's an improbable state of mind that leaves my legs feeling like jelly and my stomach somersaulting, while my face is so tense, I can feel the skin stretching over my muscles.

Together, we make our way over to Charles Roubert. He's in a group with two people but excuses himself when he sees me coming. The smile that just graced his face slips, leaving behind nothing but contempt. "Ah Mademoiselle Dubois. And who's this?"

"Ga—"

I knock my elbow into Gaby's side. "A friend." There's no need for GoPol to know who she is.

Charles sneers. "As if it wouldn't take us all of five minutes to find out."

A chill runs down my spine. I didn't expect him to outright drop his farce. If anything, it tells me I'm in deep trouble. In that case, though, there's no point in trying to probe him carefully. "Why did you take my whisper ghost?"

"All whisper ghosts need to be registered."

"She's a toddler." I hope they didn't hurt Petite Alix. It seems even more monstrous than what they've already done.

Charles only shrugs. "Doesn't change anything. Now the real question is, why did *you* break into my office and steal the classified file of an enemy of the nation."

"You don't have any proof Alix did that," Gaby says, her voice shaking slightly.

"Really?" Charles snorts. "So you're telling me it won't be her fingerprints all over my desk?" He looks at me, and my heart feels like it's being squeezed like a lemon. "How do you explain that the file was found in your bedroom?"

So, Cédric truly took it. Just as he truly betrayed Petite Alix's location. All to get ahead. I'm starting to feel hot and cold at the same time. "What are you going to do with her?" I don't dare ask what he's going to do with me. With my fingerprints and Cédric's invasion of my privacy, I don't stand a chance in court. He put the Chevalier away for four years. What will I get?

Charles takes a step closer, his chest nearly touching mine. "There's really only two ways going forward. Either we get rid of that useless ghost, and you go back to your happy little life, or we eliminate you. Both would solve the security risk you've become, my dear Mademoiselle Dubois."

Gaby gasps, while I just stare, my mind protesting that that can't possibly be what I've heard.

"You can't... you..." Gaby stammers, then she suddenly jerks me backward, away from Charles. "We're leaving," she tells me. "You're gonna come with me to my parents and—" She startles when Sébastien suddenly appears in front of us. "Stay away from us."

Sébastien only has eyes for me. "Are you—?"

"Séb!" his father calls him sharply. "We need to talk. Now!"

"I..." Tortured, Sébastien grimaces, then heads off to follow his father's summons. I don't even want to know what's so urgent now. Probably Petite Alix's removal. Or worse.

"Good, they're gonna be busy. Time for us to leave."

But before I can follow Gaby's sage advice, I spot Dix behind the bar. He's waving at me.

"Dix's here," I tell Gaby before I let go of her and stride towards him.

Gaspar joins me. "What just happened?"

I throw him a quick glance. "He threatened to kill me." There, I said it. This horrible, completely outrageous thing that can't possibly be real. My heart hammers against my rib cage just thinking of it.

"What the hell?"

The three women we pass throw me an irritated look, probably wondering who invited the lunatic.

We reach Dix. He throws a quick glance at his father and Sébastien, who seems to be getting harangued over me, further confirming that he wasn't the one to blame. "Did you find her?"

"Yes, and you need to go now. There's no guard at the moment. I don't know for how long."

"Let's go."

"Wait!" Gaby has caught up to me, looking distraught. She's followed by Marie, Odile, and Josephine. "What are you doing?"

"Dix found Petite Alix. I'm going to get her, and then we have to leave." And get as far away as possible from here.

Josephine takes a deep breath and nods. "Leave the two ghost whisperers to me. There's yet a man to be born who could resist me." It takes me a moment to realise what she's planning. Normally, it wouldn't work, but both Charles and Sébastien can see ghosts. I bet they hadn't counted on *the* Josephine Baker being present at this pretentious little party.

I quickly inform those who didn't hear her what's happening, while I watch her float off to charm the two Rouberts.

"In that case, someone should do the same with Cédric," Odile says. "Time for me to be the most excited sister-in-law I can be." Her face is full of regret. "I'm so sorry I didn't stop him from taking that file."

"It's not your fault."

"Be careful, okay?" Odile whimpers softly, then rushes in to give me a quick hug.

Gaby exchanges a look with Marie. "We'll stand guard."

"And I'll arrange the escape vehicle," Marie adds, as if it's the most common thing in the world.

My heart is still racing but I'm filled with new determination. I check the Rouberts, and sure enough Josephine has engaged them. "Let's go."

"Finally," Dix moans, before leading us to the staircase at the back.

While Gaby and Marie take up their positions, the rest of us go downstairs to reach a department that wasn't included in my grand tour. Two floors further down, we reach a secured metal door with a big "Restricted Access" sign.

"Is it open?" All I can see is a card reader.

"Nope. But behold the power of a whisper ghost." Dix floats through the wall, and I nearly lose my mind. Gaspar could follow him, but I'm still regrettably corporal. Though not for long, if Charles was serious.

Before I can truly despair though, the door clicks open, and a grinning Dix awaits me.

"How did you do that?" I ask as I rush in.

"There's a simple button on this side. It only takes a little energy to push it."

I'd almost forgotten that whisper ghosts are more powerful than normal ghosts. Just as I have one foot in the world of the dead, they've got one in the world of the living. "Thanks."

"No problem. It doesn't work on the cell, though."

"Cell?"

It doesn't take long for the answer to present itself. We're in a basement filled with all kind of lab equipment that I have no nerve to investigate closer. In the back of the room is another door, which Dix manages to open before stepping back with raised hands and breathing sharply.

I throw him a confused glance as I hurry through the doorway. Gaspar tries to follow me, but he hisses in pain too. His hand is flickering.

"What's going on?" I ask, panicked.

"We can't enter. It's an electromagnetic field, I think," Dix explains. "She's in there, though."

I turn my back to them, facing only darkness. By the time I've fumbled out my phone, my ears pick up a muffled cry.

The light of my torch cuts through the darkness and illuminates four human-sized glass cylinders connected to a switchboard. The other three are empty, but a little familiar figure cowers in the one to my left.

"Alix!" I fall to my knees next to the cylinder, pressing my free hand against the glass.

She looks up, her eyes red from crying. My heart aches seeing her like this. "Alix?" she whimpers, before crawling towards me and putting her little hand against mine.

Below her feet is an engraved symbol that reminds me of the Chevalier. When I look up, the same symbol covers the top of the cylinder. "How do I get her out?"

Dix looks at me helplessly. "I don't know." He wets his lips. "Try that panel."

"Don't worry, sweetheart," I tell Petite Alix. "We're gonna get you out of here."

Petite Alix starts crying the moment I leave her. It breaks my heart, but I need to find a way to break her free from this awful cylinder.

While Gaspar attempts to soothe my whisper ghost from afar—he tries entering again but can't bear it—I turn towards the control panel. At first, I'm overwhelmed by the number of buttons and switches, but then I notice the labels. Most of them are shortcuts I don't understand, but there's a group of four buttons on the left side that are labelled "RLS". It beats the identical group of buttons on the other side labelled "EXT".

My finger hovers over the button I believe to be Petite Alix's cylinder. The risk is too high, but then I have another idea. Quickly, I press the one above it. The cylinder next to Petite Alix's emits a hissing noise, then its walls slide open. Perfect.

I press the right button and hurry back to Petite Alix just in time for her to start screeching in pain.

"Get her out!" Gaspar shouts. "Quick!"

I grab the little girl around her waist and half-drag, half-carry her out of the room, while my own chest feels like bursting. The moment we step out of the room, Petite Alix stops screaming and starts sobbing instead.

Dix looks at me, horrified.

"Give her to me," Gaspar says, already reaching out for the little girl. "This way you won't look suspicious when we get out of here."

"Yes, let's get out of here," Dix says, huffing from the terror he just witnessed.

Together, we turn around, only to stop short.

"Yeah, I don't think so, traitor."

In front of us, Charles' whisper ghost blocks the door.

CHAPTER 33

"I should have known the three of you were in cahoots with each other." C-Trente looks from Dix over to me, Gaspar, and Petite Alix.

Gaspar swallows and I remember how he was thrown out a window when he last walked into C-Trente. On my other side, Dix takes a deep breath. "Alright, old shithead, let's do this."

"Let's do—Dix, what are you planning?"

"Go, History Girl. Make some history for me." And with those ominous words and a steely look, Dix pulls his ghost gun and shoots C-Trente in the face.

Petite Alix wails. Gaspar backs away, and I stare, horrified.

C-Trente's face looks like a horror show, but he didn't even stumble. Instead, he pulls his own weapon and aims at Gaspar and Petite Alix.

"Oh no, you won't," Dix says seconds before he vanishes, only to reappear right in front of C-Trente to kick the gun out of his hand. He follows it up with an elbow in his already ruined face.

For one heartbeat, I watch the two ghosts go at each other with a series of blows. Then the adrenaline kickstarts my brain, and I grab Gaspar by the hand. "Let's go."

We dash through the lab, narrowly avoiding a flying screen. Dix smashes into a desk and takes a blow to the head, but when C-Trente whirls around, Dix wraps his legs around his and sends him sprawling to the ground. Our way is momentarily blocked by the two of them rolling on the floor. I see blood glistening on the tiles.

After a moment of panic, I decide to bypass them and scramble over a table, accidentally wiping out some experiment. I turn around to take Petite Alix. "Give her—"

Gaspar strides through the table without even thinking twice. "That works too."

Glass smashes and wood splinters. I duck my head. Without looking back, I reach for the door and find it locked. "No, no, no."

"Here." Gaspar points to a button to the side that I overlooked in my panic. I press it and a click releases the door.

As I push the door open, Dix screams in pain. I hold the door for Gaspar and Alix and throw a last glance into the room. C-Trente has his knee on Dix's lower back and one arm twisted above it. With his other hand he's grabbed Dix's hair and smashes it into the floor again and again.

"Alix, come!" Gaspar is already on the stairs, his eyes wide. "He's doing this for us."

With the bitter taste of guilt in my mouth, I throw the door shut and hurry up the stairs after Gaspar.

He stops me just before we step on the last flight. "Take a moment, breathe, try to look as if you're enjoying yourself."

Because this was so joyful. I nod, though, and say, "You too. There might be more than a few ghost whisperers around."

As we slowly walk up the stairs, we come across Gaby and Marie kissing. They seem to be pretty into it, which strikes me as weird until Gaby opens an eye, looking straight at us. "Did you get her."

I nod.

"Wonderful," Marie says cheerily. "Follow me."

The two of them link their arms with mine and start giggling as we make our way across the ground floor. Gaspar follows us with Petite Alix, nodding at me. With a little effort, I manage an awkward laugh as well. "Really?"

"Yes," Gaby says, immediately continuing the farce. "You should've seen that. It was hilarious."

I have no idea what I should've seen, probably something that never happened.

"So good," Marie adds, bursting into giggles.

It takes all my willpower not to look around and look for Charles or Sébastien, or even Cédric and my sister. Instead, we giggle and chat our way through the crowd until we reach the entrance.

Gaby opens the door, announcing, "Let's get some fresh air before it's time for the countdown."

Gaspar steps through first, while Marie is still hanging onto my arm. As I follow him, I throw a glance over my shoulder—and look straight into Sébastien's eyes.

He frowns, but then a catastrophic crash draws his immediate attention. Someone has crashed the tower of champagne flutes for midnight. That someone is Odile. She stands next to it, both hands on her mouth, looking appropriately shocked.

As Hélène starts screaming at her, Marie pulls me outside. "Quick now."

Gaby closes the door behind us, and suddenly all our mirth evaporates. We hurry down the stairs as fast as we can.

"My uncle should be waiting just around the corner," Marie explains.

We burst into the cold winter air. A few people have gathered on the streets, starting the fireworks early, while very few cars are driving. Marie takes a moment to look around before quickly spotting a familiar car.

All five of us hurry towards a silver dime-a-dozen car parked around the corner. At the wheel, I recognise Paul. Marie jumps into the front seat, telling him to start the motor. Meanwhile Gaby scoots all the way to the far end of the back seat. I follow in the middle seat, taking Petite Alix from Gaspar, so he can sit next to me, then reach past him to close the door.

"Go!" Marie shouts.

"I am," Paul says, remarkably calm. He throws a glance in the rearview mirror at me and Gaby. "Put on your seatbelts, the roads are icy tonight."

It feels surreal to perform such a mundane safety measure when any moment a dozen policemen could storm out of the building next to us and set chase. "What's next?" I ask.

"You're going into the catacombs," Gaby says. She stares ahead but puts one hand on my knee as she takes a shaky breath.

"Apparently, I'm letting you use our access," Paul says, sounding quite unsure of his role in this evening.

Marie looks over her shoulder. "It's your safest bet to vanish quickly. Maybe in a few days, you could try to leave Paris, but for now, you need to get lost as soon as possible."

Get lost. I put my hand on Gaby's, stealing another glance at her face. My poor friend is fighting with tears. "It's going to be alright," I whisper, not knowing how anything can ever be alright again.

"I know," she says, a little too quickly and shakily. "You're gonna be fine. The Chevalier will take good care of you, right?"

"Absolutely," I tell her, almost making myself believe it.

The Marais isn't very far from here. I look out the back window constantly, expecting someone to follow us, but if they are, they're staying out of sight for now. Soon, we arrive at the little church.

As Paul opens the door, he says, "I need an explanation."

"And you'll get one," Marie says, "after we've sent Alix on her way."

All too quickly, we walk into the basement above the Boutique of Psychosis. There, Gaby suddenly throws herself at me. Tears stream down her face as she hugs me fiercely. "Odi and I will cover for you. And we'll take care of Malou. You just keep your head low, you understand? Don't you dare show your face up here until I've got a plan."

I hold her in my arms, not crying any less. "You're the best friend ever. Thank you so much. For everything." I look at Marie. "You, too."

She smiles softly. "I asked my cards for you before the party. Brace yourself."

Outside, fireworks explode in the sky. The new year has started.

Paul is waiting next to the open trap door, watching me unhappily as Gaby steps back, snivelling. "I'll get a message to you," she promises.

Gaspar takes my hand. "Let's go."

With one last look at everyone and a mouthed, "Thanks," I follow Gaspar down into the catacombs.

CHAPTER 34

The door closes above us and drowns us in complete darkness.

"Careful," Gaspar says, helping me down the stairs, while I fumble for my phone.

My heart is still racing from the mad flight. I nearly drop my phone when it vibrates in my hand. *Cédric.*

"Don't take that."

"I'm not stupid." If I did, I'm sure I'd hear some more of that fake concern while he stalls me and fishes for information.

With the phone still ringing, a message from Sébastien pops up beneath: *"Better run fast."* Then a second one: *"Lose the phone."*

I'm torn. Our flight wasn't exactly planned like this. I don't have another light with me. Or any other practical equipment you should never leave behind when you visit the catacombs.

"You're gonna lose reception soon," Gaspar says, who's been looking at the same text messages. "We'll leave it in the catacombs when we go."

He's right, the light is more important. Sure enough, the reception breaks off at the bottom of the stairs. I turn on the light and startle when I find Pierre Roche and Jean Moulin waiting there for me.

"You startled me."

Jean tips his head. "Josephine let me know the mission was a success. Well done, Alix."

I don't feel like much of a success. We freed my whisper ghost, who perked up upon hearing her name, but now GoPol will be looking for me. The regular police will, too.

"Let's get you three to safety."

None of the ghosts can truly help me if GoPol comes after me, but Jean's confidence helps settle my nerves a little. We walk in silence as I nervously watch the battery power of my phone deplete. I've already turned off any mobile functions and put it into battery save mode, as well as using the lowest light setting, but still, I can only watch the numbers count down.

"We're almost at the Crossroad," Gaspar says when he notices me checking yet again.

"And then?" I don't have enough battery power left to get out of the catacombs. Not on my own, at least.

Gaspar just sighs. Petite Alix has slung her arms around his neck and is resting her head on his shoulder. Her big eyes are watching me tiredly. The poor baby is nearly as exhausted as I am.

At last, we reach the Crossroad of the Dead. I look at the stairs, but Jean shakes his head. "They're all at the Monastery of the Bears, celebrating the new year." He wastes no time in leading the way, which I'm very grateful for as we arrive there with only three per cent left on my phone.

Pierre Roche enters the bunker the ghost way to let them know about my presence, since I can't remember the secret knock for the life of me. My phone flickers out as I stand there waiting with Gaspar and Petite Alix. In the darkness, my breathing feels unnaturally loud.

Just then, the door opens, and I'm blinded by the light. "Alix," I hear the Chevalier says. "We've been waiting for you."

"Have you?"

He steps aside. "Of course, Moulin told us to expect you and your whisper ghost." For the first time, he seems to notice what I'm wearing. "Is that a cocktail dress?"

With a sigh, I enter the bunker. "I didn't have time to change." I blink against the light, trying to see who's down here on an evening like this. Empty champagne flutes and a bottle are strewn across the table. The party must've finished hours ago.

Some ghosts are sitting at the listening station, while three people are lying in bed, fast asleep. I recognise Samara by her tight curls.

"I... I need your help." I tell the Chevalier and the ghosts all about what happened after I last visited the catacombs; the attack on Père Lachaise, Petite Alix's kidnapping, my plan to free her, Charles' threat, and the eventual escape.

"You should've left Petite Alix with us from the start," the Chevalier says, before giving me a quick smile. "Never mind. You're both here now and you're welcome to stay for as long as you need."

"Us three," I correct him mindlessly.

The Chevalier nods. "Right. Sorry, Gaspar. I know you're always at Alix's side."

"He's got that right," Gaspar grumbles. "I won't ever leave your side again."

Grateful, I lean into him and close my eyes for a second.

The Chevalier snorts softly. "Well, you look like you could fall asleep on the spot. It's about four in the morning. Take a bed and find some sleep, if you can. We'll talk about the rest in the morning. Or afternoon." He laughs softly. "Whenever you're ready."

Gaspar and I make our way over to the bunk area and I climb onto the top bed above Samara. I feel the tiredness in every bone of my body. My shoulders slump and my lids have grown heavy.

My heart is no longer racing. Though I might be safe at last, I can't help but feel defeated.

I'm a fugitive now. My life as I know it is over. GoPol won't simply let me get away with it. That means in a few days or maybe weeks, I'll have to leave the city I grew up in, leave my studies unfinished, and leave everyone I know—ghost or living—behind for... forever. The thought of such a future tightens my throat until I find it hard to breathe.

"Ssh." Gaspar puts an arm around me and pulls me close. "We'll figure this out. The important thing is that you and Petite Alix are safe."

Are we, though? I don't want to spend my life in the catacombs like the Chevalier. As interesting as they are, I like the sun too much, the whirring snowflakes in winter, picnics in the park in spring. And I already miss my family and friends. Malou. Hopefully, I can take her with me when I leave.

But where will I go? Is it enough to leave Paris or do I need to leave France or even Europe? Will I have to change my name? Start with nothing because anything could be traced back to me?

"We have each other," Gaspar mutters as if he's read my mind. "That's all that matters."

I want to talk more, make a plan, or wallow in self-pity. But my eyes grow heavy, and despite all the fears and doubts swirling through my head, I sink against his shoulder and feel myself dozing off.

I can't have slept more than an hour or two when a sudden boom makes me sit upright in bed. Bright beams of light slice through the room, landing on the bunk beds. Before I can even register what's happening, a coarse voice shouts, "Police! Everyone put your hands up!"

Chapter 35

They've found us. Already.

Two ghosts vanish into the wall. A guy jumps out of the bed across from me and sprints towards a doorway. Two policemen swarm him and hit him over the head with a baton. A whisper ghost holds down Samara but gets attacked by her whisper ghost. Jean Moulin kneels on the ground, bleeding from multiple wounds he hasn't carried since the day he died, muttering, "Not again. Not again."

Next to me, Petite Alix has started crying again.

"Alix," Gaspar hisses. "What do we do?"

"Take her and hide. Save us."

"I won't leave you."

"Go!" I shove him and Petite Alix into the wall.

Then I jump off the bed, nearly colliding with a woman. She ignores me and goes after Gaspar. Another ghost. The police have brought ghost whisperers.

The sudden action has left me reeling. After not enough rest, I'm feeling dizzy. My heart is racing, quickly eating up my non-replenished reserves. Yet still, I know that I can't give up. In the ensuing chaos, I keep my head low and sneak around the column, waiting for my chance.

Moulin is still cowering on the ground. Someone has kicked off his fedora and more wounds have appeared on his face. Terrible bruises. It reminds me of the Boutique of Psychosis, when we were all caught in our own personal nightmares. This is Moulin's: betrayal, torture, and death.

The ghost whisperer at the column notices him and takes a step towards him. I seize my chance and dash towards the opening.

"Hey!"

I ignore the shout and climb as fast as I can. Someone is coming after me. They grab my heel, but I kick them, hearing a pained grunt. I reach the top and pull myself up, quickly scrambling to my feet.

Just as I'm about to bolt, a pair of arms clamp down around me, lifting my feet off the ground for a moment. I kick wildly, hitting shins and toes, but the grip never lessens.

"I'm sorry," my captor says, and I recognise him as Sébastien. "But it's safer this way."

He helped me before. Why isn't he helping me now? "Let me go!"

"It's too late for that. If you don't want to get hurt, stop it."

I claw at his arms, digging my fingers in to try and pry his grip open. To no avail. He's a trained special agent and I'm just a normal history student. "Please. Please."

A policeman crawls out of the hole, readying his baton. Behind me, I can feel Sébastien lean his forehead against the back of my head. "Cooperate with us."

"Never."

"You still get to live a life," he hisses, desperation thick in his voice.

But what kind of life if I don't have my ghosts?

"You need help with that, Roubert?" the policeman asks.

Sébastien shakes his head. "I'm good. Did you find her ghost?"

"Natalie's onto it."

I start crying. All this struggling on too little sleep has completely depleted me. "How did you find me so fast?" I should probably keep my mouth shut, but I'm exhausted.

"We had a tip," Sébastien says curtly.

What that tells me is that I'm not the only double agent in the Résistance. Someone's doing a far better job than me, and their allegiance lies with GoPol. "Who?"

"Doesn't matter. Now, stop."

Just as he says it, the ghost of the woman I almost jumped on steps out of the wall, Petite Alix slung over her shoulder. Once again, I claw at Sébastien's hands, screaming my head off. "She's a child! You can't do this! She deserves an afterlife."

I don't even care about my talent right now. The thought of Petite Alix going back into that horrible room and potentially being ripped from the afterlife is too much to bear.

Sébastien wrestles my arms behind my back and handcuffs my wrists.

"I'm sorry, Alix, but I have no choice."

The GoPol agents gather. Petite Alix cries. I have no idea where Gaspar is. And there's not a single thing that I can do.

In the end, it was all in vain.

We lost.

CHAPTER 36

Petite Alix is returned to GoPol, while Sébastien hands me off to a bunch of regular police officers who are waiting at the exit. He opens his mouth to say something but must've realised that there's very little that will make any of this okay.

It's my first ride in a police car and my first arrest. Everything beyond that is a daze. I sit in a room for hours, dozing off from time to time, but waking with a start and racing heart every single time.

Finally, after what must've been hours, the door opens. "Mademoiselle Dubois?" A middle-aged woman looks at me disapprovingly. "Your sister is here."

"My sister?"

She jerks her head. "Come on. She paid your bail, so let's get you out of here."

"For how long?" I ask as I groggily get to my feet.

The policewoman snorts. "If you don't stop running into the catacombs, not very long."

Her words don't make sense, but I'm too tired to find out more. Instead, I follow her, wait patiently for my personal items to be returned, and get released with a stern warning and a promise that I'll receive information on my charges soon.

In the foyer, Hélène awaits me with a face made of stone and disappointment. She's changed into trousers and a chic slender turtleneck pullover since the party. Her hair is immaculate, and contrary to me, she looks well-rested. Upon my sight, she scoffs. "I can't believe this is happening."

Still dazed, I can't do much more than follow her to her car. I get in and put on my seat belt, but instead of starting the car, Hélène simply stares at me. "What happened to you?"

"Huh?"

"Huh?" she repeats in a much more screeching tone than me. "What do you mean, *huh*? I just picked you up from jail! I thought Cédric was joking when he woke me this morning. My little sister couldn't possibly end up in *jail* first thing in the new year. What did you even do?"

According to the policewoman, nothing but trespass in the catacombs. But the cataflics don't bother true cataphiles. They definitely don't bother running raids at New Year. "Does it matter?"

Hélène huffs. "Of course, it matters. Why did you leave the party last night?"

"Because I had something to do."

"It was a ghost thing, right?" Hélène asks, her eyes widening. "You had to do another favour. At my engagement party."

Her engagement party? "It had nothing to do with you or your party."

She laughs coldly. "Of course not, why would any of us living relatives ever take priority over your dead people?"

"Ask Cédric that."

"What?"

I'm starting to wake up from my daze, finding the anger beneath. "You should ask your precious fiancé why he prioritises dead people over his living soon-to-be relatives."

Instead, she starts the car and pulls out of the street. "What do you even mean? Cédric's not a ghost whisperer."

"Oh, but he wants to be one," I say, my voice slowly turning to acid. "So much so he's willing to throw everyone else under the bus. First Sébastien, then Papa, and now me."

"Cédric has nothing to do with this madness."

Now it's me laughing. "That's what I thought, because he always pretends to be so nice and caring."

Hélène shoots me an evil look. "He *is* nice and caring."

"No, he's not. He's a self-serving *asshole* who's going to sacrifice everything and everyone to get what he wants."

The car comes to a screeching halt. The people behind us are honking, forcing Hélène to keep driving. But she pulls into the nearest bus station and glares at me. "Get out."

I rub my face, reminding myself that I love my sister. "Léni, I'm not lying. Cédric sold Papa's secret to GoPol. He's wanted to join them since forever. Sébastien told me that. And he—"

"I said get out!" When I don't move, she hits her wheel, emitting a short-lived honk. "You've hated Cédric the moment I brought him home. While he's been nothing but nice to you, you've never given him a chance. Do you think I don't know how you called him Officer Cédric behind his back? Well, I've had enough. I will not sit through any more slander about the man I love and plan to marry."

"Léni, please. Just listen to me."

Her jaw is set. She can't even look at me.

"You want to know the truth about what happened last night? I didn't leave for a favour. I fled GoPol after being told they were going to *kill* me if I didn't cooperate."

A glance. "Are you drunk? Taking drugs?"

I can feel my eyes widen. "Wow. Wow! I'm telling you someone threatened my life and *that's* how you choose to respond?"

"That's because you sound ridiculous. Nobody is going to kill you."

"I bet Cédric would if that earned him a job with GoPol."

"Get out!" Hélène screeches at me.

"Don't worry, I will." I take off my seat belt. "But not before I tell you what a disgusting and horrible man you're about to marry."

"I don't want to hear it."

"Cédric went into my room and rummaged through my stuff while I wasn't there. Ask Odile. She saw him. He then brought the evidence he found to Charles Roubert, knowing fully well he was going to absolutely ruin me."

Hélène remains unimpressed. "So, he was doing his job."

"It wasn't his job. Usually, the police need a warrant to search a place. They can't just break in and take stuff. No, this was Cédric taking advantage of his family connections to land me in hot water so he could advance."

"But you had incriminating stuff lying around your room. What, Alix?" She glares at me. "What was in your room that shouldn't have been there?"

"A file."

"You stole a file?" And we're back to screeching.

"Yes, a file that proves how GoPol is conducting immoral experiments on living and dead, plants false evidence, and creates ghost whisperers by actively murdering their chosen candidates." Now that I think of it, I should've given the damn file to my father to expose them. "Charles even killed his own son! He'll definitely kill Cédric, but Cédric's too blind to see that. No, he'd rather sell out his future sister-in-law."

I would've thought that would mean something to Hélène, but her face remains a stony mask. "So, now you're the police?"

"Just because they're police, doesn't mean what they're doing is right. If you could've seen what they did at Père Lachaise. A ghost was destroyed! Grandma got seriously hurt."

"Oh my god—they're *dead*, Alix," she shouts. "What's so damn hard to understand about that? Your stupid little ghosts are all dead. They can't be killed or hurt."

"You're wrong!" It hurts to hear Hélène say that when I'm still shaking just thinking of the devastation in the cemetery. The shock that rippled through the ghost community. "Just because you can't see it, doesn't make it any less true."

"This has gone too far. You've gone completely mad. Can't you see that you're ruining your own life? No one else is doing it. *You* are!"

Stunned, I stare at her. "So you agree with them? I don't get the right to be a ghost whisperer. It's okay for the police to go behind my back and kidnap my whisper ghost, a three-year-old child who's scared out of her mind, torture her and then eliminate her, because guess what, it's only a ghost, right? It doesn't matter that she screams and cries because *you* can't hear her. And hey, she's already dead, so who cares? And if I complain about that, then, oh well, we'll just take your talent away. We can't have people *knowing* how wrong it is what we're doing."

"Really?" Hélène scoffs at me. "You're not that important, Alix."

"Can you really not see how wrong this is? How scary?"

Hélène grimaces furiously. "You know what will make it all less scary? When they finally take your powers away."

I gasp, speechless for a moment.

"This has completely taken over your life. You're just too blind to see it. Or maybe it's that ghost boyfriend." She over-exaggerates a shudder. "Don't you know how crazy that sounds? What were you gonna do? Marry a ghost?"

"Better than marrying a two-faced psycho."

Hélène grunts, her eyes going mad again. "You know what. I'm done with you. I no longer want you at my wedding. I don't want you anywhere. If you can't support me and Cédric, I never want to speak to you again."

A honk alerts us to the bus that is trying to pull into the bay.

"Go and ruin your life but don't drag the rest of us down with you." She reaches over my lap and pushes the door open.

I stare at her for a moment longer, but a second honk pulls me out of my stunned silence. Grabbing my bag, I swing my legs out of the car. "You and Cédric deserve each other. I never wanted to come to your stupid wedding, anyway."

The bus honks a third time as I exit the car. The driver even sticks his head out the window to shout at me. "This is a bus station! Move your ass out of the way."

Next to me, Hélène pushes on the gas and pulls out of the bay, leaving me standing on the road. I quickly jump on the sidewalk before the bus runs me over in frustration. Its doors open, letting a bunch of annoyed people out who mutter at me as if it's my fault my sister violated the road code.

"Are you getting on or not?" the driver barks at me.

I must've been staring straight ahead because his question snaps me out of it. Slowly, I shake my head. "No, I'm"—the doors close in my face—"walking."

Snow mud sprays my lower legs as the bus pulls out of the bay. Above me, the sky is grey, not a sliver of sunlight to see. It's fitting weather for my empty heart.

I couldn't care less about Hélène's opinion, but in the end, she wins. I lose. And soon, everything I fought for will be taken from me. If it hasn't already.

CHAPTER 37

I walk home from the bus station. It was the only choice, since being around humans is the last place I want to be right now. None of the people around me care for the ghosts. If they believe in them, then not in their feelings and hopes. And the only ones who know for a fact that what I see and hear is real couldn't care less about them. I've never felt more alone in the world.

Hélène's words cut deeper with every step. I'm the mad one, the one who lost her mind—or as she said, the one who ruined my life. The worst bit is I can't even blame her. Not completely. In my attempt to help the ghosts, I've dragged first my father and then Odile, Gaby, and even Marie into it. And for what?

I arrive home, half-frozen and endlessly tired. Since I fled the party in a hurry, I never had a chance to grab my coat, never mind my gloves, scarf, and hat. My fingers are so stiff, I struggle a whole minute with the keys. Still, I can hardly feel the cold. The pain inside is much worse.

Odile opens the door upstairs when I struggle with it yet again. Her eyes widen. "Alix?" She pulls me inside, fussing over my pale skin. "What are you doing here? I thought you—"

"It's over."

"What's over? What do you…?"

I shuffle past her into my room and drop straight onto my bed, never even bothering with taking off my shoes.

Odile follows me in. "What happened? I thought you guys succeeded. Gaby said they dropped you off at the catacombs and that I should cover for you."

With my arm over my eyes, I tell her, "You don't need to do that anymore."

"But why?" She sits on my bed, cautiously putting a hand on my leg. "Gosh, you're cold."

"It doesn't matter." I will warm eventually. And if I lose some toes, I don't really care. It wouldn't even compare to all the other things I've lost. "Odi, I don't want to talk about it. Could you please…?"

She sighs. "Okay but take a warm shower or something. Don't just lie there." Then she pats my leg. "It's gonna be alright."

I start crying.

Proving that she's a much better sister than Hélène, Odile puts a blanket on me and quietly leaves the room.

"You should listen to her," a soft voice from the direction of Malou's cage says.

Instantly, I'm upright. "Gaspar!"

He sits next to Malou, looking no worse for wear, and smiles sadly. Within a second, I've pounced him, running my hands all over his face and kissing him.

"You're here, you…" My heart has suddenly started beating again.

Gaspar wraps me in his arms and presses me against his chest. "I'm glad you're okay. When they carried you away, I was so worried. The Chevalier got away, and so did most of the others. They only came for you. I wanted to follow you, but their ghosts wouldn't let me. They told me to leave it be and go back to my afterlife. That I had no business being around you."

"But you're here. With me." I kiss him as if he's the only drop of water in an endless desert. "You're still here."

"They must have not done it yet."

"Do you think they'll refrain from it?" As little as I want that for Petite Alix, I'm hoping Charles will keep her hostage. I'll gladly endure whatever he wants from me if it means keeping Gaspar and all the other ghosts around.

But Gaspar closes his eyes and shakes his head. "I don't think they'll take that risk."

The tears are flowing again as I desperately try to hold onto my hope. "But they could use her against me. To silence me, for example. They don't want any of this to get out, do they?"

"No one will believe you if you say anything," Gaspar says gently. "To everyone not in the know, you'll just be some crazy person."

He's right, of course. Despite knowing better, my own sister sees me as nothing but a madwoman.

Gaspar slowly gets to his feet, pulling me up with him. Then he carries me back to my bed. He bends down to unlace my shoes but can't hold on to the laces.

I gulp and do the job for him, kicking the shoes off in disgust. "This isn't right."

He cups my face and leans over me. "Maybe it was never meant to be."

"No!" I grab him by the hoodie and pull him down on me, pressing my lips on his. I try not to think about the lack of heat in his mouth or his missing breath on my skin, but it's all that goes through my mind as I kiss him with pure desperation.

At last, I fall back exhausted. The pity in his eyes is near unbearable. He runs his hand through my hair until he cups my cheek again. "Thanks for making my transition the most beautiful time of my existence."

"Ugh." The tears are collecting in my throat, making it hard to swallow. "Gaspar..."

"I mean it. You're the best thing that ever happened to me. It makes me almost glad I died."

"Glad?" I choke on the word.

"It's how I met you." He bends down and gently kisses the corner of my mouth, then my neck, just under the chin. "And I'll still be there. Even if you can't see me, I'll be there, watching over you."

A sob tears from my throat. "Gaspar, please… I don't want to do this."

"But I do. Because in the future"—he places another kiss on my neck—"you won't hear me when I say it. So, it's important that you hear me now."

I swallow heavily, struggling to breathe through this.

He kisses my clavicle and then lies down beside me, the length of his body pressed against my side, his arm heavy across my stomach. "I want you to promise me something."

"Anything." I turn to the side, putting my arm around his shoulder and sinking my fingers into his wonderful soft curls.

"You need to stay alive. By whatever means it takes. I want you to go on living." His fingertips brush across my temple. "Don't do anything stupid. Don't come searching for me before it's your time. I promise I'll wait for you. So, promise me you'll live."

Instead, I cry harder.

"Please, my love. Live for me. Sing out loud. Dance under the stars. Hug your friends. Love fiercely."

"I don't want to do this without you," I manage to whisper.

He kisses my forehead. "I know. But you will. You're strong." He gives me a crooked smile. "You took it up with GoPol, so I know you're a fighter. And one day, after a long life full of love and adventure, I'll find you at the Panthéon."

"At the Panthéon?"

Gaspar grins. "Yes, because I know you'll be one of the greats. One way or another, you will change the world."

Warmth floods me from head to toe, and I press his lips back on mine. I cannot say goodbye to this boy. To my hedgehog boy.

"Promise me, Alix," he whispers in between kisses.

And though it tears my heart in a million little pieces, I sigh and say, "I promise."

He kisses my nose. "I love you."

At some point that afternoon, I must've fallen asleep. After more than twenty-four hours without proper sleep, all that commotion and emotional distress, my body just shut down. When I wake up, it's dark around me and I'm alone.

"Gaspar?"

The scuttle of Malou's feet is the only sound in the room.

I sit up and turn on my light, frantically looking around. "Gaspar?"

He's gone.

I burst into tears.

Chapter 38

The first few days of the new year are a blur. I sleep a ton, and when I'm awake, I cry. I don't interact with my family, all of whom check in at some point. All but Hélène. Odile keeps me hydrated and somewhat fed, but food has lost its taste and I never manage more than a few bites. All I do is hold Malou and cry.

The weekend before we go back to class, Odile knocks on my door and sticks her head in. "Gaby called me. She says to charge your damn phone."

I haven't looked at my phone since I picked it up at the police station, still depleted from my useless tour through the catacombs.

"If you don't, she'll drag you out of bed tomorrow. This is her last warning." When I don't react at all, Odile sits down on my bed. "Everyone is worried about you. Well... never mind."

"What?" I ask tonelessly.

She sighs heavily. "Hélène says you brought this on yourself."

"I know."

"She also said you're dead to her."

"I know."

Odile groans softly. "Don't do this to me. I don't want to be in the middle. That's your job."

I don't have anything to say.

After a while, Odile sighs again and gets up. "Charge your phone." Then I'm alone again.

Gaspar made me promise to live, but I don't know how to do that anymore. My life feels so empty without my ghosts. What am I supposed to do now? Give tours at the Panthéon with no one around? Visit Père Lachaise to lay flowers on an empty grave? Go to class and learn about dead people without talking to them?

"I'm sorry," I whisper into the nothingness around me. "It's too hard without you." I try to imagine Gaspar in my room. He'd be sitting next to me. Or he'd be holding Malou and spoiling her rotten. But I can't. Even in my imagination, the room remains as empty as it is now.

Minutes turn to hours without anything ever changing. Outside my room, I hear steps passing by and muffled conversations, the clattering of dishes and then laughter. The living keep on living and the dead remain dead. And I am lost in the inbetween. Part of neither world.

A knock on my door pulls me from my daze. This time, it's my maman. "Darling, you've got a visitor." She addresses someone outside my room. "Give her a few minutes." Then she looks at me. "You might want to get up."

Why would I get up for Gaby? She's seen me in pyjamas before. I don't know if I have the energy to face her, but that won't stop my friend, of course. With a sigh, I push myself upright. "Better?"

Maman cocks her head, her eyes full of pity. "It's gonna be alright, sweetie." Clearly, it's not better at all.

Then she leaves me alone, leaving the door open for my visitor. It's not Gaby. Instead, with an awkward knock, Sébastien appears in the door frame.

Electricity shoots down my spine, forcing me upright. I haven't heard from him since he handed me over to the police. He's certainly not on my list of people I ever want to see again. But Sébastien isn't alone.

His hand is holding a much smaller one. Next to him, half-hiding behind his leg, stands Petite Alix. My whisper ghost.

"How?"

My brain short-circuits. How is she still alive? Why is she with Sébastien? If I still have my whisper ghost, am I still a whisperer? But then where is Gaspar?

Sébastien swallows. He doesn't look all that great either, haggard with dark shadows under his eyes. "She was scheduled for elimination."

I hang onto every word from his lips. "B-but?"

"Dix went rogue. They're looking for her. For both of them. And they'll eliminate him. Alix, I need your help."

Afterword

Are you still with me? That was intense, wasn't it? I'm kind of glad I put all those happy scenes in the beginning because we sure needed that at the end. I'd love to say this is Alix's blackest moment, but I'm not sure I can promise that with all the stuff still waiting ahead.

Sébastien had a bit of a rough ride, too. I'm sure you hated him for at least some portion of the book, but here's hoping he can redeem himself in book 4. He definitely didn't deserve Alix's harsh words, but he hasn't exactly come through for her either. I hope you'll give him another chance. As for his father, hate away.

I can't wait to get into book 4 and explore this new dynamic between Alix and Sébastien, now that he's followed Dix into rebellion. Meanwhile, Alix will come back stronger than ever, building her own trusted team. How cool was that girl power rescue mission? There will be more hedgehog content (sorry, Malou wasn't all that present in this one), more emotional dilemmas, and more action. Of course, we'll also have to find out what happened to Gaspar. I promise it's going to be a doozy.

The next book is *Ghosts of the Opera* and... yes, we're totally going Phantom of the Opera for this one!

If you can't wait to read it and really enjoy exploring European cities, you should try out the *Spirit Seeker* series. Like Alix, Rika can see things others don't, with her empathy being her biggest strength. *A Force of Nature* takes place in Berlin and starts an action-packed supernatural sightseeing adventure through Europe.

A big thank you to all the FAKAs and my amazing beta readers. You know who you are. Keep kicking ass. Love you all!

And, of course, thanks to all the wonderful, amazing readers and followers on Facebook, TikTok, my newsletter, and wherever else I've picked you up. You continue giving this series life. Thank you for joining the Malou hype and making her the best-loved literary hedgehog ever ;) See you all back for *Ghosts of the Opera!*

Love, Janna

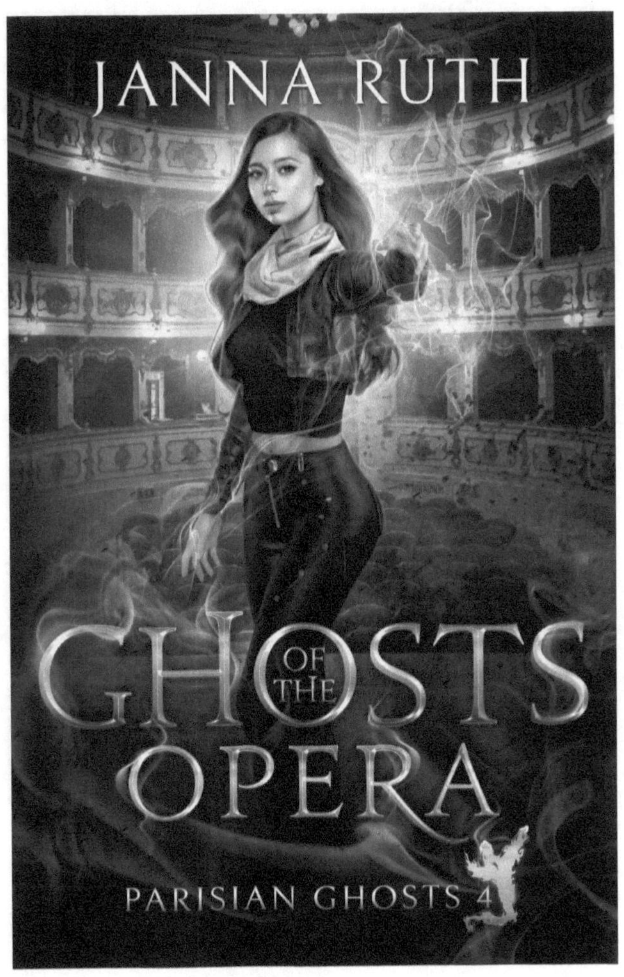

Book 4: Ghosts of the Opera

A supernatural adventure through Europe

Magic, Demons and High School Drama

About Janna Ruth

Once upon a time, Janna Ruth studied the plate boundaries of this world. Now, she's creating her own worlds. Born in Berlin, Germany, Janna lives in Wellington, New Zealand, writing both English and German books.

Janna's writing career kicked off when she won a writing competition for German publisher Ueberreuter. Her first self-published novel "Im Bann der zertanzten Schuhe" (Melody of Curse, coming in June 2022) went on to win the 2018 SERAPH for "Best Independent Title". She debuted in English with her witchy novella "Witching with Dolphins" in 2020 and has since published urban fantasy, YA sci-fi, and contemporary coming-of-age novels and series.

When Janna isn't writing, she has a plethora of hobbies, such as aerial acrobatics, cake decorating, drawing, reading, and anything crafty you can throw her way.

Find out more about Janna and her books here:

- **Website:** www.janna-ruth.com

- **BookBub:** www.bookbub.com/authors/janna-ruth

- **Facebook:** www.facebook.com/authorjannaruth

- **Facebook Reader Group:** www.facebook.com/groups/storyseekers

- **Goodreads:** www.goodreads.com/author/show/16513923.Janna_Ruth

- **BlueSky:** https://bsky.app/profile/janna-ruth.bsky.social

- **Instagram:** www.instagram.com/janna_ruth

- **TikTok:** www.tiktok.com/@jannaruthwrites

- **Pinterest:** www.pinterest.com/jannaruthwrites